GOOD TO BE GOD

GOOD TO BE GOD

TIBOR FISCHER

ALMA BOOKS

ALMA BOOKS LTD
London House
243–253 Lower Mortlake Road
Richmond
Surrey TW9 2LL
United Kingdom
www.almabooks.com

Good to Be God first published by Alma Books Limited in 2008

Printed in Great Britain by TJ International, Padstow, Cornwall

ISBN (HARDBACK): 978-1-84688-071-1
ISBN (HARDBACK SPECIAL EDITION): 978-1-84688-074-2
ISBN (EXPORT PAPERBACK): 978-1-84688-072-8

For Louise

GOOD TO BE GOD

You know when you're in trouble. You know you're in trouble when you phone and no one phones back. You know you're in trouble when you get back home, the door's been kicked in, the only thing stolen is the lock (it's the only thing worth stealing) and your burglar has left a note urging you to "pull yourself together".

This isn't funny when it happens to you.

I tried to live my life decently. For a long time. I really did, but it didn't work...

"Well," says Nelson. I haven't seen him for a few years. He's waiting for me in the Chinese restaurant, patiently turning over the menu. With your school friends, you tend to think of them as they were, and it was unnatural to find Nelson there, not just on time, but early.

Nelson was the school friend my parents liked. He mastered manipulation young, and my parents were reassured by the state of the nation when Nelson, his hair immaculately combed, would greet them with excessive courtesy. This opposed to the inevitable grunts of my other associates. My mother was often more pleased to see Nelson than I was.

Only once did my mother have suspicions. One evening, as I walked out to join Nelson in his car, she mused, "He does look too young to be driving." That was probably because Nelson was indeed two years too young to have a driving licence, but since the car was stolen that didn't matter much.

Nelson, Bizzy and I would roll through south London. You'll never be able to enjoy driving as much as when you're fifteen and in a stolen car. We'd stop off and have an expensive meal (prawn cocktail, steak, black forest gateau) on one of Nelson's stolen credit cards. We did this quite often, and we only had trouble one night, but not from suspicious waiters or the police. Nelson – normally a conscientious driver – accidentally cut up a vanload of heavies, twice our age, size and number. We were chased around for an hour, and it was the only time I saw Nelson scared.

"How you?" asks Nelson. It's a perfectly reasonable, expected question. But it's one I wish I wasn't asked these days.

"Fine," I say. We both know this isn't true.

Every school has a Nelson: the kid who phones in the bomb threats, who steals teachers' bags and exam papers, who goes off on exotic holidays with complete strangers paying for it or foreign governments arranging for his travel back, under that famed practice of deportation. From the age of about twelve to eighteen I don't think Nelson went a day without committing an incarcerable criminal act. Yet he never spent five minutes in a police station – in England. It seemed to us that he was destined either for the gallows or stardom in international skulduggery. What happened to Nelson? What happened to Nelson was that life kicked the shit out of him.

Married with two kids, Nelson now works as a rep for a company that manufactures handcuffs. The company does some other things, but its staple is handcuffs. Nelson has some piquant stories about his overseas customers who, for example, ask for their money back when blood jams the cuffs and they can't get them off the bodies.

We share the same birthday and this makes him an outlandish

mirror. We reanimate that night we nearly got mashed and other choice japes. To have a really good laugh about them we need each other. Have we seen anyone from the old days? We haven't. Not for years. But even if we had, they wouldn't have evented enough to produce a good anecdote. Nothing much happens when you're forty.

Not that I need reminding, but when I look at Nelson I see how punishing this marathon is. He's not slow or lazy. "I haven't bought so much as a shirt for myself in four years," he tells me. His daughter wants to be a doctor and he has to save up. We both express horror at the price of everything, especially food. He can barely afford a restrained night-out in a cheap local Chinese restaurant, and I can't afford it at all. That's middle age for men, less hair and more stinginess.

"Why can't they do proper coffee in Chinese restaurants?" he reflects as he pokes his liquid with a spoon. "You know, my wife does my hair." He makes clipper movements with his hand. Is ageing a reverse process? You get a few moments in your twenties when you wangle some clout, but then it all closes in on you and you're back in a saggy version of childhood where you can't do what you want and someone who doesn't know how to do it is cutting your hair.

Nevertheless, I'm well behind in this game. Nelson may have a huge mortgage, but he's got a mortgage. He has a dire job, but a job. A pension. He has kids. Everyone we know, even the truly dim and unpleasant, has something.

"Let me pay for this," says Nelson, and I don't even feign protest, just in case he changes his mind.

"So, women?" asks Nelson.

"No." Nelson anticipates I'll be fleshing out this answer, but I don't.

"You're not lucky are you?" If you think you're unlucky, you may or may not be. It's hard to gauge the bumps, and typically thinking you're unlucky is self-pity. But when your friends start telling you you're unlucky, you're really in trouble.

We're silent as we wait for the waiter to return Nelson's card.

"Miami next week," Nelson sighs.

"What's the problem there?"

"If I were on holiday, Miami'd be great. What it means for me is a generous helping of road rage, a day on a plane, four days in an air-conditioned box dishing out my cards to members of the law-enforcement profession who'll be behaving as badly as they can get away with, and who, if they were interested in my stuff would know where to get it anyway. My liver's shot, so I can't booze. Then a generous helping of delay at the airport, another day on a plane, a generous topping-up of rage on the drive home to be battered by the wife because I was in Miami and she wasn't."

A skeletal Chinese man wanders in with a large shoulder bag. From this he produces a fan of pirate DVDs which he submits to the various diners. He doesn't utter a word of English and I wonder if he has any idea where he is.

"I'll happily go for you," I joke. Nelson studies me.

"Why not?" he says unjokily. "Yeah, be me."

"I can't pretend to be you. And I've lost my passport."

"Think about it," continues Nelson. "Know what I want? I want to sleep. I want to stay in bed until lunchtime, maybe some golf in the afternoon. I want to do that for a week. I was even considering having a sickie to get out of Miami. You. You can go out there, stay in a nice hotel, hand out a few cards, have some fun."

"What about the passport?"

"Take mine."

"I don't look like you," I say, but I look at Nelson and I realize while we're not identical twins, we both have shaved heads and porky, defeated features, and whose passport photo looks like them?

The more we chew it over, the sounder it sounds. I use Nelson's passport and credit card and do enough in Miami to create the impression Nelson went.

"So is it cata, pole or blow?" I ask.

"Strictly cata. We don't pole or blow."

Two things will happen to you if you're a salesman, regardless of what you sell. One: you'll end up at a trade fair in some awful German town. Two: you'll end up plying drinkers with drinks. That's the entry level. After that, it's a question of company policy. You can restrict yourself to dishing out catalogues ("cata them up a bit") or you can take prospective clients to pole-dancing clubs ("bird-watching") or if you're in the right city, brothels ("pipe-cleaning"). Selling, sad to say, isn't a sophisticated business. One year my former company hired a string quartet for their stand at the trade fair. They never did it again.

Outside we loiter over goodbye and survey the dingy high street where in the distance a sextet of hooded teenagers lumbers towards us, but then retreats howling about something it deems worth howling about. It's bracing being on the street with an old friend you can count on: a jokefist, Nelson's contribution to any fight would be to drain his assailant's energy by absorbing blows, but he wouldn't run. He'd never run and leave me. He wouldn't like it, but he wouldn't run.

"Look after yourself. And remember," says Nelson in parting, "you can't have the commission."

I go back to my place. It's depressing at the best of times, because a shitty bedsit in a shitty neighbourhood always is. It's always depressing to come back to an empty home. It's not where I want to be. It's not where anyone would want to be.

There's an elderly, prick-puce alky who sits outside all day, clutching a can. He's so purple it defies belief he's alive. The differences between him and me are few (and diminishing). Most importantly, he has the gift of making his money stretch to all-week sipping (I still have a weakness for food). In addition, he's quite happy. Unlike the innumerable winos, junkies and beggars of the neighbourhood who want to be as large as possible in your life, he remains silent and serene. It's extremely annoying. My colour's better, my clothes a little less worn, my day more active, but otherwise I'm his understudy, his successor, as I currently appear to be as employable as His Puceness. Very few things are as destructive as a long dose of unemployment.

I almost didn't call Nelson, because one of the worst aspects of being fucked is having to pretend that you can handle it, because of course you can't. If you have one compartment that's air-tight, you can stay afloat. But when money, marriage, job, home and health go...

I don't give myself airs: I know I don't have a great intellect. I don't know any languages, I don't know the dates of battles or kings and queens. My technical knowledge extends to changing the oil in my car. I can't sing. I can't dance. Eminence at my golf club has eluded me, but... but I always thought I had some smarts, something, a little fox in the box. And of course the question that comes to mind as you return once more to your sweaty mattress in a shitty bedsit, is if you're so clever, how come you've ended up here partnering His Puceness?

I really had no choice about accepting Nelson's suggestion, because I need to do something. If he'd offered me a week cleaning his toilet, I'd have accepted. Doing anything is better than doing nothing. Nelson may have saved my life.

✈

Bulbs belong in the garden. That's what they told me on my first day at work. Lamps. Luminaires. Never bulbs. Otherwise, the secret of selling lighting is rather like sprinting, where a hundredth of a second will win you the medal: just knowing a candle more than the buyer will win you the contract.

I did my job well. Not very well. Not brilliantly, but past okay. You don't grow up wanting to be a lighting salesman, but for fifteen years I visited factories, offices, shops, schools, clambering around taking measurements, and I realized it suited me. Then business boomed enough for the company to need someone else working my territory. I chose the new rep.

Some interviewers relish the process. They get off on the grovelling and pleading. I didn't. I disliked having to interview job-hunters who were mostly decent and desperate for work, because I knew I would disappoint all but one. Clarinda turned up for the interview in a miniskirt so short I couldn't look.

From Singapore, she was the most qualified for the job, she was the most ruthless of the interviewees, and she had a miniskirt. The lighting business is very male, and Clarinda may not have been the only woman in it, but she must have been the most attractive. Then the boom, as booms do, stopped. It's annoying to lose your job because you did your job, and it's annoying to have hired the one who gets your job. Despite my seniority, Clarinda stayed and I went. I don't think the miniskirt was a decisive force – the clincher, I'd hazard, was her living with a lawyer considered the foremost expert on employment law.

Of course losing your job shouldn't total your life, but it did. You remember how the big, shiny, billion-dollar space shuttle disintegrated because of one titchy bit of foam?

I won't bore you with the story. Highlights include disastrous investment, divorce, fire, an embarrassing medical complaint, lawyers, a substantial selection from the bad-luck catalogue. You turn away for a second and that thing you called your life has gone. You probably don't even need to turn away, it could do it right in front of you even as you're fretting over it. And I came away without any funny hard-luck stories. At the very least bad luck should give you some anecdotal might.

There are places that are waiting for you. You may not have learnt this, but there are.

At immigration, I join the queue manned by a scowling official with a feeble moustache who is suffering a rancour overdose. This becomes clear as he fusses over two Venezuelans, an innocuous mother and daughter. He processes so slowly you can't tell he's processing, holding the Venezuelan passports with his fingertips as if they were rotting.

On my right the queue is run by a jolly, white-haired retiree type with a successful moustache who whisks visitors through every two minutes with a grin and a joke.

After ten minutes I know I've got a bad case of wrong queue. On my right, a bespectacled woman who was loudly discussing her Caribbean cruise and who had been six or seven holidaymakers behind me has now reached the fingerprinting pads.

Change queue? But I guess that the Venezuelan crisis has to be coming to an end soon. When after twenty minutes it hasn't, I decide there's no point moving, because it really can't go on much longer; this is a decision I bitterly regret ten minutes later when the Venezuelans are still struggling to maintain their polite smiles.

It's a simple class in human nature. My misfortune has made me a connoisseur of discontent, but I don't need my bitterness skills here; my prospective interrogator has a grievance stoop. Things are not right at home: his boiler has exploded or he's discovered his wife on a bukkake site, and now as an immigration official, he's in an ideal position to make someone pay.

For another twenty minutes I consider changing queue, but I fear the second I'd switch the grinster on my right would stop work and be replaced by another monster of bureaucracy. After an hour in the queue, after a long flight, I'd happily give up and go back if I could transport myself instantly, even though I have nothing to go back to. That's how much fight I have left.

After a long hour and a half, when I reach the desk I'm apprehensive as I hand over Nelson's passport. Up to now my outlaw file only lists cheeky parking and sundry joints; this is a big step up in the imprisonment stakes. But, immediately, I see there won't be a problem. I've memorized Nelson's passport, all his details, rehearsed the cover story, but I'm not asked one question. A profound satisfaction reigns in the official's eyes; he's had his workout with the Venezuelans, and as all his colleagues on duty have processed ten or twenty times more visitors, he's probably concerned about his work rate. I'm nearly outraged.

Miami airport is the standard carpet-n'-plastic anywhere. But once you've picked up your luggage and you get out, it's different.

Suddenly the heat. You're force-fed light. I know about light, and I've never seen light like this. It doesn't even look real, it's so white. As the taxi takes me to the hotel, I realize that this city has been waiting for me, this is the place for me, but I was too stupid to find it. Heavy with light, light-heavy Miami.

My hotel is right on Miami Beach. It's clean and cheerful, although I can see from the neighbouring establishments that it's not the most luxurious, but I'm impersonating a handcuffs salesman, not a rock-n'-roll star. I check in and the speed with which Nelson's credit card is seized by the receptionist assures me everything will work. This is a city where they want to take your money.

Crammed with light, my room is perfect. I inspect the balcony and stand in the sun. It purifies me. I have the same problems as when I left home, but I don't care.

I'm not kidding myself, I really don't care. And not caring about your problems is as good as not having them. The light scrapes out the black encrustations at the back of my skull. It's as if I've died and gone to heaven. In pretending to be Nelson, I've been given a new life.

I order a club sandwich and a coconut milkshake from room service. Having expensive food brought to you at someone else's expense is such a kick. Still bright outside when I've finished eating, I have no temptation to venture out to explore. The unexpected bliss has exhausted me. My room is such a fantastic alternative to my previous existence that I'm quite keen to stay in and enjoy some early unconsciousness. And it is the first decent night's sleep I've had for years. No sweating, no sour dreams, no pre-dawn gut ache: I sleep the sleep of the successful.

In my morning grooming, I surprise myself in the mirror: it's as if Tyndale Corbett has died without leaving a corpse. I'm a different person. What's that line about how travelling won't leave your problems behind? How wrong they are.

Am I nervous about selling something I know nothing about and letting Nelson down? No. Not a bit. I take a healthy appetite to breakfast. The buffet is of that faux-healthy variety (aka cheap). I'm examining with incredulity the minuscule cereal packets and dollhouse bagels when a voice rumbles out:

"They must think we're little tweety birds."

The commentator is so fat he's taking up a whole table. He has a whole tray of some chocolatey sweet, probably tiramisu, in front of him, and when I say tray I do mean tray, as in one of those large objects you see in a display case in a confectioner's. He has worked his way through at least a quarter of it, enough to, say, nauseate the average family. Also, since there's no other tiramisu in sight, it means he's either confiscated the hotel's entire supply or he's brought his own.

"Hey, come on, sell me something or at least gimme a T-shirt. You got extra extra extra extra large?" he urges. I was wearing one of Nelson's company T-shirts. That's how I met Rehab.

I was a little uncomfortable sitting next to him, because I hate chocolate. I can't bear it, the sight or smell of it, but being different in any way puts people off, and though the nakedness of so much chocolate made me queasy, I sat next to Rehab.

Within two minutes of my first day pretending to be a handcuffs salesman I was plugged in.

Rehab was an undercover cop from LA, although how much work he did for his employers was an intriguing topic, since as Rehab was quick to explain he did actually spend a lot of time in rehab. Cocaine was his first addiction, then heroin, then bourbon followed by weed, a habit he only managed to break thanks to crack. His compulsive gambling had lasted for a brief two years, before he had got hooked on tiramisu.

Three hotels had been designated as the "official" hotels of the conference. There were many responsible policefolk at the conference, I'm sure, individuals with so much rectitude that no one in their family had received a parking ticket for a hundred years, but they weren't the ones who were staying in my hotel, having fun with Rehab.

Every business has its wideboys. My business did. Singer, for example, who, sharing a hotel room with a colleague, famously left him dead in his bed for two days because the prospect of the paperwork and the awkward calls were too much ("I was being sympathetic to a bad hangover" was his excuse).

I'd imagine the efficacious cops would be unlikely to be sent to a conference in Miami. Would you want your top thief-taker carousing for days? The good news about Rehab's sidekicks was they were all extremely friendly and open to other cultures (particularly their female representatives). There was bad news.

Normal names were out: Pussyfiller, The Pan, Earmuseum, Unibrow, Clingfilm, Shootastic. This might have been for the same reason that criminals have street names, so no one knows the real one. Many of the nicknames were giveaways however: The Pan had a frying pan fixed on the back of his jacket, and Pussyfiller was mostly interested in that.

The only one of Rehab's circle with a normal name was Larry. Rehab had a massive transparent plastic container next to him, the sort you'd fill up with potato salad for a picnic.

Inside was a large spider. Bigger than my hand. Certainly the largest I've ever seen, and I've been to a zoo or two. The large spiders I saw there, the tarantulas, were immobile and as exciting to watch as a tired pebble. This spider was drumming forcefully on the sides of the container in arachnid fury.

"Yeah, that's right," said Rehab. "You know how they say wild creatures don't want trouble? They'll only attack you if they're threatened? They only want to be left alone? To be wild and do natural shit? Not Larry. He'll attack you because you're... there. And if you're not there... he'll come looking for you."

For the next two days I didn't sleep much. Highlights included heavy cop betting on Larry, as he had a number of fights. Larry vs white mouse. Larry vs rat. Larry vs an especially hefty rat Clingfilm and I spent hours searching for in a drainage ditch. Larry vs boa constrictor (this was much duller than it sounded – the boa was huge, but lifeless, despite encouraging kicks from its owner). Larry vs an insultingly small spider Unibrow found on a plant and bet on simply to annoy Rehab (it was adjudged a draw, although nothing happened and Rehab insisted, "It's too small for Larry to see.") Finally, Larry vs a pitbull called Loco. Larry took out the pitbull with one bite and did a runner, several members of the audience getting above head height in palm trees in their ardour to give Larry plenty of clearance.

Three times a day a delivery van would present Rehab with a tray of tiramisu. The whole time I never saw him eat anything else or drink anything but cognac. I did my stuff for Nelson: I spent the float he'd given me. I gave away his catalogues, although we only went to the conference proper for half an hour because Rehab needed to borrow money. Two Costa Rican prostitutes I found in my bathroom recounted to me something of their country's history, of which I was embarrassingly ignorant (apparently it's one of the few countries that doesn't have an army), before I redirected them to Pussyfiller.

We had a lively session at a shooting range, which had a long list of rules displayed in several places in head-sized letters. There was only one rule we didn't break, but when the owner of the shooting range is your friend who's counting? I shall always remember fondly Shootastic blasting the ash off The Pan's cigar with an armour-piercing round from a hundred feet (admittedly, it was a freakishly long cigar...).

One of the most memorable moments, however, was ostensibly trivial. I was helping Earmuseum and Unibrow carry a sofa out of the lobby of a snazzy hotel – we weren't strictly speaking stealing it, because it was for a bet Earmuseum had made with The Pan. Earmuseum had been scathing about hotel security, and the low calibre of the employees. "Man, we could just walk in there, pick up a sofa, and walk out." He was right. He collected fifty dollars from The Pan and another hundred from the driver of a pickup truck who liked the sofa.

But as we were carrying the sofa out, although the security staff weren't in evidence, I noticed this man looking right at me.

There was something familiar about him. Forties, stocky, shaved head. Actor? Politician? He was dressed Miami-style in a turquoise guayabera, and jewellery peeked from his chest, though I couldn't tell whether the necklaces were some cultural-heritage crap or straight bling. But he looked right at me and he knew what we were doing.

As The Pan collected his money, I couldn't stop thinking about the guy. You grow up in a big city you can recognize someone heavy. A cop? Possibly, although frankly he appeared too intelligent. Much as I had cherished the company of Rehab and the boys, I hadn't undergone any intellectual intimidation. The police force tends not to attract the finest minds because you get paid very little, the worthless spit at you or try to kill you, and unlike the army you're in trouble if you kill them back.

Bullet-headed and dark, I would have pegged him as a Turkish bus driver, Bahamian school football coach or Peruvian bricklayer, but for his presence in a luxury hotel, and the posturese of a summiteer. That aura comes to men when, although they may not have been as successful as they'd like, they've made it to a summit with a good view. High in their habitat. Content to sit back.

You may not be the most renowned gynaecologist, but you have the house, the holiday retreat, the right car, the boat, kids in good schools, money fattening in the bank, so you only work a few days a week: you're a summiteer, you can sit at home and chuckle. Or take an insufficiently auctioned painter, whose work hasn't made it to the biggest galleries, who hasn't conquered the covers of magazines, but has a comfortable slot teaching, and was fêted enough to sleep with dozens of art students. Sitbacker. Sure, we'd all like to go up another rung, to have another helping of chocolate (okay, not me), but the important work has been done.

I wanted to go over and say, "I'm sure I'd be better off knowing you." But you can't do that without looking gay or mentally ill. And I had a full programme with Rehab and gang. But his stare stayed with me.

Adieu time came the next morning. All the cops were leaving, but I got one day extra in Miami, I suppose in case there was any bonus post-conference ingratiation to be done. I pass Nelson's home details to Rehab. He's still a little down about Larry's escape. He takes his special tiramisu spoon and shovels up a mega-mouthful. "Where am I going to find attitude like that?"

We shake hands in the lobby. Enthusiastically, Rehab explains how keen he is to come and visit. I wonder how Nelson would cope with Rehab on his doorstep. I'm tempted to spill the truth, because it's distasteful deceiving, even in a small way, someone you like. Fifteen minutes later, as I exit, Rehab is still in the driveway waiting for a taxi. I think he sees me but pretends he doesn't.

Now, I'm not feeling so great. The solar high and eight-legged excitement of the last few days are fading. The prospect of return is in my face. Apart from some dirty bed linen I really have nothing to return to. The country already has more lighting salesmen than it needs. One of the seventy job applications I've written in the last month might have coughed up a lead, but I doubt it.

I was mulling it over, but I now announce it formally to myself: I'm not going back. If I'm finished, I might as well be finished with a tan.

I have a few friends, but they're like Nelson, weighed down with family and job. They're good for an appearance down the pub twice a year. And I'm not likely to get a job. The unemployed are always suspicious. *Why* are you out of work? The time you'll be offered a job is when you have a job.

Then, although I have some faith in my abilities, companies can give a job to someone fifteen years younger than me who's probably not as good as me, but not much worse and whom they can pay half the salary, and who will work harder than I would. At my age, I should be high up the tree, hanging on grimly and voiding my bowels on those below.

I'm not going back: they'll have to shoot me.

I consider suicide. I haven't thought about it for a while. It's something I used to do for hours, like watching daytime television, or fantasizing about beating Hollis with a choice bit of iron piping. Suicide's chief appeal is that it's easy.

Going through with it isn't. That requires some drive, but the mechanics are simple. Which of the following is easiest? Filling in a ten-page job application form which contains several questions you don't even understand? Moving house? Getting a qualification in computing or engineering? Trawling through the lonely hearts columns hoping for someone with decent conversation? Building up a business in executive toys on your own by working twelve-hour days for six years?

Or swallowing some pills?

Suicide panders to our laziness. And laziness, laziness always wins. Sooner or later. That's the only law.

And why not kill yourself when you're in a good mood? Why go out miserable? Why not quit when you're ahead? The notion of checking out in a good mood in a good hotel suddenly appeals to me.

The main reason I ponder suicide a lot is because I know I won't. I have the problem of being a coward and a weakling.

But I'm not going back: I'd sooner die here than return to the aged urinal that's London. Evidently I've been doing something wrong with my life. It just hasn't worked. There's no unfacting facts. In a modest, scarcely noticeable way, I've tried being sensible and honest. Forget that. I don't know what I'm going to do next, but forget that.

Strolling down Collins Avenue, I abjure reason and jettison honesty. It's fantastic. I resolve to laugh at qualities such as reliability, compassion, punctuality, patience, industry and the truth. I let off a cackle as proof of my determination.

I immediately decide to bribe myself. It's rather pathetic, but since I still control Nelson's credit card, and since my diet before Miami was toast and scrambled eggs, I'm buying myself an obscenely expensive snack, goose liver and caviar with gold flakes, something like that. When in doubt, call in the goose liver and caviar.

I head for the Loews. Everyone should stay in a luxury hotel once. Staying in a luxury hotel removes the hankering to stay in a luxury hotel. It's delightful to sit by the swimming pool with someone world-famous, so you can go on about having sat at the swimming pool with someone world-famous, but you only need to do it once.

Curiously, the thicker the luxury, the snottier the staff are, and unless you own a country or are one of the ten most fame-heavy figures in the world, they won't take you seriously. By some process the staff come to believe they are rich and powerful. The best hotels are the good three stars, spick and span with cheery staff.

As I transect the cavernous lobby I notice a board listing the meetings and events the hotel is hosting. *The American Society of Golf Course Architects* are in town, *The Organization of Competitive Eaters*, some entity called *Whomp-Bomp-A-Loo-Bomp A Womp-Bam-Boom Boom Bam, Baby* and a talk on "Not Being".

The menu is not as extravagant as I was hoping for. No ortolan-and-panda sandwich. I settle for a tuna ceviche, and while I'm waiting for luck and debating which would be the more dishonest, walking off without paying at all or using Nelson's card, I see him.

I see him disappearing into a doorway, with a model-grade woman looping around him like an eager assistant. It's him, the Sofawatcher. In a hotel full of the self-important and wealthy, he's cornered all the gravity. I have to find out more.

Outside the doorway is a sign "Not Being – A Guide to Vajrayana Buddhism with His Holiness, the Lama Lodo". On the stage I can see the Sofawatcher getting ready to talk in the way that talkers getting ready to talk get ready. So, he's a salvation salesman. That's a surprise, but I go in.

You probably have to register or pay some fee for this, but of course, I don't do stuff like that any more. I settle in at the back, and check out the audience.

Two or three students. One little old lady. You could give a talk on any subject, anywhere in the world, anytime, and there'd be one little old lady. The obligatory nutcase is in attendance, twitching away, pulling at his beard. A woman with a humourless stare (and with her face I'd be humourless too) fiddling with a notepad, who's probably the local journalist. A couple of couples who look like concern is their major concern.

Then, more significantly, a group of well-tanned, well-off women in their thirties, say one marriage down, seeking some shoring. One sitting three rows in front of me reaching down into her bag has a section of back exposed: a hard, fat-deprived coccyx with half a Chinese inscription showing. For forty seconds or so, I have an imaginary, largely physical affair with her.

They say marriage is being stuck in a room with someone who irritates you. It's no use trying to avoid that. The best deal is finding someone who doesn't irritate you very much, and who sporadically gives you something in return: money, an amusing comment, support for your exercise regime, a tasty meal. "Are you sure about this?" I'd said to my wife as she walked out. She was.

In the past they understood things better. I remember my grandmother saying, "For years I kept hoping your grandfather would die, but now we need the money." This was when he came out of retirement to ride with a boiler fitter, who was a tremendous boiler fitter, but who couldn't read or write. My grandfather accompanied him to do the paperwork. Customers loved it, since they had the impression they were getting more service with two fitters turning up. My grandmother was of a generation that understood you weren't here to enjoy yourself. You didn't divorce, you hoped for a bus with bad brakes. But she stuck it out and got what she wanted: peace during the day and a few extra quid.

I think my wife was wrong. I think I was right; but I've noticed that being right doesn't do you much good. Being right doesn't improve the quality of your life, any more than wearing yellow socks.

"Move down to the front, please," says the Lama, "It's an ancient Tibetan belief that sitting in the front row is excellent for the karma." The Lama couldn't be more showbiz if he had a backing band, dry ice and laser beams. Within a minute, he owns the audience.

A brief history of Buddhism follows. I know nothing about Buddhism, apart from the involvement of Buddha and head-shaving. The Lama informs us that there are several brands of Buddhism. I'd always thought there was the man, the teachings, you sign here. But no, there are several brands, most of which the Lama disposes of elegantly. Of course as soon as you get the crowd in, the squabbling starts. No business is about business, it's almost entirely about backstabbing. Whether you're selling enlightenment or dog food, the paramount concern is to plant your boot on your colleagues' windpipes.

"What sets us Tibetans apart is our belief in reincarnation lineages and our tradition of termas and tertons," explains the Lama. Tertons, being scripture-drivers who find long-lost or long-hidden scriptures, terma, mind-treasure. I find it hard not to laugh. Not that I've ever paid much attention to religion, but I know from casual television absorption history is cluttered with maniacs brandishing updates and shopping lists from God.

"And as in many other cities, many here in Miami have become ensnared by intoxicants such as alcohol and narcotics," says the Lama with a frown.

"Cocaine: Toot. Nose candy. Blow. The Old Bolivian Marching Powder. Foo Foo. Merca. Mojo. Coca Puffs. Heaven Dust… Green gold… Mujer… Tutti-Frutti… Charlie." He pauses.

"Coke: that tropane alkaloid also known as White Lady… Snow White… El Diablo… Yeyo… Sleigh Ride… Soft… Studio Fuel… California Cornflakes… Vitamin C… Aunt Nora. Bazooka."

Pause.

"Henry VIII… Florida Snow… Inca Message… Cabello. Working Bags. Merck. Dama Blanca. Reindeer Feed. Jolts. Grout." Pause. "Azucar… Freeze… Double Bubble. Devil's Dandruff. Carrie Nation. Coconut. Love Affair. Basuco. El Perico. Scorpion. Zip. King's Habit… Chicken Scratch. Nieve. Esnortiar. Happy Trails." Sniff. "Sugar Boogers. Ghostbusting. Mighty White. Copter. Gift of the Sun God. Rich Man's Speed."

Pause. "And I'm sure you've heard many other names."

I've never understood why heavy drinking or methodically doping yourself is so attractive. Getting wrecked with your pals, once in a while, when you're younger: okay, indeed, hooray. But my indifference to booze and drugs stems from their failure to change anything: your woes wait for you. Finally, frankly, I'm too impoverished to spunk money on intoxicants. When it gets too much, my solution is to be unconscious. Go to sleep, it costs nothing, and when you wake up your luck might have changed.

"You must not think of non-being, because non-being is merely another form of being. You must think of non-non-being," says the Lama with a smile. He gives that digestion time. We're getting deep here if you start thinking about it. What's interesting about religions is that they all view, this, this here ride, as a bit of a nuisance, a dreary obstacle course, a ghastly bit of gum stuck on our soul.

I ponder what sort of non-being Hollis was aiming for when he drank the wine cellar at the club I had invested in. It was the sound of "club owner" that made me invest. It conjures up hedonism and beauties in skimpy clothing, international gangsterism, liberating luridness, everything that is the opposite of being an eker and a disappointment.

I didn't invest very much, because I didn't have very much to invest. I owned one per cent of the equity, so that was the ashtrays and two of the smaller chairs, but it was all the savings I had, and most significantly, I invested against the loudly expressed wishes of my wife.

Investing in a club or a restaurant is notoriously risky, like marriage. In every age, in every land, couples have made a stand against eternity, and individuals have bound themselves together in the hope of profit. I'm still proud of my younger self for having that gush of adventure: as when you're fourteen and you sneak into a club and cross the dance floor to ask the girl with the fabulous breasts for a dance. You're fearless because you don't understand that girls with fabulous breasts not only won't dance with you, they won't talk to you. I didn't understand that I wasn't allowed to invest in clubs.

You see others successfully breeding their money in trout farms, in pomegranate conserves, in revolutionary golf bags, and you say to yourself: I can do that. But you can't.

At first, we liked Hollis a lot.

We liked him because he hired beautiful waitresses. This is the great secret of being the manager of a club: hire beautiful waitresses, because you might get to sleep with them and it'll make you popular with the owners. Beautiful waitresses might also prevent anyone noticing that you spend nights in the wine cellar emptying the most expensive bottles, the venerable burgundies, the thirty-year-old whiskies, the cognacs whose price makes you go whoa. Hollis's drinking didn't destroy the club, but then a small hole in a keel doesn't destroy a yacht either, it's the ocean that does the job. In our case, the banks. Despite Hollis and incompetent accountants (who, like Hollis, had come highly recommended) we were very, very close to making it, but the banks pulled the plug.

Wives are very unundestanding about you losing money they told you you would lose.

Altogether, it was a very dispiriting venture. Apart from the waitresses, all present were rather ugly and unglamorous. The only perk to come out of it is that I'm well prepared for the end of the world. Should our civilization perish, law and order expire, my first act would be to get an iron bar and laughingly beat some bankers to death, and if they're reasonably young and juicy, eat them, even raw if I could still get the right seasoning. I'd also be hunting for Hollis and our accountants. Loader too.

"What about Tibetan divination techniques?" asks the beard-puller, as questions are invited from the audience.

The Lama smiles. He's been here before. He answers with a smile, although I suspect he has little time for the fairground side of Tibetan culture.

"Let me tell you the story of the bear and the weasel's shoulder blades," he says. He elaborates about the dough ball and the butter lamp, while I admire the fine cotton of his pale-blue shirt. Is it some ancient Tibetan shirt? It's certainly expensive.

"And if you're setting out on a journey," continues the Lama, "and you see a funeral procession, that's a bad omen." Is he having a laugh? Finally you never know. A car pulls up, the driver leans out and says to you: "This is your lucky day." He's selling some leather jackets or a hi-fi. You know the goods are murky, but you actually do want a leather jacket or a hi-fi, and the question still remains: is this your lucky day or not? Who will get the best deal? Will you have a hi-fi that self-incinerates in a week or a bargain? And deep in our innards, we reckon we're owed a lucky day or two. We're waiting to hear some good news, and if you're not listening how will you hear?

"What about the Chinese invasion of Tibet?" asks the beard-puller. He fancies himself as a bushwhacker; he's been waiting forty minutes for this. "How come your divination tricks didn't see one billion Chinese coming?" He twitches exponentially in satisfaction.

The Lama smiles. "Our divination tricks did see the Chinese coming. They foresaw it with perfect clarity, far in advance. But when one billion Chinese invade your country, predicting it doesn't help you much." The Lama smiles, but some darkness resides behind it. I can imagine him catching the beard-puller in the car park later on and giving him a thorough Ancient Tibetan kicking.

Books and DVDs are on sale. I have to say I like the Lama. He's a salesman and he shields the nothing well. Also for all the celestiality of his talk, he's a lad. He's a fan of clapping loins. In the Lama's hotel room, the jacuzzi is bubbling, the champagne is chilling, the sports channel is on, and the Ancient Tibetan art of muff-diving is practised.

On my way out, he catches my eye. He nods.

I know now where I've seen the Lama before: in my future.

I review the unfortunate facts that are called my life.

Most people don't understand how easy it is to lose everything. This isn't a criticism, I envy them. Luck. Everything's luck. You can't cross the road without it. You can't get out of bed without it, and if you disagree, just wait. Everything's luck, and if your luck is bad, there's nothing you can do about it.

Nevertheless, self-pity must be the most pointless of the vices. To begin with, at least, most vices are fun, but self-pity does you no good at all, and isn't, as far as I'm concerned, even enjoyable. On the other hand if you don't feel sorry for yourself, who else will?

I'm sitting in Silver Sushi, waiting for my luck to change, eating sushi. Silver Sushi on Washington Avenue is my favourite sushi place in Miami. It's the only sushi place I've been to in Miami, it's the first time I've eaten here, but I've nominated it as my favourite place, because when you live in Miami you have to have a favourite sushi place, and I now live in Miami. They have cool art books lying around that you can flick through while your fish is readied; it's a small, cheap touch, but it makes a difference and I approve.

Chief among the unfortunate facts: lack of ability. I don't have any skills. I'm too old to sell my body, and my mind's pretty bare. I wouldn't even be much good at menial labour (not that there isn't stiff competition from Haitians, Cubans and other boat arrivals on that front).

This may sound obvious, but one of the reasons I was never successful was that I never aimed high enough. I wanted to be successful, who doesn't? But I didn't do anything that might have put me on course for the thick chocolate. I worked hard as a salesman, but with the business I was in, and the commissions I was on, I could have done okay, but there was no chance of summiteering.

I used to say to my customers. "You can have anything you want. Anything. But you have to pay for it."

You can have Cleopatra-shaped luminaires. Rainy-morning-shaped luminaires... Anything is possible technically, but you have to pay extra. Predictably, everyone hugged the rut. Everything was carefully calculated, products priced to be just affordable by the clients, products with just enough commission to make them worth selling. The cheese was no bigger than required by the trap.

My investment in the club was another example of my lack of mission. Even if the club had been a success, I wouldn't have made anything astonishing out of it. Not with one per cent. It would have been pocket money. A good holiday. New suits. No, to make it, you need something that can grow uncontrollably.

You tend to end up where you start. I know of two cases of

honourable travel from nothing to abundance. A young lady who married money, and one of my neighbours who was a composer. He used to force me (and anyone else he could lure into his home) to listen to his symphonies. They weren't the worst things I've ever listened to, but close.

Desperate for money, he composed a jingle for a television quiz which was syndicated all over the world and made outrageous sums of money. He moved into a country mansion, but was more miserable than before since he was celebrated as a jingler, and he eventually topped himself.

I swish a morsel of cuttlefish into some soy sauce, and I choose the religion business.

It's one of the few businesses where not having an ostentatious car or cathedral-like showroom isn't a hindrance, where, in fact, beggary is cool. For a person of holiness, lack of progress up the power tower can be regarded as a triumph.

It's true I know nothing about it. It's true I have little interest in it. But its great appeal is that you're selling nothing, and when you are selling nothing you have no product you have to invest in or to make sure is in working order; joining the God squad is about being convincing when you say "it'll be all right" in reply to the question "do you think it'll be all right?"

Religion never has to deliver, it only has to promise to deliver. Delivery is always round the corner. Down the road apiece. What the Lama was offering was refuelling. He was a refueller, refuelling. It's about being convincing, and I can be that.

In my defence, I was honest and decent. For a long time. I wouldn't dismiss honesty and decency if they gave you a stable income, but they don't. They're why I'm sitting with someone else's credit card in my pocket and a persistent and extremely embarrassing medical condition.

And what's more, I might well be able to deal out some wisdom; it's difficult to set yourself up as a preacher if you're twenty, but at my age I can dish out heartfelt counsel on vicissitudes. And if you'd like some more "non" on your non-non-being, I'm your supplier.

Then I realize I'm doing it again. I'm plotting small, I'm thinking like a drudge. First of all, I'm at a big disadvantage in the God game, compared to say the Lama, who has all that Ancient Tibetan stuff to draw on, and who has been at it for decades. It will take me years to get to the stage where I'll be holding forth in a plush hotel pushing the merchandise, should I manage it at all. And just because you're in a plush hotel pushing merchandise, it doesn't mean lurid take-home pay.

I need to do what a gambler on a bad run is supposed to do. Double up. Lose, then double up. Double up, until you get back to where you started. Except I don't need to double up, I don't even need to quadruple up, I need to do something like centuple up, thrice. I can see everyone laughing at me back home.

When you think they're all laughing at you, you're in serious trouble. Because either it means they are all laughing at you, or you're going mad.

I tweezer my last piece of sushi, and I decide to be God.

Have ambition. Aim high. Cut out the middleman. Don't be holy, be divine. Don't act as a scripture-driver explaining the hard-to-follow manual, give them an evening with the main man. I've pretended to be a handcuffs salesman with great success, why not up the ante? Of course, pretending to be God: tall order, but what a potential pay day. Considering my failure as a human being what do I have to lose by acting worshippable?

Excited by my idea, I return to the counter to order some coconut ice cream to aid me in my plans. The counter is staff-free.

I wait for a few minutes, disappointed by the decline in service in my favourite sushi place.

In the back room I can hear the staff jabbering away in a Miami standoff between Spanglish and Korish. There's something funny about speakers who are keen to argue, but don't have enough of the language to let rip, like watching two fighters ten feet apart trading punches.

I call out a couple of times. The invective hobbles on in the back room. My impatience grows. No one has forced you to open a sushi bar in South Beach, but if you do open one and attract customers inside, you should at least take their order. I was always on call, late at night, in the bath. I always did my job, I humoured the many mentally ill and unpleasant customers I had, and yet I find myself penniless in a sushi bar, with a persistent and embarrassing medical condition, unserved.

But that's going to change. The old Tyndale would have fumed. The new Tyndale overcomes. The new Tyndale is unidirectional. There's a phone by the counter; I reach for my little black book and phone England.

There's only one person I know who could help me with my plans. But one can be enough.

"Hello?" It's Bizzy's distrustful voice.

Bizzy and I go back to the first day of school. Let me tell you about our trajectories.

The last day of school, I went out and spent all my savings on a suit for my first, proper job, in a travel agent's. At weekends I'd worked in a supermarket, stacking shelves. So had Bizzy. But unlike me, Bizzy spent his time stealing or helping his friends steal. I'd always felt grateful to my employers for giving me employment, so I never lifted anything. Thus Bizzy had thrice the cash I had.

He also needed a suit for his first job. He went to the same place as me. As he was twiddling with the suits, someone sidled up to him and asked him which one he liked, then told Bizzy to meet him outside. Bizzy, who had thrice the cash, got a suit twice the price of mine for a third of what I paid.

We lost touch, but eventually I heard Bizzy was running a snooker hall. I went to see him, in a shitty area, where I found the snooker hall dark and locked, although the info on the door said it should have been open. After hammering for a while I managed to raise Bizzy. Bizzy smelt off, the hall was dingy and empty apart from a pair of three-legged, leprous tables and a rusty beer keg.

"Are you renovating?" I asked.

"No," Bizzy replied. I left feeling sorry for him, because it looked as if he had been quarantined from luck. Six years later I heard he had retired from snooker-hall management and had bought a twenty-room mansion in Scotland, with a hundred acres. I wasn't sorry for him then.

Once I visited him. He never left the property and when his wife and two daughters did, they wore body armour and were accompanied by a squat guy with a flattened nose and no conversation. The whole family spent hours at their very own shooting range.

"My old boss had an unusual problem: he found himself with too much cash on his hands," Bizzy had explained to me, cradling the rifle he carried everywhere. He had run a string of snooker halls where no or imperceptibly little snooker was played, but which had been unimprovably profitable. Happiness was universal for six years. Bizzy's only headache was snooker players wanting to get in and interfering with the money-laundering. Happiness was universal for six years. Then it wasn't.

I left not knowing whether to feel sorry for Bizzy or not. But he's the only person I know who was into big-time multinational illegality. And just as I know lighting experts in Ljubljana, Seoul or Buenos Aires, it occurred to me Bizzy might be able to help me out in Miami.

"It's me, Tyndale."

"I don't know any Tyndale," Bizzy replies.

"Yes you do, Bizzy,"

"I'm not Buzzy or whoever it is you're looking for," says Bizzy.

"Yes, Bizzy you are Bizzy. And I'm Tyndale."

"I'm not saying I'm Bizzy, but what proof do I have you're this alleged Tyndale?"

"Bizzy, I'm out in Miami and I need an introduction."

"Unknown stranger who's misdialled, let me tell you, I hardly know anyone in America."

"I need... how shall I put his?... I need someone not too honest."

"Listen, Mr Weirdo, why are you asking me, me of all people, a question like that? How would I, a man with no criminal record, no appearances in court, a man whose tax returns make inspectors weep with joy at their naked probity, why would I know of someone not too honest? I have spent my whole life avoiding anyone even suspected of the teeny-weeniest wrongdoing. I abhor illegality in all its forms and I'm not just saying that because someone might be listening to this conversation—"

"Do you know anyone in Miami or not?"

"Well, lunatic caller whose identity is a complete mystery to me, and whose questions are deeply offensive, I only have one contact there, but he might be what you want."

"What's his name?" I ask, poised with pen and paper.

"Dishonest Dave."

Dishonest Dave's shop is on the quiet, less affluent end of Fifth Street, away from the glitzier blocks of South Beach, flanked by a couple of porn shops and a Haitian restaurant. The shop has a big neon sign in front, "Dishonest Dave's", and underneath it in smaller, but still unmissable lettering, "We fully intend to rip you off."

I wonder how dishonest you can really be if you're warning your customers you aim to gimpli them. Inside the shop, one half is devoted to music in various formats, the other half is a miscellany of furniture and household items, rocking chairs, squirrel cages, microwave ovens.

With a jutting name like Dishonest Dave, I expect the holder to be large in frame, large in manner. But he is average height, wiry, dark, fortyish. He greets me quietly but warmly.

"So you're a friend of Bizzy's? Frank. Ella. Pharoah."

I have no idea what he's talking about. But as always when you don't understand: smile. Sometimes smiling when you don't understand will get you a smack in the mouth, but the odds are with you. Dave shows me around his premises, pausing to assure one elderly woman studying a photocopier that it's "a hundred per cent stolen".

"Business looks good," I say, because you say that even if it isn't.

"I do okay. I'm lucky. I got this place ten years ago. Now, here on the beach, I wouldn't be able to afford the doorknob."

"So the sign works?" I ask, gesturing at the rip-off neon.

"It does. The public notice. Some are infuriated, but mostly, the upfrontness is liked. We're only saying we're a business and we're out to get the best deal for ourselves. Customers appreciate not being clintoned."

"You from Miami?"

"Port-au-Prince. I've lived here for twenty-five years. There are a few who've lived here longer than me, but I've never met anyone from Miami. That's what Miami is, a city you come to, not from. When I arrived here, it was decrepit Jews, some folks from the Midwest who'd got lost, furious Cubans and Haitians with their derrières hanging out of their trousers. Now you can't cross the road for the bankers and galleryistas."

We go into his office, where he offers to make me some coffee. I notice a jug half-full of coffee.

"I'll have that cold."

"Okay. I like it that way too, better than fresh, better dusty a little, fermented a little, yeah." He grins. I've passed some test. He puts his feet up on his desk. "So how heavy are you? You as heavy as Bizzy?"

He's not talking about my body weight. I shrug, which he accepts as an answer. It's amazing that he hasn't clocked me for the failure machine that I have become. It's wonderful to be mistaken for someone; that's one of the worst things about unemployment – the conclusion you're nothing. Probably in the great scheme of things we all are, but you don't want to feel it.

"So what can I do for you? I can get you anything you want in a couple of days. Except a nuclear weapon. There's a waiting list for that."

"There's nothing I need yet. I just came to say hello, but I will need some advice later on."

"Make sure you ask the right question. You heard about the alchemists? They wanted to turn shit into gold. But the real question was not whether you can turn shit into gold, the real question was is it worth the effort of turning shit into gold?

Otherwise, you can have pretty much anything you want... if you're willing to pay for it."

"I've noticed."

I debate how much to tell him. I outline my interest in holiness without giving too much away. In any case how damaging could it be to be denounced as a fraud by someone called Dishonest Dave? Dishonest Dave fixes me up with an acquaintance who has some rooms to rent cheaply, no deposit and no questions. I leave Dishonest Dave's with a Duke Ellington compilation (the music was playing in the background and when I commented favourably on it he insisted on burning one for me) and a punchbag (eighty per cent discount) which he swears will change my life.

A large man is protesting angrily to one of Dishonest Dave's assistants that the toaster he was sold is not as advertised. Wearily, Dishonest Dave wraps a tea towel around his right fist and tests the tension. "It's always the toasters."

I phone Nelson to tell him I'm stealing his credit card and to give me four hours until he reports it. "Okay," he says, "I'll get myself something too. Have a good time, did you?"

"Yes I did."

"You see, no one can be unlucky all the time."

I rush to the nearest most expensive boutique and buy myself a charcoal-grey suit, some shirts and additional underwear. When you have a persistent and embarrassing medical condition and you want to impersonate God you need some sartorial backup. Normally, I have no time for grey, but the cut of the linen suit is so perfect, I can't resist it. It was waiting for me. I put it on straight away and bag my old clothes.

Enjoying a new suit this much makes me a little ashamed, but the suit makes me feel new, heavy and holy. It just does. It is ridiculous that it can give me this much propellant, but it's good that it does: a surge of self, however undeserved, shows that I'm not entirely beaten.

But it is discomforting, the pleasures that stay with you. I don't really enjoy golf any more, and you can't say it's because I'm bad at it, because I was always bad at it, but I used to enjoy it. Your body can cause you a lot of embarrassment, yet it gives you some reliable joys: a good shit, the drawing-out of a constellation of snot from the depths of your nostrils. Ignoble, yet frustratingly pleasurable. I wish strenuous exercise or absorbing some master-piece of art could gratify me as much, but they don't.

Downtown on Flagler, I take out as much cash as I'm per-mitted from an ATM, then, catching my new suited self in reflections whenever I can, I make for a dingy stamp shop and purchase their most expensive stamp, one with Benjamin Franklin. Nelson's card is now litter. I stroll across the street to another dingy stamp shop and sell it for cash that I stuff into my wallet.

The address Dishonest Dave gave me is in Coconut Grove, away from the water, and the house is impressive in scale and style, although major reconstruction is under way.

Sixto, the proprietor, shakes my hand in a formal way. He's short, dressed in a long-sleeve shirt with tie, which in this heat is fairly radical; he has a faint moustache, presumably grown to add gravitas to his face, but failed in its mission. He resembles a fourteen-year-old dragged to a family photo shoot.

The room on offer is huge, but bereft of any furniture; the swimming pool's not bad, the rent is moderate. Cash only. I can't move in for two weeks.

"I'm having some alterations done," says Sixto. "Are you around during the day? You might find it disturbing."

Am I around during the day?

"What is it you do?" Sixto asks as I hear Dishonest Dave's voice saying no deposit, no questions. What is it that I do?

"I... I'm in the illumination business." I say hoping to be convincing. Sixto doesn't laugh or enquire further. I realize he's being polite. He doesn't challenge me on my ludicrous statement. I turn it back.

"And you?"

"Project manager." I'm not tempted to ask more, as I don't really care, and it's always good to save some small talk for emergencies later.

"I'd like to move in now if that's okay."

"I can't get the bed out of storage today."

"No, it's okay. I can sleep on the floor." It takes Sixto a while to grasp I'm serious, and he gives me that look you give people whom you thought were all right but then show signs of worrying weirdness.

We dodge past some workmen to get into the kitchen, where I meet another lodger.

"Hi, I'm Napalm. My girlfriend is a dominatrix," he says.

Let's consider the evidence. First of all Napalm is too old to be calling himself Napalm. He's well into his thirties. Furthermore, I'd wager he's not a musician, tattooist or hired killer, professions where a preposterous name is a plus.

I'll never be the focus of an ad campaign, but Napalm... Napalm is especially unfortunate. I would describe Napalm as a twelve-year-old lesbian. With a beard stolen from a burly fisherman. Not a good start, and Napalm tops it off with a basin haircut, binocular-thick glasses and one of those large-mesh vests popular with very muscular black men that makes his depressingly white skin more depressing. In my entire life, I've only met one other person so far from the accepted standards of allure, and when I described him no one believed me.

Immediately, I want to help. It's so unfair. I want to give Napalm some money for contact lenses or a haircut, some fashion tips, grooming suggestions, but I can already see he's disqualified. You don't want to tournamentize, but Napalm's disqualified.

It's impossible he has a girlfriend. Women can get very desperate, and can be very compassionate too, but this is not on. Even paying for it, Napalm will struggle. He's not even sinisterly or intriguingly ugly. Merely no-use ugly.

"Can I make you a coffee?" Napalm asks. All his top teeth are struggling to form one big tooth, and they are covered in a delicate yellow film.

It gives me a boost. I may have a persistent and embarrassing medical condition, but clothes cover it, and I still have a chance. No matter how unlikely, I'm still in the game.

"I have my own business. My company produces high-end custom-made waterskis for the blingers and the jocks," Napalm explains. "You've probably heard of us."

Love the *us*. Love the *probably heard*. Truth: I have a shed where I fiddle with fibreglass. Napalm selling anything is questionable. No one with a tan, athletic ability, success at any level would tolerate Napalm's presence in the same room. Sixto is shuffling around, anxious that Napalm will scare me away.

"Why isn't the water boiling?" asks Napalm.

"You haven't plugged in the kettle," I point out. Napalm was nowhere in sight when the good stuff was handed out. But he's still game. I admire him for that. He's fighting when there's no hope. That takes uncommon courage.

The coffee, when Napalm has coaxed it into being, is terrible. I don't know what he's done wrong, but it's undrinkable. I long for an opportunity to pour it down the drain but Napalm gives me his full attention.

What galls me most about failure, is the amount of effort I've gone to to achieve it. I was given the manual. I followed the instructions. Shake hands firmly. Look people in the eye. Buy your round of drinks. Help with the washing-up. Tell the truth. Keep an eye on elderly neighbours. Remember birthdays. Be polite. Save your money. Don't drink and drive. Recycle. It's like getting a computer, following all the instructions, but the computer refuses to work. A computer you can at least shake, or kick around. Sadly you can't do that with your existence.

This reflection I banish as weakness. A wobble. Be uni-directional. Towards deification. You're well ahead of Napalm.

"Let me show you round the neighbourhood," proposes Napalm. "Being the boss of the company, I can take time off whenever I want." The old me would have politely agreed.

"Thanks, no. I need an early night."

My room is completely bare and white. There's an agreeable purity to it. A big white womb that will give birth to great things. However, Sixto may have been right about the bed. The floor is concrete and cold. A few blankets won't do. But I want my base. I don't want to waste money on a motel.

I take an unhinged door from the corridor, some empty paint pots and create a makeshift bed. It's much better than it sounds, though I lie awake for hours seeking sleep.

But that's nothing to do with the bed. I often journey through the night awake.

Revenge passes the time. I think about how I paid taxes all my life, how my parents did too. Then when my mother was ill, how nothing happened at the hospital. You pay tax, and you get nothing. No, that's not true, you get shit. I ponder how my bosses didn't like me taking time off to look after my mother. How that helped get me fired.

I think about revenge. Pointless weakness. I strain to submerge the thought. Be unidirectional. But the rage bobs back up time and time again. My guts are fermenting. I fart rage. I can't stop thinking about how I'd like to have half an hour with my former bosses and an iron bar. Revenge colonizes our thoughts. Stories on television, at the cinema, in books, they're usually about revenge. Why so much about revenge? Because in reality it never comes to pass.

I abandon consciousness wondering whom I would track down and kill first if civilization collapsed.

I wake up early, beaten. What am I doing here? Sleeping on a door, far from home, wanting to fool everyone that I'm God.

I pray. I pray because there's nothing else. I don't pray for myself. I pray for everyone. I pray that God will set everything right. Save me, sure, but save everyone else. Why do we have to go through all this? All this... and all this... all this... trampling? Unluckily for me, deep down, I'd like a world with a smattering of justice.

In the bathroom mirror, I inspect my face. To regular observers of Tyndale Corbett there's no doubt he's cracking up. "Portrait of a man about to go pop" could be the caption. I plant myself on the toilet in an attempt to jettison the hopelessness.

Napalm's waiting for me in the kitchen. "How about some coffee? I do great waffles." I have to laugh.

"Thanks. But I have a meeting."

I need to get plotting. A full stomach is the best start to plotting. I get in my car to locate an expensive breakfast. As I hit the ignition, a black youth, stripped to the waist, cycles past, handlebars unused, because he's using his hands to snort something. I admire him because he's having fun. The bike is so shoddy it couldn't get stolen, and his trousers are rags, but he's relaxed. It's all about attitude. It really is. If you don't care, you don't care.

On my way over to Ocean Drive, I again briefly consider suicide, but as I tuck into my eggs benedict in the sun, my spine reforms. I need to draw up a business plan for becoming God. How? How fast? How best? Should I concentrate exclusively on getting divine, or should I make some money? Even with a liberal application of frugality my funds won't last more than a few months.

I have to get on with it.

At the table on my right a very ogleworthy woman gets up. She's mid-thirties, a soupçon of time-inflicted sourness, but still confidently publicizing her breasts. She has the same travails as Napalm: doubt, betrayal, loneliness, dry skin. But she's travelling first class. This is what is so unfair. She may die alone and miserable, but it's unlikely. I've known some beautiful women who were unhappy, some inexplicably unhappy, but I haven't known any who were alone or poor.

Fumbling with her purse, she spills some coins which spiral all over the ground. I retrieve two quarters for her that have rolled to my feet. It's a great opportunity for conversation. We could meet up somewhere for a drink or a meal, get to know each other, hit it off, tumble into bed; but then where would we be?

Without paying, I smile and walk off.

Finding work isn't so easy.

Without a work permit, the choice isn't so great. And even if I can get some fake ID, it always takes time to find a job. But I want to be doing something. I know how easy it is to drown in yourself.

In a T-shirt shop selling rubbish to tourists, I almost get work, but the missing staff member turns up just as the cash register is being explained to me. After two days of tramping around. I find myself in a small shack on an unfashionable section of the beach, selling refreshments.

I open up, feeling good. The weather is overcast and, for Miami, cool. I'm in charge of three tubs of ice cream, some water, coke and some burgers and buns. I have five dollars in change and was left by the owner, a Mr Ansari, to whom I gave a deposit of fifty dollars, with the injunction that if I cheated him he'd find me and kill me.

There aren't many people around. After forty minutes, a stubby woman with a five-year-old child turns up. That I only have three flavours galls her. She's ugly, and I've noticed this with the ugly, because they've had so much shit, they tend to go to one extreme or the other; either they become very jolly, or they don't.

On top of that, there is nothing more ruthless than a mother with a small child. This is a working mother, on her day off, swindled by the weather. Exasperated about the lack of flavours. After consulting her kid, she asks for some pistachio.

I reach for the new tub; opening a new tub is strangely pleasurable. I reach for the scoop, and then encounter a problem. The ice cream is hard, completely immune to the scoop. Even with straight-from-the-freezer tubs I can usually tease off some shavings. But not this pistachio. I don't know what they did with this tub, but it must have been involved in some extreme refrigeration activities for years.

I smile. Always smile. "It's really hard," I say to the mother in the hope that she'll acknowledge my predicament and say "we'll come back in ten minutes". She doesn't. I decide to put the tub on the hotplate for burgers, but either the hotplate doesn't work or I don't have the ability to switch it on. I push the scoop as hard as I can. The scoop gets a slight veneer of grease. I push again until I sweat. Is this stuff really ice cream?

The mother watches me with contempt. This is worse than being shouted at. This isn't my fault, but it might as well be.

"Where's the ice cream?" the kid asks predictably.

"The man's just making it for you," the mother replies. This is what's interesting about kids. They believe. They believe the man's making it. They believe we can fly.

I push the scoop so hard my vision goes, and the scoop buckles. Out of curiosity, I examine the other two tubs. Like rock. I smile at the mother. There we are, attendees at an unfortunateness.

My mishap with the ice cream persuades me not to mess around any more. I need to get on with my mission, and to trust that money will come from somewhere. Unidirectional.

Pondering how to give off hints of divinity, it occurs to me that a house of worship would be rich in believers and where God-grade actions would be appreciated (I'm not wasting my time trying to persuade people who don't even believe in God). I hang out in a few local churches to get a picture of piety in Miami and I can see that the mission won't be at all easy.

If you want something, you can work hard to create or to earn it, to assemble it day by day, week by week, year after year, or you can go out and steal one someone else made.

The big churches are well organized, they have skilled pulpiteers. Like any successful business they are well placed to repel boarders. St Mary's Cathedral puts on a great show, but it would take me years to work my way through the ranks. It's the pyramid scheme all over, you have to pay before you get. And I suspect that the Catholic Church would be rather upset about God turning up and wilting their authority.

The smaller congregations, on the other hand, seem too nutty, too poor to bother hijacking, but are also quite jealously controlled by cult masters.

I spend an afternoon strolling down the Miracle Mile in Coral Gables. No one I talk to knows why it's called the Miracle Mile, but then it's very likely the staff in the shops I browsed in have only been in Miami a month longer than me. The Miracle Mile is a row of glitzy shops, but has nothing out of the ordinary about it. Would it be too corny to simulate a miracle on the Miracle Mile? On the other hand the copy would be prewritten for the journalists. I've got to make my act press-friendly.

Turning off the Miracle Mile, I saunter into Books & Books, which I assume is a bar with an odd name, as a bar is what greets you in the courtyard, until I see they also do books. Are there any short books about becoming God?

As I'm hot and tired, I sit down and order a drink instead. The walking's drained me, and I also spent the morning thrashing the punchbag Dishonest Dave supplied. With Sixto's permission, I fixed a screw into a tree branch in the garden, and hung the punchbag.

I've never had a go at a punchbag, but immediately discovered I had a vocation for violence. I beat that punchbag senseless. Punches, jabs, elbows, roundhouse kicks (in a lame, forty-something way, but it was fantastic). I couldn't believe how much I enjoyed hitting it. I was enjoying it so much I was certain someone would come and stop me.

My vocation for violence is, however, a vocation for violence against the inanimate. I've had two fights in my life. The first was at school when I was six. One kid had swapped my new chair for his crappy chair. I was tugging back my chair, when the teacher spotted us. Instead of stopping us, she said, "Go on then, slug it out." I won and got my chair back, but I wasn't happy. I wasn't happy because I'd discovered I was in a brawn-ruled world.

My beer is served by a tall blonde. Generally, I have no interest in attractive barmaids, because the standard attractive barmaid has no interest in me, and attractive barmaids are constantly accosted by glibber, more appealing or more obsessed customers than me.

The poise of hot barmaids makes them as approachable as a mountain peak. But this barmaid fumbles over every order, which makes her more charming. Her unrevealing attire also suggests she must be some grad student who started on the job fifteen minutes ago. She's friendly and conscientious not because she's being paid to be, but because she is.

Dedication is sexy. I hate laziness and sloppiness. We chat and I get a wobble. Suddenly, I get a burst of loneliness, and my uni goes off in another direction. I want a life with the barmaid, to take some poorly paid job in a warehouse that wouldn't matter because I'd be with her.

"Any chance you're free for dinner?" I ask not with any expectation of success, but because if I don't ask the regret will be a stone in my shoe.

"Hey, if I were single…" she says. I suspect this isn't true, but it's a decent way of saying no. That future has gone to where all the other unused futures go. I'm surprisingly undeflated. The wobble's over. But if you're not too bothered about the no, you're not too bothered about the yes.

I briefly scan the section on religion, but there's no book clearly marked "How to Fool Everyone You Are God" and so I give up.

On the way home, I get lost and hungry. Near the Government Center, I stop at an unfancy Cuban restaurant where the waitress is dejected and the menu is laminated. The whole place is run on an easy-to-wipe-down basis. Even my chair is plastic. I order a pork chop.

The pork chop is simply done, but it's so good, so unimprovable, it's terrifying and unnatural. It's as if I've been waiting twenty years to eat it. The mashed potato it comes with is unfancy as well, but it's the best mashed potato I've ever had. I realize it's one of those useless miracles.

These miracles occur when you get exactly what you want – usually without you knowing what you want. Seeking to repeat the experience, you might enjoy it, but it will never be as good, because perfection is only once, and perfection is even more perfect when it is a surprise.

Across the room at another table, I catch the talk of an old guy, talking to two ugly sisters. Not plain, ugly: they're never going to sneak into beauty for a night out. No nose job, gym membership or implant will make a difference.

They're not at Napalm's level of disassociation, it's not the end of the world. They probably have doting husbands, satisfying jobs, pride-making kids, but no man is heading home to beat off in remembrance of them. Women go on about love, tenderness and how disgusting those pictures are, but most, at heart, like the idea of men oinking for them. And the sisters aren't going to get that. It's unfair, because there's nothing you can do about that; it's not like being poor, or not very smart, or being born in an agricultural region: you can compensate for that.

It's unfair in the born-without-an-arm way, and there's nothing you can do about that. The one-armed, no-legged often say they don't mind, but I don't believe them. I'd be furious. I'm enraged enough about my life as it is. The reincarnation crew say you get a handicap like that because of your actions in a previous life. I have no idea whether that's true, but it's a great explanation. They deserve it. There's reason. That's what scares us more than punishment however harsh, a reasonless blow from the dark. The dicemare.

The old guy with the Ugly Sisters, he's in the God business. I spot the dog collar. Dressed in black, short sleeves. Shrivelled, balding, he is painfully trad, but for the huge dayglo orange crucifix on his chest.

"Do you pray hard here in Coral Gables?" he asks. He's working his audience, working them hard, which means he's not very successful. The Lama had that insouciance of a man with a mile-eating, house-costing sports car revving at the traffic lights, knowing he couldn't be beaten – occasionally challenged, but never beaten. The best salesman doesn't have to pretend he doesn't care: he doesn't.

The Ugly Sisters are getting some pep talk from him. By the time they leave, I've finished my cafecito and I wonder if I should follow him. He has left some pamphlets at the table. You're in trouble when you're leaving pamphlets on easy-to-wipe tables. "Free Health Check on Your Soul" I read. "See Hierophant Gene Graves".

I leave a generous tip, but the waitress is too depressed to care. I always have this strange desire to be friendly to waitresses, receptionists or taxi drivers. I want to say I know you have to deal with oafs all day, but I'm not one. I want to be liked. Why?

Back at Sixto's, Napalm is waiting for me.

"I've got some brochures for the Shark Valley Trail out in the Everglades," he announces, and suggests we go cycling there at the weekend. I'm considering taking up his offer, because I've got nothing planned and because I might as well explore.

Part of me, though I'm ashamed to admit it, would be embarrassed to be seen with Napalm. At school, you'd walk through a burning building to avoid being seen with Napalm. As you get older, you get more relaxed about being around failed individuals who are of a lower value than you, because it's understood that they can't be your friends, they've just drifted into your presence. You never lose that sentiment of caste. We're all at it. The best players at my golf club would barely say hello to me. Why? Because they had no need to. Because there was nothing they could get from me. They talked to good golfers or the powerful. Politeness is what happens when you're figuring out people's value.

I'm in big trouble, but I can't see a way out for Napalm from his life. Maybe I'm wrong. He's maybe five years younger than me, and perhaps by the time he's my age he'll be deliriously happy and successful. Maybe his worldly goods won't be a few clothes and a persistent and embarrassing medical condition.

What can I do for Napalm? As Tyndale: haven't a clue. As God: haven't a clue. Shouldn't I be able to help him? Yes, this should be a simple task, but I haven't a clue. Shouldn't I be thinking about my policies as God? I should have some positions on matters such as Napalm.

The doorbell rings and I find Dishonest Dave outside.

"Thought I'd show you around a bit... show you the sights. Yeah. Hit some clubs." I think about asking Napalm, but because I know he'd say yes, I quietly close the door behind me and tiptoe to Dishonest Dave's car.

We go to the pawnshop, where we're obliged to queue up outside for a few minutes, even though Dishonest Dave is on the guest list and since it's early the club is empty. Two Cuban bouncers are on duty.

"Bishop to Knight Two," says one.

"Bishop to Knight Two? Are you shitting me? You sure?"

"You heard. Asswipe."

"Okay. Pawn Bishop Four then."

"It'll end in tears, maricón. You'll chicken out first. I'm castling and you can eat my fianchetto." They're playing a game of mind chess, which is one way of passing the time, while we all go through the process of letting some minutes elapse so the club's dignity isn't besmirched by simply letting customers in.

I'm touched that Dishonest Dave has taken the trouble to companion me. He's also very generous with the drinks, purchasing three rounds to my one. He talks a lot. He talks animatedly, although what he talks about I can't really say, since the music is very loud and Dave talks very fast and waves his hands a lot. It's hard to act engrossed in something you can't understand, but I smile and nod a lot, hoping he'll dry up so I can just ogle the women and enjoy my drink.

I catch something about black women. "Black women. Black women. They'll do anything for you. That's what you need." Then a little later on, "Electromagnetism – they just don't understand it. They ain't got a clue." Several times I indicate to Dishonest Dave that I'm tired and want to go back home. He hears what I'm saying, but he's not listening; my information is not germane.

Eventually I realize I'm so drunk it's no use in refusing his offers of more drink or fighting to get home. I'm so drunk I could be robbed, stripped naked, cudgelled and left in a ditch, and I wouldn't mind one bit. Dishonest Dave is still holding forth.

At six in the morning when we're the last drinkers thrown out of the club, Dishonest Dave answers his phone and placates his wife. I'm experiencing quite a strong hatred towards him now as it's clear he's been pulling the old "he's a stranger in town, I have to show him round" ploy to flee the coop. It's not about showing me the town, it's about getting off the leash. I've known quite a few husbands like that: who've arranged a business meeting in a bar which will only last fifteen minutes, after which they'll go boozing with friends or romp with their secretary for three hours, so they don't have to lie to their wives about having a meeting.

Dishonest Dave is jigging around as if he's about to go out for the evening. I can't see a taxi anywhere, and I don't have any money left.

"Please. I'm begging you, take me home."

"Not till you've had breakfast. I know a place that serves the best breakfast in Miami."

"Honestly I need to sleep."

"After breakfast. A great breakfast will set you up for a great sleep." We walk a few blocks as Dishonest Dave talks breathlessly about elections in Haiti and by this stage if I had a gun I would have shot myself. Perhaps this is my punishment for not inviting Napalm along, which in a way would be comforting since it would suggest justice is paying close attention to everyday events. But it's funny how it's always punishment and not reward...

A ginger-haired guy sidles up to us and says, "Listen..." I never found out what he intended to say since Dishonest Dave hits him. Or I assume he hit him, since there's a loud cracking sound and our interlocutor is lying on the ground rug-style. Dave's that fast.

Dave bends down and picks up a knife I hadn't noticed, which is lying by the barely conscious mugger. Then Dave reaches inside his jacket and extricates some papers.

"I want you to know," Dave says to the guy, "that I'm not some knucklehead. That's my bank statement. See? You see that? That's my money. All that money is mine. And this," he says unfolding another bit of paper, "is my doctorate in Caribbean studies. You do know what a doctorate is? So, not only can I kick the crap out of you, I'm way way richer and smarter."

"Well, time to go home," I say.

"No," says Dave. "I'm not letting this spoil my breakfast." He makes the guy strip naked and throws his clothes over a wall.

We reach the restaurant as Dishonest Dave complains about being mugged all the time. "I know people who've lived here twenty years, they've never had so much as a harsh word. I get this every other week." I can see why in a way; like most of the very dangerous people I've known, he doesn't look dangerous. Average height, light build, accompanied by a drunk, tubby guy; you can see that it would be tempting.

Dave orders an Ecuadorian omelette for me despite my protests, and then holds forth about *noirisme* and how Papa Doc tried to make himself into a God, something I suppose I should pay attention to, but I can't.

"Power is the drug that destroys the strong," he concludes. "You aren't eating your eggs."

"I'm sorry, I'm really not hungry."

"We're not leaving until you eat your eggs." He's not joking. I push my food around on the plate while Dave lectures on the role of the army in Haiti. "Haiti is the smallest democracy in the world; there's only one voter: the army." I attempt to get the waitress to call for a taxi, but Dave countermands my request by saying something in Spanish which makes the waitress smile. Fortunately Dave goes to the restroom and I swiftly bin the eggs.

"Okay. Home time," I say with relief outside. My vision is fading.

"You look terrible," says Dave. "What you need is a good shave. I bet you've never been shaved, proper old-fashioned, at a barber's."

I look up and down the street, desperate for a taxi. One glides past unavailably with a passenger.

"You promised," I say, fully aware I sound six years old.

"After a good shave. You'll be amazed how good it'll make you feel. I know the best barber in Miami."

Dave's car draws up outside a huge sign that says "WANT A FIGHT?" Am I hallucinating? The last thing I want is a fight.

"How can you call a barber's 'Want a Fight?'"

"This is Miami. You can do anything you want. That's why I wanted to check up on you. Visitors here, they just loco-fy. Hard-working, churchgoing family men, they come here and it's like one of those stop-motion films, you can see them growing horns in front of you. A day or two here and they're holed up in a motel, surrounded by empty bottles, on the phone to Bogotá and moaning some chiquita. We're craziness central. When they flew those planes into the World Trade Center in New York, you know what we were saying down here? We're in on this. Don't know how, but we're in on it. And we were. All craziness checks in to Miami."

We're seated, and as our bristles are removed we watch on the huge screens above us the last round of Tyson vs Holmes. Then at Dave's request they put on the Rumble in the Jungle, Ali vs Foreman. He stares at the screen open-mouthed with such childlike joy that I forget how angry I am with him. There's something enjoyable about watching someone enjoy themselves, but nevertheless because the chair is so comfortable, I fall asleep.

Dave wakes me up. "So how about one for the road?"

The next day I draw up outside the Church of the Heavily Armed Christ, in a run-down sprawl of Miami Beach that isn't yet billionaire-heavy. Three blocks away cranes and new steel are on the skyline, but here there's a burnt-out restaurant opposite, and a string of boarded-up premises that were thriving concerns forty years ago. Finding a parking space is no problem.

Above the doors of the church there's a skilfully painted image of Christ, looking, well, Christ-like, but nursing a rifle with a freakishly large magazine. The church itself is an unimpressive building, a prefab hall, unimaginatively rectangular and dull. A little sooty on the outside, with blotchy paintwork. This is the sort of church that could be hijacked. Own premises, but not too successful. No hardened freeloaders ready to protect the trough.

The door opens. So far, so good. That's as it should be, though as I enter it also strikes me there's nothing worth stealing. Some vased flowers. Two small piles of hymn books. There are five rows of pews, so a maximum congregation of sixty or so.

I make my way to the back, where a door is marked "Hierophant's Office". When you're selling there are basically two tactics: you sell (or appear to sell) cheaply. Generally this is the most winning argument, but the other trick is to insist you have something better, something unique. There's little point in calling yourself Father or Reverend; that's been done. Christ's been depicted with children, puppies, sunbeams, rosebuds, but I haven't spotted him lately toting major firepower.

All morning I'd debated whether I should do more research and plotting, but... laziness always wins. Time for some events. Strong-arm. Strong-arm events. The Hierophant is cleaning a window; he glances quizzically at me. He labels me a tourist in need of directions or some municipal plod in search of a late payment. But I'm not that. I'm the commodity any church desires most. A walk-in.

"I'd like to talk about my soul."

"I'm rather busy at the moment," says the Hierophant.

"But I need to talk. I've done something..." I planned to let the silence do the talking, but the Hierophant jumps in.

"Have you killed someone?" The hopeful way he poses this question makes it evident that the penitent murderer is right at the top of his wish list. I'm annoyed I wasn't ready for this, since conjuring up a non-existent stiff in a far-off country wouldn't be that difficult, but instinctively I opt for the preconsidered story of the abyss tribulating me.

"No." I add, "Not yet." Since that's easy to add. "The abyss is drawing me in." Which isn't a lie.

"What's your name, son?"

"Tyndale."

Up close, the Hierophant is well mad. His glasses are cheap and his remaining hair is regimented not in the lamentable, denial style of older slapheads, but because everything is locked down. The emblem of the Marine Corps is perched on a shelf. He's retained that military spickness. He's a fighter, I'd guess, and as someone who's not... I admire that.

Being a fighter is often not much help. I've noticed that. Mind you, there was Gus, at my golf club. He played every day. Rain, cold didn't matter. The coaches made a fortune out of him. He was obsessed, and made all the effort, but he wasn't any good. He simply wasn't. Even I managed to beat him. His ambition was modest: to play for the club in local competitions. For years and years, he waited. I greatly admired him for not giving up, because it's easy to keep going if you get a whiff of success, but when you're given bitterade year round, that takes stones. Gus did get his moment. The club's team was swallowed up by the ground (new course, old, disrespected mineshaft) and while they ate hospital food, he represented the club. But that's the exception.

"Tyndale, the abyss is drawing us all in. We have to fight every day. Let me tell you about a young man who was standing where you are a few months ago. Dan. Dan was governed by the abyss, by decades of abuse of alcohol and drugs, by violence, by theft, but he got down on his knees and changed that."

Some short-sleeve shirts are hanging in the ajarness of a closet. Even at a distance I can see the shirts are spaced out precisely and they are ironed to perfection. I've got to say, as a slob, I'm impressed by discipline. Before I left for Miami, brushing my teeth was almost a full day's programme.

"Dan got down on his knees and arose a new man. He even had time for reconciliation with his three sons... although the reconciliation wasn't as long-lived as it should have been, because of his fork-lift truck accident the next day."

Is Dan and the fork-lift truck quite the advertisement the Hierophant intends? The Hierophant invites me to sit and I give out a carefully edited list of facts about myself. Mystery enriches. Keep it subcutaneous.

"I was called here," I say.

"We have special soul-clearance techniques here," the Hierophant replies. "Tyndale, we can make sure every chamber of your soul is cleared of malcontent and darkness. We can start right now."

I haven't eaten for two days now. Improbably, I feel great. Of course, there's a huge difference between fasting by choice as I'm doing and, say, not eating because you're stuck in a disaster or because you have no money.

I've been fasting to impress the Hierophant. Yes, I could have pretended to fast, but holiness grows on you. Also, it saves me money, since food is my main expense. And since I came to Miami with something of a gut, I can afford to evade some calories.

I've become the Hierophant's right hand quickly, overnight really. Who wouldn't like an unpaid henchman? I gave him some guff about the abyss and how his pamphlet came into my life at just the right time.

The Hierophant believed me. Why? Because he wanted to. Wouldn't you want someone who agrees with you all the time, who sees how right you are, who does what you want and who doesn't ask for any money? I told him I'm staying with friends and that's stemmed his curiosity about why I don't have a job or money or other calls on my time.

I placed myself at his disposal. I collect dry-cleaning. I climb onto the roof to fix leaks. Everything's going great at the Church of the Heavily Armed Christ (his arsenal includes armour-piercing denial, the Kevlar of service to others and the magnum force of the holy word), although I can't see yet how it will help me, and our average congregation could fit into a car. But it feels right and it's creating radiance: *oh, Tyndale, he always helped others*. Soon my radiance will be noticed.

Curious as to how weak two days' fasting has made me, I seek out the punchbag and take a few swipes at it. I am very weak, physically at least.

Sixto comes out of the house. "Tyndale, you here this afternoon?"

I've got to know my landlord over the last couple of weeks. Sixto may be the only person in Miami who was actually born in Miami. His father fled Cuba after Castro blah, blah, blah. Sixto and his sister spent most weekends stripping guns and cleaning them blindfolded, out in the Everglades. "Man, every fucking weekend it was eating snakes and bugs and blowing stuff up with plastique we made in the bathtub. And my father was always pissed because I couldn't shoot as good as my sister. She could put a standard NATO round through an ace of spades at four hundred yards, day or night."

"What does she do now?"

"Market research for a pet-food company."

For five years Sixto's father stopped talking to him after Sixto refused to play groovy guerrillas in his leisure time. Warmth was only re-established when Sixto took a vow to shoot Castro like a dog if he ever got the chance, and that whatever happened in the future to one day make the journey to Cuba to piss copiously on Castro's grave in the event of his father predeceasing El Beardo.

"I need someone to be here later to take a delivery," Sixto walks towards me and gazes at me oddly.

"Tyndaaaaal," he says. He stops and, as he quivers a step backwards, I identify the odd gaze. I run towards him, but before I get to him, he's folded up on the ground and twitched over into the swimming pool. It's not a big pool, but big enough to drown in if you're having an epileptic fit.

It's really not easy getting him out; if he'd been a bigger man he would have drowned. I put him in the recovery position, while searching for his tongue with my fingers, but so much vomit comes out I can't catch it. It's indisputable however he's alive and breathing properly.

I'm terrified and half drowned, but Sixto, no surprise, is in a much worse state. "It's okay," he whispers, but he's shaking badly.

Later, we drink some Barbancourt Rum. "I should have told you about the fits," he says, "but you know… it's so boring going through all that." I sympathize. I had a girlfriend who had minor fits. It was tedious for her, though I'm ashamed to say I was always hoping she might have a fit during sex, just to see what that would be like. I consider mentioning my persistent and embarrassing medical condition, as a sort of bonding, consolation thing, but only for a second. I've bonded and consoled plenty, and some information is best unaired.

"I'm draining the pool," Sixto says. "It's not as if any of us use it." He now hates the pool, irrational though that is. "I don't suppose I have to tell you I owe you. Gratitude is a big deal for us Cubanos," he says as if he sincerely wishes it wasn't. "You can ask me for anything."

"Don't really need anything. Some part-time work to earn a few bucks would be nice. Could I help out at your company, maybe?"

Sixto groans. "You would ask for that, wouldn't you?"

I tug on a door and it opens. I advance through the darkness, as I can hear music further on. I am now a successful cocaine dealer. I hope.

"There are only two types of dealers," Sixto had told me. "The unsuccessful. They have interesting lives. Shoot people. Get shot. Get arrested. Have girlfriends who snitch. Feature on television. Spend years doing strange things for bigger men in jail. If they survive, they write hilarious memoirs. Then there are successful dealers. If you're a successful dealer, your day is more boring than a postman's or a pizza delivery boy's. Postmen get bitten by dogs, pizza guys get ripped off."

Sixto isn't being entirely reckless or generous about letting me in.

I know nothing.

I know nothing about who he works for. I know nothing about where it comes from. My job is simply to take packages to certain people and bring back the cash. Very often I don't even get cash. Basically, Sixto has given me the most tedious part of his job. True, it's a risk on his part, but since, as he confided in me, he is training to be a psychotherapist, he doesn't have as much time to drive around town making the drops.

And he's right. It is like returning a book to the library. Sixto only does business with old acquaintances and in bulk. I make brick-sized drops. Like this one.

"It's a club," says Sixto. "It's one of these so-trendy-we-don't-bother-telling-you-about-it places, but if you can find the door we might let you in." Finding the door wasn't easy, because the door didn't have a number next to it, nor was the name *Three Writers Losing Money* anywhere in sight.

I enter a huge dance floor with a bar at the end. This must either be the club or the local circus.

Behind the bar is, I assume, the barman. The barman, in addition to a generous scattering of tattoos, has a variety of metal stalagmites and stalactites fixed on his face – but that we've all seen before. He's shaved his head and fixed onto it a number of thin, bright-blue rubber strips. It gives the effect of a blue dreadlock wig, but a very badly made one. It's as if he cut the strips himself, but got bored with it after a while, and gave up on uniformity; some strips are hairs, some finger-thick, some long and some short.

It might have worked in an haute-couture way, but for the fact he's a twenty-year-old twat with acne. Next to him is the DJ nest, and behind the decks I see a monkey. It's a small monkey, but I note the monkey has a gun.

It looks like a real derringer and the monkey carries it in a spangly holster. The monkey is changing discs with practised ease. Two hefty guys on the other side of the counter are watching the monkey in a tense, hostile way one wouldn't associate with monkey-watching, which is meant to be entertaining.

"Does the monkey have a licence for the gun?" I ask sunnily.

"It's a monkey, it doesn't need a fucking licence," replies the barman in a tone they didn't teach him in bartending school. "And who are you?"

"I've come to see Bertrand."

"Is he expecting you?"

It's very tempting to be sarcastic, or indeed violent. Fasting gets you high as the buzzards, but it does make you bad-tempered. I could take the barman easily, but the other two are very hefty. And it wouldn't be very radiant. I suppose it's a repetitive-strain injury from years of visiting strange workplaces. I always had an appointment. Shall we think about this? If you want a favour from someone is it a good idea or a bad idea to turn up unannounced? And what's amusing is that while many of the clients I dealt with were self-important dullards, the receptionists were always the worst.

Now, I'm doing Bertrand a favour. I have enough poisonous alkaloid with me to keep the whole club's gums numb.

"Yes," I say. "I am expected." And I remember to smile. Always smile.

Bertrand's office is up on the second floor. He's on the phone when I enter, and as there's no one else around, I flash him the brick. He waves me in.

"It's a simple question," he rambles on. "It's a simple question. *It is* a simple question. So why didn't they ask me? Why didn't they ask me? Wh-y? Wh-y? All they had to do was ask. They ask me the question, I give them the answer. That's not difficult is it? So, why, wh-y didn't they ask me the question?"

I peer out the window and scrutinize Miami. I see the light and the roofs. I love this city. I look out for several minutes as Bertrand gases away, and soon, much as I love looking out on Miami, I have to work hard to look as if I'm really keen on looking out of the window and not very impatient.

"Okay, Opium Garden is big, it's what's you or I would call

big, but it's not right to say that it's really big. It appears bigger than it is, because of the way it's divided up. But if you count up all the bars in Mynt, it's bigger than Opium Garden. It doesn't look bigger, but it's bigger. Now, no... no, no, I'm not saying it's a lot bigger than Opium Garden, but it is bigger. No, no, no. Let's take Crobar. Crobar is actually the same size as Opium Garden. Yes it is, if, if you take into account all the stairs—"

I make some I'd-urgently-like-to-hand-over-the-brick gestures, but Bertrand retorts with some wait-wait flapping.

I stare out of the window pretending I'm savouring the view and not fuming. I think of my old boss, Bamford, and three years on, I understand why Loader asked for his telephone number.

There are events and conversations which sometimes take me a year, five years, ten years, twenty years to unlock. I don't know why, but suddenly the answer tumbles out.

Bamford was a no-nonsense man. When his wife went mad – not a little peculiar, but dead-end insane – he had a week off work (and he took it as leave). One week off. He had his wife certified, found boarding schools for his kids, and never said one word about it. I've always admired those who could eat their greens without a murmur, because I can't.

The highest compliment from Bamford would be to call you a cunt, as in "I can't believe you made that sale, you cunt". That was if he liked you. If he didn't like you he wouldn't talk to you. Yes, he was from Yorkshire. On the other hand, if he was wrong, you could simply tell him to fuck off. His was a style of management almost extinct even then. Almost everyone liked Bamford, he was how you wanted God to be really – hard but fair.

Bamford's retirement lunch was one of the first times I had doubts about the whole running of the universe. What happens when you've worked at a company for thirty years, when you've essentially built the company? You get a retirement lunch and a farewell present. The retirement lunch was faultless, everyone turned up, colleagues who loathed each other were cordiality itself, the food was great. He got an expensive dust-gatherer to put on his mantelpiece. Loader, the new boss, shook hands with Bamford, and told him, "We must do lunch."

Normally when someone says to you "We must have lunch" or "We must have a drink" it means precisely the opposite. If you want a lunch or a drink why not arrange it, why shove it off into the future? It's like someone calling you "my friend". It's precisely people who aren't your friend who will call you "my friend", individuals who are either ripping you off or about to rip you off or kill you. "My friend, you have nothing to worry about" is a phrase that should make you run as fast as possible.

What frightened me most, however, was, the second, the very second Bamford walked out of the restaurant, he was gone. Everyone rushed off to further their interests, and he was nothing. Finally, we all are a dense nothing, but it's not nice to be reminded. It was a dress rehearsal for death.

Bizarrely, despite the "we must have lunch" brush-off, Loader did invite Bamford for lunch the following month.

Everyone in the company had heard how Loader had once ended up in court on charges of theft, as a large amount of company gear had been found in his flat. The favourable interpretation of these facts was that the stolen stuff had been in the room of his lodger, who also worked for the company. Bamford went to court to testify on Loader's behalf, though there was debate as to whether this was because he believed Loader innocent or whether he couldn't stomach losing his best salesman.

The day of the lunch, I saw Bamford waiting in reception and said hello. It occurred to me I should mention I had seen Loader go out minutes earlier, but concluded it was none of my business, and I assumed Loader would be coming back. The new receptionist also thought about that, but she had been strictly briefed never to give away the movements of company personnel, so she couldn't tell Bamford that not only was Loader out having lunch but so was Loader's secretary – so no one could explain to Bamford he had been forgotten.

Bamford sat there for an hour, because he didn't give up easily. So everybody in the company filed past and witnessed his stranding. The lunch never took place. Ironically, I was more upset by Loader's behaviour than Bamford was. Loader had quite liked Bamford (just because you're a sack of shit doesn't mean you don't have emotions) and he forgot him not because he wanted to forget him, but because he had no need to remember him. Bamford had attained the invisibility of those unable to dispense benefits.

A year or so after, Bamford's name came up, and Loader said to me: "We must have that lunch. What's his number?" I was confused. Everyone knew Bamford's number. He had lived in the same house for forty years.

It's only now I grasp that Loader had to believe that there was some difficulty with Bamford's number: that was the only scenario that would permit him not to see himself as a shit. Loader is close to the top of my list in case civilization falls apart.

I check my watch. I've been in Bertrand's office for forty minutes now.

"Okay, okay. The ceiling is higher. The ceiling in Mynt is higher, but that doesn't do you a lot of good, now does it? No, if you take out all the furniture…"

My job is to hand over the package, but Bertrand is pushing his luck. I'm not interested in being nothing. If Bertrand had just once uttered "sorry" or "hang on" it would have been different. I take a piss on one of Bertrand's pot plants, because I need one, and perhaps this will get his attention. It doesn't. I stroll out in case that gets his attention. It doesn't.

Downstairs the barman is now yelling at the two chumps. "Yeah, I have to feed the monkey, but the monkey does the job."

"We did the job," responds a chump.

"We had fifteen people in here last week," shouts the barman. "Fifteen. And ten of them were my friends."

"You can't fire us," says the other chump. "You didn't pay us, so you can't fire us."

"You're right. I'm not firing you. What I'm doing is giving somebody else the opportunity of using your turntable skills."

"The monkey can't do the job."

"It's true it took him two hours to learn how to use the decks, but I'm willing to nurture his skills…"

The monkey yawns. It opens a large, leather-bound book which has a biblical appearance. It skilfully rips out a thin page, which it then begins dexterously to roll into a joint with weed taken from a pouch. It lights up and puffs mellowly. I suppose anti-marijuana legislation doesn't apply to monkeys either.

I've seen enough. I exit, and as I'm basking in the sun wondering where to go for an expensive sandwich I have no intention of paying for, the two chumps storm out, and attempt to slam the door, which they can't, since it has one of those slow-close mechanisms. They charge up to me. I feel fear. Am I going to be mugged?

"He's fired us," says one to me. Does he think he knows me? That's the price you pay for usual features. The two of them are wearing white T-shirts with a picture of grapes. My interlocutor has large sideburns: one is dyed purple, the other is dyed yellow.

"He's replaced us with a monkey," says the other one. "A monkey called Stinky." If I had been fired and replaced with a monkey, particularly a monkey called Stinky, I don't think I would go round telling the world.

"It's not about the strippers. No one comes for the strippers. They come for the music. Without the music, man, the strippers are nothing. What does a monkey know about music?"

"Yeah," I say sympathetically, trying to load the word with all the things they want to hear. The two guys are twenty, beefy, and they're standing very close to me in a blocking sort of way. Is this a preamble to a beatingful robbery?

"You're Bertrand's dealer, aren't you?"

"No," I say, surprising myself by how convincing I sound. Denial, outrage, surprise, a hint of menace – all present.

"I knew it," says the other one. "I knew you were."

"You've got heavy connections, right?"

"No."

"Oh, man. Which cartel do you work for?"

"I don't work for anyone."

"We want to work with serious people."

"We want to work with serious people, not monkeys," says the other.

The one with technicolour sideburns reaches into his pocket. I'm alarmed for a second, but the trousers are too tight to conceal a weapon. "I'm Gamay," he says. "This is Muscat." He hands me a crumpled card with the inscription "DJ Gamay and DJ Muscat – Rhythm Gods".

"Hey," says the other one, handing me another card with

an identical layout that reads "DJ Muscat and DJ Gamay – Rhythm Gods".

It's taken me a while, but I grasp that they are that stupid. It's partly youth, but mostly stupidity. Of course, I've never regarded DJing as a job. Where's the skill or enterprise? You buy a record, which in most parts of the world rarely involves a journey of more than a few miles or the investment of an hour. You play the record on a turntable. Indisputably, some technical ability is needed: plugging the turntable into a power source, but frankly, Stinky rests my case.

"Give us a chance," says Gamay.

"Guys, I work at a local church."

"Give us a chance," says Muscat, going down on his knees. "Phone us anytime. We need to be big-time. We need to be nationwide. "

"Thank you. If I need any DJing I'll call you first," I say. I drive off. Now I'm worrying about Bertrand. Will my walking out cause serious repercussions? Will there be bloodshed?

By the time I get back to Sixto's I'm sweating about my decision. I know nothing about the practice of this profession. Sixto is in charge of everything in Miami. The house itself is a money-laundering exercise for his bosses. Buy ruined house, spend fortune doing it up, sell it for bigger fortune, claim decoration skills, all legal. Sixto's renting out rooms to earn some pocket money for himself. But just because I've saved his life doesn't mean he'll let me do anything I please; however, when I tell Sixto what happened (omitting the pot plant) he says: "Bertrand's fantastically irritating. We can live without him. You should have walked out straight away."

Doubtless my being asked to come along is a mark of approval, an acknowledgement that an apprenticeship has begun. Hierophant Graves drives us out to Opa-Locka to visit a family who aren't members of his congregation, but former neighbours of his former neighbours, who are in need of tribulation-easing. I contemplate the rosary that Hierophant has had fitted on his dashboard so he can knock off a couple of prayers when he's stuck in traffic. That's religion, there's really a lot of praying. They have lots of differences, but I can't think of one that doesn't go in for prayer. Right rite. Rite right.

I've become a fan of the Hierophant's grit. He's an also-ran. Granted, so am I, but he's taken thirty years to build up a church with an average congregation of twenty, he's not very smart, and I can't see him upping his game.

The Hierophant talks of the end of time and nuns' arses. He's of a generation for whom humour means nuns and farmers' daughters. But there comes the point where you have to stop talking of the end of time and nuns' arses and get out of the car and deal with a dying child.

We're here to tackle the big one. The mollification of the really unjustifiable. I'm sure this former Marine's sergeant would be proud of the way he hits the beaches of suffering, rushing straight for the hardest section.

The Locketts are a young couple. Balvin is an unemployed jai-alai player and his wife, Nina wants to give up her job as a food-standards inspector to look after their three-year-old daughter, Esther, who has leukaemia and, they say, a few months to live.

There is of course, nothing the Hierophant or I can do to alter the injustice of their daughter dying, but he is good. As I listen to him pastor, I grow more confident and optimistic. Our ears tend to be more open to sentences we want to hear, and there is something soothing about someone telling us again and again, with confidence, that it may be all right.

The one problem with turning cynical and dishonest is that you can never succeed completely. I dislike children. I dislike children because they're typically noisy and smelly; you have to spend your whole time escorting food in and out of their bodies, but you're expected to be charmed by them.

The problem with Esther is that she is completely charming. She sits quietly on her own, playing with some strange counters on a board, smiling, looking perfectly healthy and happy. Why are we all equipped with such honest joy at the start? It's so radiant even I am momentarily invigorated by it, before knowledge of her illness defoliates me. I believe I would give her my life if I could (or at least I feel as if I would, who knows? I'd probably chicken out at the last moment if it could actually be arranged), mostly because I don't have much left anyway, and because she is bright and good-natured and won't mess up like the Hierophant or me.

We leave. I'm weighed down by how astonishingly hard life is, and my opinion of the Hierophant is considerably raised. It's easy to talk about benevolence when the sun is shining and bank accounts are full, not so easy when the torture's going on. He may have done some good, and if he didn't, he was trying. There is a season for bullshitters.

On our way back, the Hierophant suggests we do some shopping. We stop off at Publix. It's important to keep your shopping holy at all times, because you never know who might snoop into your basket. The Hierophant is doing the weekly shop and his trolley is heaped with spare rib, but I have only a loaf of bread and some price-reduced papaya in my basket. Like everything else, if you make frugality a habit it's quite easy, and it makes the splurges all the more enjoyable.

As we join the queue for the checkout, four aisles over, I spot the Krishna. A group of four. I don't think I've ever seen a devotee solo. Probably they need one person who knows the way to the supermarket, one person who knows the way back from the supermarket, one to steer the trolley and one to deal with the cashier.

"Don't look," the Hierophant whispers to me. "Act natural."

As our items are processed I wonder what acting natural in my case would involve? Act like an unemployed lighting salesman? Act like an unemployed lighting salesman acting like he's God?

Outside, we load our goods into the car, but the Hierophant doesn't start the car up. He smears some dirt on the number plates. He ushers me into the driver's seat and then surveys the exit. He fiddles in the glove compartment and produces a Miami Heat cap and a pair of sunglasses which he dons; he fiddles some more and finds another one for me, and produces a pistol.

"Tyndale, I can't see any cameras out here, can you?" I look around. If we're on camera, I certainly can't spot it. "Drive as I tell you," he says ominously.

The Hare Krishna appear and load up their people carrier. The Hierophant cocks the pistol and says, "The .22 is a weapon that is appropriate for a holy man."

I'm shitting myself. I've already been courting decades in maximum security and if I end up behind bars I want it to be my fault and not someone else's. We trail the Krishna and then the Hierophant leans out and fires three rounds through the length of their people carrier, rounds, I assume, designed to shatter the glass rear and front, to terrify rather than injure. We speed off in the opposite direction.

"I can't help myself," says the Hierophant. "You know how at school there's always a kid that everyone beats on, and you feel sorry for the kid. And then there's another type of kid at school everyone beats on, and you just want to get your licks in too."

As far as I'm concerned (as long as I'm not jailed) the Hierophant could take a chainsaw to them, because I'm humouring the Hierophant, because I'm not hugely bothered by anything much these days and because I still have vivid memories of being overcharged for a dismal carrot salad at a Krishna restaurant.

"This poor sinner believes the Hierophant is right."

Back at the church we prepare some turkey subs. We're going to distribute some eats to the needy. "We don't want to get there too early," the Hierophant explains. "Hector takes care of people at 6.12."

We arrive where the homeless congregate, round the back of the Omni, about twenty past six. Two guys are munching some enormous empanadas, which even from afar give off an irresistible meaty aroma. Half a dozen trolley-pushers gaze at them wistfully. "So where's this Hector?" I ask.

"He was here at 6.12," says the Hierophant. "He could feed a thousand people if they turned up at 6.12. You can have almost anything you want. One time he even had caviar and freshly buttered toast. But woe betide those who come at 6.16. Some say he hates handing out food and some say he hates the unpunctual."

Hector had been in the open sea for two weeks on a raft from Cuba that had gone badly off course. He had been moments from death when he made a deal with the Santeria divinities: save me, and every day for the rest of my life I'll feed anyone who needs it. He was picked up by a fishing boat at 6.12 p.m. within a minute of making his pact.

"He kept his vow," says the Hierophant. "But you have to with the Santeria divinities. They won't take any shit. I don't even believe in them, and they scare me. So Hector gives generously every day, though of course some also say that, while he gives generously every day, he never promised exactly how long he'd be generous for every day."

I've been with the Hierophant now for over a month and I have to say I don't really understand what his church is about, or rather how it differs from the mainstream churches, apart from the fact that it's his church. He's had a new leaflet printed with the catchy strapline "Affordable paradise: what are you waiting for?" I suggested handing out some of the leaflets along with the food, but the Hierophant wouldn't let me.

"That's cheating," he said. "They know who I am if they want to find out more."

The turkey subs are welcomed. The easiest way to spot the homeless or mad in Miami is to keep an eye out for winter clothing; those boys love to overdress (and it is mostly men, another testament to womankind). There are some old guys who badly need the food, some younger guys newer to destitution who are cooler about it; but it's pleasant to do something helpful.

"Nice shoes," says a simple-looking guy to me. My shoes aren't especially fine, but you forget that you can sink to the point where an unruined set of footwear looks good.

A very tall black man comes up to me. I immediately christen him the Prophet. He's wearing a headdress and carrying a magnificent walking stick, made out of some dark, gnarled wood. His clothes are ripped up so regularly you'd say some garment-grater had been at work. Sunglasses, and his most distinctive feature, a gas mask, hide his face. I doubt this is to protect himself from his stench, which pokes me in the eyes, since one of the great mercies of existence is that you're immune to your own fug. I'd say the gas mask comes under the heading of inappropriate concern; when you have no job, no money, no home and only an approximation of clothing, car fumes shouldn't worry you.

He is incredibly straight-backed though, which makes me push my shoulders back. The years accumulate a stoop on us. I pass him a turkey sub. He stares at this, perplexed, as if I'd given him a clockwork rabbit.

The turkey sub is very simple – turkey, lettuce, tomato, butter – but quite good if I say so myself. A white guy with an afro who's sporting a black overcoat (although he's naked underneath) asks me what it is.

"Turkey," I respond.

"I want ham," he says. I wonder if Christ had this problem with the fishes and loaves, the crowd at the back asking for cheese or spare rib.

There is a part of me that yearns to say, in the style of my erstwhile employer Mr Ansari, "Take the turkey or I'll kill you." But I can't do that. I hand him another turkey sub, which is wrapped up so tight you can't see the turkey. "There you go," I say. He walks off without opening it. Tell the hearers what they want to hear. It may not work for long, but it does work.

Only one of the recipients expresses thanks. "Great sub," he says. Young guy, doesn't look homeless, he looks more like a student who's stayed out late. "Hey Fash," shouts the shoe-admirer, "let's go. Let's go."

I'm surprised to see Dishonest Dave approaching us, and he's a little surprised to see me.

"He's not here," says the Hierophant to Dave. As I suspected, Dishonest Dave is one of those people who knows everyone.

I sense from Dishonest Dave's posturese he doesn't want to talk about why he's here. So I don't.

"How are you?"

"Doing good. All going to plan?"

"Fine," I say. The Hierophant has ambled off to issue the last subs. "There's one thing I wanted to ask you. Do you know any corrupt doctors?" I'm confident Dishonest Dave will have a couple on the books.

"No." He says. He then says nothing more. I feel he has said this too quickly. I want at least to hear something like, "Let me have a think…" or "Maybe…".

"You don't know any corrupt doctors?" In one way, you sound stupid asking the same question again, once it's been unequivocally answered, but I have found that asking the same question three or four times on occasion can get you closer to the answer you want.

"No," says Dishonest Dave, torpedoing my first attempt at a miracle. "Let's go for a drink some time."

Developing my deification has to be my top priority now. I've established myself as a mysterious, austere figure, who doesn't drink, smoke, shoot up, chase women or boys; who hardly eats (in witness-heavy circumstances). Calm, patient, willing to clean windows and to hand out leaflets. A great sitter in church. Wholly holy.

God-grade worship starts with miracles. A few discreet, not too publicized miracles would get me going.

Curing the sick is a standard one. Curing Esther would be great, but for the problem I can't do it, and even I wouldn't want to engender any false hope. Curing the sick is in fact a very tough one. You see cripples bounding out of their wheelchairs or tumour sufferers boasting of remission, and a part of me thinks, well, I could be wheeled into a mass and then jump up, and as for the genuinely sick getting better, they do that all the time, despite the doctors (although not, apparently, if you have a persistent and extremely embarrassing condition like mine).

But healing is a real crowd-pleaser.

The easiest way to get rid of an illness, is to get rid of one that isn't there. What I need is a sufferer, what I need rather than a straight fake who might flake, is someone upright, someone for whom the tumour is real and who will then love the cure.

Persuading someone they're terminally ill is cruel and largely unforgivable, but not if you do it to a banker or a lawyer. What I need is a morally depleted doctor who, when some unsuspecting banker or patient he hates comes in with a sniffle or rash, persuades him (and it will have to be him – no women, no kids) to take some tests. The test results are tweaked to be disastrous; more tests are done with equally doom-laden results. Then in steps a mysterious, austere figure recommended by the doctor as a spiritual counsellor. Hey presto. I must talk to Dishonest Dave again about his medical acquaintances.

I go downstairs where two attractive girls are mopping the floor. They are wearing skimpy bikini bottoms, and nothing else. It's the scenario that you long for when you're sixteen but you've given up on by the time you're forty-something, because you know it'll never happen, and even if it did you wouldn't be able to do much about it.

"Are you the holy guy?" one asks.

It's working. I'm pleased that I'm radiating, but I'm blowing it by gawping at their breasts. However, they are unembarrassable.

"Sixto told us about you," says the other. Bearing in mind the work I carry out for Sixto, I fear he's having a laugh. "Do you really sleep on a door? I'm Trixi and this is Patti."

In order to preserve my holiness, I retreat back to my room. Later, when I've heard them leave, I return to the kitchen to fix a snack.

"Sixto, I've just met your cleaners," I say when he appears.

"Yeah, I'm furious about that."

"Why?"

"I told Patti she could clean up. I didn't ask her to bring a friend." Patti, Sixto elaborates, is the younger sister of his girlfriend, who had been hassling him month after month for some blow. Sixto judged it immoral to sell cocaine to his girlfriend's younger sister. He judged it immoral to comp her even one line. But because she was so relentless, he agreed to let her earn some by doing housework.

"To instil the work ethic, you know?" Sixto had been taken aback when Patti had shown up with Trixi. He had also been taken aback when they stripped to keep their clothes clean. "Man, I told them to put their clothes back on. I fucking begged them. But no, they were too worried about their clothes getting grungy. And you just don't have any authority when you're talking to fifteen-year-old breasts."

"Fifteen?"

Sixto inspects the ground. "Why did I do her a favour? Why did I want to help her out?"

I have visions of twenty topless fifteen-year-olds fighting over the right to clean the hob for a toot. The whole school rolling up.

It's hard to be bitterly disappointed when you're forty-something, because you have basically given up. But I do have that one-step-forwards, ten-steps-backwards sensation. I can't conceive of any anger-diverting way of Sixto explaining to his girlfriend how her younger sister scouring his surfaces, coked-up and naked (and that's how it will be in his girlfriend's mind, it won't be any use him highlighting the bikini bottoms as mitigation) was originally a disciplinary measure. We're down for one of those five-hundred-year sentences in maximum security. This is what happens when you do favours.

Driving over to join the Hierophant, I consider how all these white-powder escapades could put an uncorrectable dent into my plans. I can't believe we haven't been arrested yet. It's Friday afternoon. The cops will probably wait till Monday morning. What can I do about it? Nothing.

I meet the Hierophant at the public swimming pool. The Hierophant did three tours of Vietnam (they wouldn't let you do any more) and gets some military pension, so he could be taking it easy in a trailer somewhere less chic in Florida, hooking marlin and so on, but he ploughs most of his money into the church and has this part-time job at the pool working the ticket desk. His energy is remarkable, especially since I doubt the job pays enough to buy a newspaper.

Three rotund middle-aged ladies buy tickets. "Where are you from?" asks the Hierophant, because, naturally, they won't be from Miami. "Toledo," says one.

"Do you pray hard in Toledo?"

The Hierophant is wearing a T-shirt with the inscription "Work Harder – Millions of People on Welfare Are Depending on You" and a baseball cap. Some wear a baseball cap because of fashion or because it is the badge of a certain group. The Hierophant wears it because it's cheap, useful headgear.

A woman comes up, carrying one kid, with four others, two very young, in tow. She's horribly poor. She has to spend the whole day counting her money and recalculating her purchasing possibilities.

"Hi," she says. "Do you have a family rate?" Of course, there isn't one. The misery is caked on her. Her husband died somewhere struggling to make money in some foreign shithole, no insurance, leaving her with the creases of widowhood. They've driven for days to have a holiday, to stay on someone's floor. That's why there's so much stuff about being kind to widows and orphans in scripture, because it's so fucking awful. You get a taste of how hard life can be, and you also know that an insight like that is of no benefit, it's like stepping into a squishy turd. You just want to wipe it off.

The Hierophant lets them in for the price of two kids. I'm proud of him. No one has been done out of anything. It was a little wink of decency.

"Everyone has a breaking point," says the Hierophant, "and everyone's wrong about where it is."

This is what's funny; the characters who go on about caring for others are nearly always the most selfish. I had some dealings with the union reps at work and they were all, almost without exception, the most greedy, self-centred and vile types you were ever likely to come across. You should see their expenses. Beware talk of brotherhood and justice. Whereas those, like the Hierophant who trumpet the stand-on-your-own-two-feet creed are the most likely to give you a hand…

I wake up with the dawn and I pray hard.

I pray hard for everyone. I don't even pray for myself. That's how pure my prayer is. I've been praying hard for some time, begging unashamedly for a better world, because I'm appalled by the one I'm in and I haven't noticed any difference. It occurs to me that probably many others have been on the beseeching trail; surely if prayer had any effect we'd have noticed? On the other hand, just because something doesn't work for you doesn't mean it's not working somewhere else. If I had to start a fire by rubbing twigs, I'd be nowhere, and I'd have some chance of pulling off a stunt like that.

Breakfast restores my spine. How confidence-rich a doughnut can be, how character-forming coffee. Time for a miracle. Time to radiate.

The Hierophant needs to be seeded with intimations of my supremacy. He will serve as the chief witness of my divinity, so he has to be fed some amazing information, so first I need some amazing information.

I grab myself a terminal at Kafka's, and see whether there's some good stuff on the net. I immediately find an interview with the Hierophant conducted by a Virginia Hawthorn, the journalist at the Lama's talk. She's evidently hot on religion. I mark her down for cultivation.

Then I drive over to the Church of the Heavily Armed Christ, where I sweep up, even though since I swept up yesterday, there's nothing to sweep up. I leave a terrifically phallic blue pen on a top shelf in the Hierophant's office, which should garner me amazing information.

The next day, I arrive early to filter the mail, in case there's any amazing information. Sadly there is no letter informing the Hierophant of a visit from a long-lost friend or relation. There is no news of a large fortune bequeathed to him. There is nothing that could be even considered respectable information. There are bills and ads for gardening equipment, and since I've opened the envelopes clumsily, I have to ditch all the mail to conceal my tampering.

I then plug in to my pen, which can record up to eight hours of conversation. The trouble with recording up to eight hours of conversation is that you then have to listen to it. The material is as junk as the mail.

I discover the Hierophant sighs a lot in private. Every few minutes or so a heartfelt "aaaah" is released. Papers are shuffled. He sighs more. It's reassuring to learn that the assured aren't so assured, but the sighs rapidly become exasperating. There's also a great deal of scratching, although I can't identify which part of his body is getting the nail.

Finally, a conversation. The Hierophant explains to an unknown caller that he bought a watch that morning. He went into one shop, checked the price of the model he wanted, then went to another shop where the same model was a hundred dollars more. The Hierophant returned to the first shop and bought the watch.

Not a stunning anecdote, and the Hierophant doesn't tell it well. He doesn't tell it any better to caller "Mitchell" and caller "Ellen". He pads it out explaining how he expressed his outrage to the assistant in the second shop that they were selling the watch for a hundred bucks less in the first, and expressing astonishment to the assistant in the first shop that they were selling the watch for a hundred more in the second (I'm précising here).

It's unfair to knock someone's repartee when you're eavesdropping, but I doubt if I can carry on bugging the Hierophant, not on account of any ethical discomfort, but because it's so tedious. I've snooped on four and a half hours of the Hierophant's privacy and I'm drained.

"See this watch?" the Hierophant asks me the next day, relating that it was one hundred dollars cheaper in the shop he bought it in than anywhere else. I resist the impulse to correct him by saying he only went to one other shop. Who knows, if he'd tried somewhere else he might have found it for a hundred and twenty dollars less, though I doubt it since the market does curb abuse.

But you don't know. You don't know whether there is another shop with a better deal. You don't know whether there's another shop. Laziness always wins. Sooner or later. How much roaming and asking should you do?

If you spent a week going to forty watch retailers and succeeded in saving a hundred dollars, or even a hundred and twenty, would it justify your effort? You don't know. That's what's so frightening: you walk into one shop and they sell a watch for one price, and another shop sells that watch for another price. There is a conspiracy. It's called the world.

"Tyndale, it's time for the Hierophant to hit the fan."

The Hierophant requires me to hold a rickety ladder for him, while he climbs up to fix one of the fans. The church doesn't have air conditioning (too expensive and troublesome), but five propeller-style fans (cheap but more troublesome). Holding the ladder while the Hierophant spouts some non-God-based profanity, I suffer a powerful attack of futility as I realize that I am holding a rickety ladder in a hut in a run-down part of Miami while a demented ex-Marine fumbles with a fan so old it should be gracing a museum.

That's my job: rickety-ladder-holder. For which I'm not paid. The despair grows so strong I can barely stand up.

I attempt to amuse myself by imagining killing, but it doesn't work. I'm too aware that imagining killing is a trait of the defeated, and that my romps of violence will never happen. Not only will I never beat Loader to death with a handy bit of metal, I probably won't so much as tread on his toe. I'll never get to see him luckless and broken. You just don't get an opportunity for revenge. I think of all the people who've shat on me and I've just never once had a chance to settle up; they've never once walked in front of my car on a dark, rainy, witness-poor night.

On the other hand, while I've never managed to get even with my malefactors, I've never been able to get even with my benefactors either. True, the latter category is dishearteningly small – family excepted – countable on the palms of my hands really. Bamford, for instance, who pulled me out of the shit, who saved me, all I could do was to say to him "thank you". A sound isn't much.

We nothing along with no real power to touch those we want to. I'm here now in Miami, holding a rickety ladder with a persistent and embarrassing medical condition, my other years of no consequence.

I arrived here with no baggage, nothing to help me or hinder me. Born again, the same start whether I had spent my previous life giving stray kittens milk and running errands for the elderly, or microwaving puppies and strangling the old. Your moral bank account is a currency that can't buy you anything.

"What was Vietnam like?" I ask to make conversation.

"Hot," replies the Hierophant. I wait for more detail, but it's not coming.

"Did you get to the jungle?"

"Yes."

I wait. After two more minutes of fan-fiddling, I try:

"So what happened?"

"My watchstrap rotted. Everything rots there. Your uniform. Your nutsack. Everything."

More silence follows. Finally, the fan jerks into motion.

The Hierophant packs away his tools. "Do you want to know the most astonishing thing I saw while I was in 'Nam?"

"Go on."

"There were lots of bars and whorehouses. Lots. But one bar had this sign outside saying "Giant midgets". I never went in. But my question to you, Tyndale, is this: if they really were giant midgets, how could you tell?"

Picking up the pen, I leave the Hierophant. In my car, I suddenly get pangs of hunger. I should be holy and not bother with food, but I'm so beaten I hang up the holiness for the day. I ponder where I should go for a meal.

There's a greasy, hole-in-the-wall place on the next block I've noticed, with a greasy, sweaty guy surrounded by greasy bits of scrawled-on card listing his dishes that I've never tried because everything about the enterprise said don't. I now realize I'm too hungry to venture further, so I saunter over and buy a chicken sandwich.

When I bite into the cheap sandwich, I learn how wrong I was.

The fried chicken is unimprovable: happy chicken, ideal batter, fresh roll, one crisp leaf of lettuce. A simple but unbeatable sandwich, made with reverence for the reputation of the fried-chicken sandwich. A testament to good ingredients and the power of man to create tastiness.

In any job, it's easier to go through the motions, and in any job going the extra mile rarely gets you anything. The roll could have been stale, the chicken stringy or oily, but they're not. This guy gets up early to do the job right and it's unlikely it'll get him ahead of the stringy-chicken gang. Eventually he'll get ill or old or broken and there will be no record, no memorial to his home-cooked triumph. I salute the valour, the unbowed courage of this lone chicken-sandwich seller.

"Great sandwich," I say.

The sandwich-maker shrugs and wipes his counter.

This unforeseen attack by quality restores my faith in life. Part of my joy lies in the fact that I'm ahead. I've given the sandwich maker a small amount of money and he's given me bliss.

As you get older you understand that emotion is like the weather: despair, rage, self-hatred, delight, they all pass (even if they leave some damage). Knowing this doesn't help much, just as knowing on a cold, rainy day that the cold and rain won't last for ever.

It's embarrassing. Holding rickety ladder: down. Eating great fried-chicken sandwich: up.

I wish I could control my mood, spurning fried-chicken sandwiches, repelling rickety ladders, but I can't. Perhaps that's where holiness comes in. If you can have the fried-chicken bonus without the fried chicken. But if you could have the fried-chicken bonus without the fried chicken, what's the point of fried chicken and what's the point of skipping it?

I buy two more sandwiches to take home, aware that the hit won't be the same as the first.

Dawn kicks down the door of my unconsciousness and I pray hard. I pray hard for everyone before I get up, and then, gradually, the selfishness takes over.

How am I doing? That's the question, but what's the answer? How am I doing? That's what I'd like to know. Maybe I'm holding a rickety ladder for an eccentric ex-Marine, gratis, but maybe given the luck I've been allocated, maybe that's the best I could do. Maybe I'm not a failure; perhaps I'm viewed as a failure by many, but to the contrary, I have triumphed over several realms of adversity.

You don't know. It would be interesting to have a hotline to the Supreme Being to ask: how am I doing? But if you could, would you? What if the answer's not one you want?

I've only ever made two mistakes: too much or not enough. Too much determination or not enough determination. Too much trust, or not enough. Too much optimism or not enough. Or, if you want, I've only ever made one mistake: not getting it right.

Victory, Bamford used to insist, was not achieved soaring joyfully over the winning line, with the competition in the distance. Victory, he said, was usually a matter of crawling on all fours, cursing and dribbling, your ankles gnawed by your enemies. If so, I may be on the road to victory, as I'm definitely crawling.

I resolve to get into the church early to check the pen.

Out in the driveway I find a dog crapping. It's an old corgi mix. The dog growls with gusto. Why do old, small dogs yearn to pick fights? I locate the owner standing several yards away, smoking a cigarette dreamily; one of those dog-owners too lazy to walk their dog, content to let it off the leash and let it crap everywhere.

I don't know why I commit the error of being reasonable. Perhaps because I assume the owner is a neighbour and one wants cordiality on the block. Perhaps the holiness is getting to me.

"Might be a good idea to keep the dog on a lead," I smile. Always smile.

"My dog is no business of yours," he says. Immediately I see him. Smug self-feaster. High on his I. Bureaucrat. Not gifted enough to be a banker or businessman, but safely ensconced somewhere doing something where results don't matter, but you still get good holidays and reasonable pay: drugs counsellor, or human-rights monitor, so he can claim he's not part of the system, while getting pumped full of comfortable blood.

He'll have Congolese thumb-piano music to show how open he is to other (chiefly less affluent) cultures. He will bore you about the environment and the crimes of governments and multinationals, the sweatshops of Asia and the battle against malaria, but he smokes and lets his dog coil out a biggie on someone else's driveway. Uncanny, how fast you can hate.

The dog, too fat and ailing to jump, half-jumps up on my leg and barks at me in the best frenzy it can muster.

"What's wrong with you?" says the smoker to his dog in an amused, sing-song, talking-to-a-small-child tone. I've noticed this with dog-owners. They never apologize.

"If—" I start to raise the matter of the dog log, when the dog bites me. A nip, but still painful. I glare at the smoker waiting for an apology. I wait. He takes a drag on his cigarette.

"Your dog just bit me."

"No, it didn't."

Now he could have said this in a dishonest, I-don't-want-to-accept-any-liability-for-this way, in case I had two lawyers hiding in a bush nearby, but no. Although his dog bit me in front of him, in excellent daylight, he sincerely doesn't believe it. He is outraged by this vilification of his dog.

I'm so angry I can't hit him properly, and I punch him in the face, which is a mistake, because you'll only damage your fist. But I suppose I go for the face because it's the seat of the mouth. My knuckles get a twinge of hot ash. After his dog shat in my driveway, attacked me and he called me a liar, it would have been a crime to just walk away.

Here's the remarkable thing: as my fist closed in, there was an expression of surprise on his face. It's also remarkable how much scheming can fit into a second: although I was exploding, there was that part of me, having grown up in a big city, that calculated it was safe to hit him.

My fist sits him down and, now that violence is being dispensed, the dog slinks off to a safe distance.

I get into my car and drive to the church, although I'm so angry I drive through a red light and almost do it again. I'm angry I'm on the same planet with idiots like that. I'm angry because I can't win. If I hadn't punched him, I'd be furious with myself for not hitting him, but I'm also angry because I hit him.

Hitting him makes me marginally less angry than not hitting him, but what makes me churn and churn is that the smoker will now be amassing sympathy by telling anyone who'll listen how he was peacefully walking his dog when he was assaulted by a lunatic and what is the world coming to when a man can't walk his dog in safety. Thinking about it makes me so angry I want to go back and thump him again.

Bulging with rage, I attempt to listen to the pen. This time the pen has captured something worthwhile. I hear the Hierophant talking about going up to Rhode Island and then an odd conversation about investing in cobia, apparently some deep-sea fish that loves to be farmed, that gets off on captivity, regular feeding and a warm tank. I was considering how to infiltrate this information into our dialogue in a godlike all-knowing manner when the Hierophant strolled in.

"Good morning, Tyndale, I may be going up to Rhode Island for a few days." So much for two hours of listening to sighs. I remember the newspaper profile said the Hierophant came from Rhode Island, so I decide to bowl that info.

"Back to your roots, Gene? You do have a Rhode Island air about you."

"Hardly. I come from Cleveland." Never believe anything you read in the paper. I take a breather, make some coffee and then take another route.

"Gene, I had this dream about you and fish. You were like Christ multiplying the fish and feeding everyone, but making lots of money. The fish had this weird name, kopia or something."

The Hierophant sighs. He takes off his glasses and polishes them. "I knew this would happen. It always does. Tyndale, son, Miami's full of it, you've got to stay away from that stuff. Okay? Just stop. You can't help out here if you're on space patrol."

"No—"

"Don't say a word, Tyndale. I understand, I really do. We're all weak. We all sin. Let's pray."

I have to sit through a lengthy, custom-built homily on narcotics, then we settle down to preparing sandwiches for the homeless. As we load up, across the road an argument starts up. Two black guys, one black woman. It's heated. Then one of the guys wallops the woman, open-handed, but we feel the boom. It's a real connecter.

The group is, however, far away enough from us for us to be able to pretend it's not happening. In fact, there's a couple of Sikhs unloading some boxes halfway between us and them, Sikhs who are giving the unloading of those boxes their deepest concentration. And we don't know what's going on. Maybe she deserved it (you never know). I have no interest in getting involved, because there's nothing in it for me, but the Hierophant straightens up: "Let's sort this out."

He strides over purposefully. This is the last thing I want to do. The two guys are door-sized and either one could turn me into pulp. Having grown up in a big city, I know heavy when I see it. But if I chicken out now, bang goes my credit with the Hierophant.

My jaw is tingling as if it's already been jigsawed as I tag along behind the Hierophant, close enough for him to accept that I'm backing him up, but not so close that the yellers would automatically assume so. I tell myself the guys won't beat us up. They'll probably just shoot us. I'm willing the Hierophant not to say anything foolish or provocative such as hitting women is wrong.

He smiles. "Do you need to pray by any chance? We have a church just across the way if you need one. We're always open for hard prayer." It's the last line they're expecting. The woman tells us to go to hell. The guys laugh: the engine's been switched off.

As we walk back it occurs to me the Hierophant had the advantage of age. If he'd been twenty or so, the same age as the guys, no matter what he would have said would have been seen as a challenge, they would have had to mash him; but he's a ghost from another world. Did the Hierophant know this?

Back home, I listen to the pen again. The exchange about the cobia is quite clear. They can't wait to be farmed. The Hierophant has balls, but he's losing his marbles.

I'm very tempted to give up on the omniscience front, but I have the inestimable gift of not being able to afford giving up; it's God or bust. The following day, I return to the pen, and prod myself lightly with a knife to offset the tedium of listening to the sighs and scratching.

I hear an exchange about sigmoidoscopy. It sounds very serious and medical. The Hierophant's voice is unprecedentedly dejected. Googling, I discover that sigmoidoscopy is arse invasion. The Hierophant has gut problems. If he drops dead is that a help or hindrance? The callousness of my reflection pleases me.

I ruminate on some clever way to divulge this info, but can't. You either have spooky knowledge or you don't.

"You know, Gene, I do get these premonitions. I wouldn't say anything about it, but I had this dream and I'm worried about you. You had some stomach problems. I know you'll think this crazy, but why don't you have a check-up?" I say when he comes in.

"Had one a month ago," he declares. "Scared the doctors with my health. You can forget about your premonitions. Thirty push-ups every morning and my turds are award-winners. However, I've had some not so good news. My mother's in a bad way." Sigmoidoscopy, I'd wager. "Truth be told, she's just about done."

His mother is bedridden, terminal. The Hierophant's returning to Cleveland to care for her. It's a situation where so many would find so many reasons for not rushing to the bedside. For sending money instead. The Hierophant has bad taste in clothes and jokes (Marine jokes pioneer new levels of tastelessness), but he has no fear. I really do admire him. He is a decency-heavy individual and that's why he has a small, congregation-light church which he's about to lose to me. It's strange how when you're getting what you want, you still try to ruin it.

"Can't you bring her down here?" I suggest, realizing that would counter my progress.

"She's never left Cleveland in her life. I doubt she has much idea where she is, but it would be wrong to move her. She'd want to end there." Again, he shuns the easy road.

"This is very difficult for me," he continues. "Her friends have been helping her, but she needs round-the-clock care now. I hate to leave my flock here, but I have to go. But in a way I'm lucky. I'm very lucky because I have you. You know, Tyndale, I get lots of offers to help out, a lot, but they rarely translate into actions, but you're the only who's been a pillar. You're here day after day, never asking for anything, always willing, you're quite something. The only reason I can go to be with my mother is because you'll be here ministering for me."

So, it's official. I have my Church. I feel enormous guilt. The Hierophant's faith moves me. Tears breed in my eyes. Why is it you always get what you want in a way you don't want it? He makes me sub-Hierophant, the first in the history of the Church.

"Any advice you want to give me?" I ask.

"Yes. Don't do it."

"Sorry?"

"Don't be a pastor. Don't run a church. That's the best advice I can give. Don't do it. One other very important thing. If Mrs Barrodale invites you to lunch, don't go. Her food's terrible."

The next day I retrieve the pen and hit on a conversation. The Hierophant is explaining he's off to Cleveland to nurse his mother. "No, I'm not closing the church. There's a follower who can run things for me. He's a bit strange, and he may not be right, but I have to give him a chance."

This is my punishment for bugging the office. We're never quite as loved as we hope we are, but, mulling it over, it's even more touching, if he has doubts about me, that he's willing to praise me up and give me a chance.

Enough dabbling in omniscience.

I wake up in the dark, drenched in an unpleasant sweat. A giant hand is squeezing my guts and I curl up into a ball. I feel far from home, and utterly beaten. With a total lack of dignity, I moan. Perhaps we are all far from home and utterly beaten, and the trick is not to feel it. Lying on a door in an empty room, soon-to-be mentor to a handful of Miami's foozlers, with a few hundred dollars to my name, I feel it keenly.

I pray hard. I pray hard for everybody, because there's nothing else to do.

You should never study your congregation too closely. It's often a dispiriting prospect. The Hierophant has entrusted me with his greatest hits to read out in his absence, which suits me fine, since I have no desire to sit around composing sermons.

Now that the Hierophant Graves is away, I not only conduct the services but I am responsible for the "surgery" afterwards. As I go into the office I am a little disconcerted to see that half the congregation has stayed behind. Should this be interpreted as a vote of confidence in me or a lack of confidence in the Hierophant?

First in are Mrs Shepherd and her son, Peter. Mrs Shepherd is one of those dumpy, uninteresting women who do the sweeping and acquisition of flowers for churches, and let's face it, it's important work, even if you don't want to do it. I've done the sweeping several times, when everyone was around, to demonstrate how humble I am, but that was enough.

Warmly, I offer her a seat as I want (and I'm sure the absent Hierophant wants) the sweeping and flower acquisition to carry on uninterrupted. She reintroduces me to her son, a powerfully built lad who hands out beach towels at a hotel. They are both extremely cheerful, so I can't foresee major quagmire here.

"We were hoping you could help us."

"Of course," I reply. "That's my job." So far, so good. Assurance is easy and should always be swift.

"We asked the Hierophant before, but he said no."

Terror lurches in me. This isn't going to be a sunny walk in the park, this will be something nasty and is certain to be something that will get me in trouble with the Hierophant. This is a trap. I smile.

"And what exactly did he say no to?"

"Me and Peter would like to get married." The family resemblance is so strong I find it hard to believe...

"Peter is adopted is he?"

"Don't be ridiculous," Mrs Shepherd replies indignantly. I am stumped. The Shepherds' indifference to millennia of global, ecclesiastical, cultural and legislative convention is word-removing. Is this a hoax? A test devised by the Hierophant? Dodge.

"Why do you want to get married?"

"My husband died last year, and I'd like to get married again."

I suddenly realize how ignorant I am. If you looked at the Shepherds you'd see nothing remarkable about them at all. But there's something going on here. Rock-solid stupidity? Something I have no appetite to learn any more about. The world frightens me.

Smile. Always smile. "Rona, I'll have to think about this," I say.

In reality, I've already thought about it. If the Hierophant comes back in a week or two, it's off my plate. If he's away for longer, I may have to strike a deal with the Shepherds. I'd like the sweeping and flowers to carry on. Whatever is taking place in the Shepherd household is taking place, and a benediction from me isn't going to make any difference.

As they leave I reflect that they probably have an important job. After some terrible planetocidal disaster you or I would be too distraught to carry on, too squeamish about survival, but the Shepherds would be out there repopulating, until nature reintroduced sophisticated features like intelligence again. Mrs Shepherd and her son are our backup.

Next, the elderly Mrs Garcia hunches in. My job is about listening, but even I get tired of listening as she takes twenty minutes to get to her whinge. Her neighbour's cat is making her miserable: shitting in her garden, trashing her plants, eating her hummingbirds. After the Shepherds I'm delighted to be presented with a simple feline matter. I advise Mrs Garcia to trust in the power of prayer and tell myself that if I can't dispatch one rotten cat I might as well give up now. The cat's description carefully noted, I hustle her out.

The Reinholds come in last. Mike and Sue. Regular, money-earning, middle-aged couple. Comfortingly uninsane. Mike is only a few inches away from a lucrative career as a dwarf, but he's me. He works at the waterworks, and I know he will always be passed over for promotion. He's certainly too assiduous. Turns up early, gives it his all for a modest salary. Will never be promoted. I imagine he spends his evenings reading up on new theories of water management to be ahead of the game, but he will never be promoted.

Why do they attend this church? I have an urge to tell them to get some proper religion. What's their problem? His promotion?

"Our daughter, Alexa..." Mike begins. He falls silent. "We don't know what to do," picks up Sue.

It's that old perennial. The bad-boy problem. They have a sixteen-year old daughter Alexa who fallen for a bad element, three years older than her, the neighbourhood biker. The biker is always older because women tend to be more mature, and those extra years can seem very impressive in terms of greater experience in knowing where the seedy bars are and joint-rolling.

I am moved by the Reinholds. You spend sixteen years cherishing, bodyguarding your daughter, you read bedtime stories and help with homework when you're exhausted, you forgo good golf clubs so you can pay for guitar lessons, you queue interminably to collect medicines, you make sacrifice after sacrifice, because you know your daughter will be the only value in a creation which refuses to promote you. Then your daughter drops school, and spends all her savings (Granny's legacy) buying clothes for the neighbourhood biker and, worse, disappears for days to let him plant his principality wherever he wants.

The Reinholds have tried all the parental ruses, shouting, begging, bribery.

They're in a difficult position. If Alexa were younger they could get legal. If they were better off they'd have a chance of buying her off with a three-month tour of Europe or India. They're also battling the most powerful force in the universe: pleasure, the old white eye. Chatting with your friends, listening to music, going shopping, all these pastimes (never mind education or volunteering to wash up) fade away when you discover intersecting loins.

I'm eager to help the Reinholds, although I doubt I can do much. Parleying with the daughter is a non-starter. If they can't slow down her pleasure I have no chance. But her idol... they give me the telephone number for Cosmo, the injectioneer in question. I promise to have a heart-to-heart talk with him.

My first attempt to make contact with Cosmo fails. He's "too busy" to see me. I knew I wouldn't like Cosmo, but now, dislike seriously takes root. I can only have respect for those who tell the truth or who lie elaborately. I would have rated Cosmo more highly if he had told me to drop dead. The Reinholds have informed me that apart from feeding their daughter thrusts, Cosmo has no job and spends his time drifting from couch to couch, subsisting on others' fridges.

Much to my surprise, a few days later, when I call again he agrees to meet me.

"Don't bore me," he says. "And bring a bottle of Barbancourt Rum." I suppose he has agreed because he's flattered by the attention, that a spiritual advisor has been called in to wrangle his phallus. And because he doesn't have much else to do. And could use a bottle of rum.

I drive to the address he gives me, (getting lost several times in the traditional Miami manner), but it doesn't make sense. It's a brand-new money-shrieking block up on North Beach. They say Miami is the hottest property market in the world and you can believe it as these colonies of giant jack-in-the-boxes spring up everywhere. I check my note twice, but it's the place. Cosmo is either tending someone's guppies or visiting a friend, because he couldn't afford to live here. As I approach the building, an attractive realtor walks out.

When I buzz in, I have no idea what to say.

A half-dressed Cosmo admits me into a vast unfurnished condo. I immediately guess he is doing the realtor too and is taking advantage of unsold space. One of the few benefits of being a salesman is that you do get a knack for sizing people up quickly. I hope Cosmo will show some weakness or opening I can exploit, but he doesn't. I see a shiny leather jacket on the floor, which cost (the Reinholds told me) a thousand dollars.

"Where's the bottle?" Cosmo asks.

"I'm sorry," I reply. "I'm not allowed any money." I enjoy saying that because it sounds so pure and it's so untrue. There's no comeback.

"Don't bore me, Your Holiness," he says sauntering out onto the balcony. There's another deadbeat perched on the balcony rail. On closer inspection, I perceive that his trousers have been lowered to his ankles. "Did he bring the rum?" he asks.

Cosmo now drops his trousers, and manoeuvres his rear over the balcony rail, hanging on in a quite precarious way, considering that we are on the twelfth floor. He and his friend are shitting on two sports cars below, tough targets at this distance.

"Why are you wasting my time?" he demands, fine-tuning his position. For no good reason I respond with a subtle threat.

"You're causing a lot of upset."

"Not my problem. Couldn't you get me a drink?" His face grimaces as he struggles to squeeze one out.

"Distress has a way of working around; if you cause distress, eventually the distress comes to you," I say with my most mantic voice.

Cosmo grunts and voids one. "Big miss," his spotter announces.

"Do the cars belong to anyone you know?"

"You're boring me. You'll have to go."

Cosmo isn't hard. He's seen some rough things, he's an accomplished delinquent, but in a city like this, where executions are gleefully carried out for a few hundred dollars, he's froth. In Liberty City, they'd spread him on toast. He's a skinny creature and I'd even fancy my chances in a fist fight, since I must have fifty pounds on him. That morning, when I had smacked the punchbag, I was again surprised by how enjoyable, how familiar... how righteous it was. I consider sucker-punching Cosmo.

"Do you love Alexa?'

"Woah, I'm not a one-woman man." Of course not, his vasa deferentia must be on call round-the-clock. His sideshitter shakes his head, agog at my crass remark.

If it weren't for his sideshitter, this would be the perfect solution to the Reinholds' problem. Effortlessly, I could just upend Cosmo completely and over he'd go. I'm glad his companion's there though, because I probably would have chickened out otherwise, and I'm glad I don't have to worry about the probability of chickening out.

"You'd better not insult me by offering anything less than twenty grand to stop seeing her. She's into expensive presents, and her pussy is pencil-sharpener-tight, yeah? I told them, twenty grand and I never take one of her calls again."

I doubt the Reinholds have twenty grand to spare. Even if they danegelded Cosmo he would be unlikely to keep his side of the bargain.

"Why should they pay twenty thou, when a motorbike accident only costs one? A young man like you, you'd make a wonderful organ donor." This is the first time I've ever threatened to kill anyone, and it's fun. This is not what Cosmo's expecting. He's unnerved by the turn of the conversation.

"Alexa's old man wouldn't have the cojones to park illegally, let alone kill anyone."

"You're right. He wouldn't. Others would."

I can tell what Cosmo is thinking. He can't believe this ancient old turd has just threatened to kill him. I may represent a strange church, but I appear to be a man of the cloth, a promoter of holy writ and instead of a dreary homily on fornication or a hug-in, he's hearing about murder.

He's furious, and I have to concede that I might not win a fist fight with him. But he's not sure either. This is jungle stuff. Okay, you have this ancient turd calling you out, the ancient turd probably can't back it up, the ancient turd looks lame, but what, but what if he can? You guess wrong and you're some teeth short. A little belatedly it passes through my mind that Cosmo and his chum could do a good job of throwing me over the balcony. They wouldn't do it deliberately – they're too frothy for that – but they might want to scare me and mess it up. On the other hand, they'd have no ideological objections to giving me a thorough kicking.

I bet right however. Cosmo waves his hands and compresses ten minutes' worth of abuse and obscenity into my leaving, cursing me as best he can with his limited vocabulary. But he keeps his distance. As he rages, I take stock of my new fondness for high-risk gambling. It's not a good new hobby.

"Hey, I have friends. I have friends." Cosmo keeps on shouting.

"No. You don't," I counter. This is always a good line to throw in, because even the biggest egos have a hairline crack on this one.

Outside, I switch on my phone. I acknowledge again what my mistake has been: too reasonable. The cat and Cosmo will have to be dealt with. But they're no problem. When you're God you can do anything.

I call DJs Gamay and Muscat. I had almost thrown their card away, because I couldn't conceive of ever needing to talk to imbeciles of their magnitude again. Real water bottles. Walking water the pair of them. But that's one lesson I learnt as a salesman: contacts are everything, and just because you don't need an imbecile now doesn't mean you won't need one later.

Most importantly, they're big, beefy imbeciles, much bigger and beefier than Cosmo, and you don't tender your services to a major multinational criminal organization unless you're prepared to get rough. And if they want to work for a major multinational criminal organization, that's what I'll let them believe.

"That's a great suit, Tyndale, you look so cool," says Gamay as he and Muscat enter. As flattery, it's feeble, but I acknowledge the effort. I give the DJs a pad of paper and tell them to write a one-thousand word autobiography, and to give me the names and addresses of at least twenty friends or relatives.

Apprehensive as they arrived, they now look freaked.

"Why?" Gamay spokespersons.

"Here's the deal. The deal is non-negotiable. You don't ask anything. You never ask anything. Ideally, you never say anything. You do. You do or you leave. Do or leave."

"Okay. Totalism," nods Muscat.

They settle down with the paper. This will be difficult. Are they appropriate vessels? I doubt if Gamay or Muscat have written anything longer than a cheque. Next, counting up to one thousand will be a challenge, and as they can't be more than twenty-one, they can't have too much life to recount. All application forms are designed to humiliate and subordinate the applicant, and I have added a touch of genius by giving Gamay and Muscat the additional burden of having to invent the questions.

Truthfully, I'm also inspired by one of my former neighbours, an Iraqi exile, who had been imprisoned, tortured, mock-executed and whose entire family, apart from his daughter, had been executed. He used to give me advice about torture which I never imagined I could put to good use. "Before they start the beatings, they make you write. They make you write about yourself and no matter how clever you are, you always give something away." In the end he strangled his daughter, since he felt she wasn't dressing demurely.

As I go out to the pool to do some laps, Patti and Trixi come in from their swim to resume their clothing. Gamay and Muscat's limited compositional skills expire. They undergo a formidable stupefaction in the presence of The Dream... the big house, the nymphs gambolling around naked. Their imaginations weren't lying. I make a point of not introducing them to the girls.

After my half-hour in the pool, I return to find little progress. Even holding the pens stretches Gamay and Muscat.

"Tyndale, where should I expect to see myself in five years?" asks Gamay.

"What did I say about asking?"

"I'm not asking. I'm only curioso. When do we get some major disfrooting?"

It's recognized that part of the ageing process is viewing the young as useless, listening to terrible music and drivelling away in some outlandish cant, but no one will disconvince me that Gamay and Muscat are anything but useless strange drivellers and perpetrators of terrible music. I reinstruct them to do their bios and go out for a walk.

It's at least two hours before I get back. Gamay and Muscat are as uncomfortable as two manatees in a sandpit. But that's okay: to make people happy, it's beneficial to make them unhappy first. Their autobiographies are woefully brief and Muscat has drawn a smiley face on his paper, presumably in an attempt to placate my wrath.

Can I trust them with solving even Mrs Garcia's cat problem, never mind Cosmo? But they're all I have. It's easy to succeed with proper help. Buddha? Mohammed? Jesus Christ? Did they have to work with dumbos? You bet. Anyone can work with the talented. Can you do it with dumbos? It's what sorts out the illuminators from the droners.

To impress upon Gamay and Muscat the gravity of their signing-up, I get them to put a fingerprint on their bios, then I take a shot of them with Sixto's camera, then a real close-up, for purposes of iris recognition I explain. I warn them that they'll probably end up dead or in jail, and they look unconcerned. Stupid or tough? Stupid. I consider teaching them a secret handshake, but that would only get them into trouble.

"You have a long way to go before you're in," I say. "Remember, I'm the hopmaster: when I say hop, hop." I make them hop up and down on one leg for three minutes. They're bulky, and not in condition. By the end they're gasping piteously.

I outline their tasks, simply and slowly, and emphasize how complete discretion and reliability is required.

"We won't kennedy you," says Gamay.

"We won't kennedy you," seconds Muscat. I think I understand what they mean. They sit there watching me watching them watching me.

"Okay. Off you go then."

They look at each other. "You know that stuff you want us to do?" says Gamay. "Would you write it down for us? And is that stuff about the woman and the cat... like some sort of code?"

Two days pass. I have given them all the information on Cosmo and the cat, and then I've been busy with holy work and thinking about some miracles. They're relatively easy to fake, but hard to fake well.

I ask myself when Gamay and Muscat are going to check in. I can't chase after them – that would look undignified – but I have to say I'm annoyed at their failure to ring in and apologize for their failure. I doubt real criminal organizations would be tolerant of such slackness.

But finally, out of curiosity, I phone Gamay.

"So?"

"Things are great, totally cool," he says.

"You had a chat with Cosmo?'

"Not as such."

"And the cat?"

"It's right there on the list."

"What have you been doing for two days?"

"Well, yesterday I was out of it. Someone must have spiked my drink, cos I was feeling bad all day. All day. Today I had to go and see my stylist, Roxanne, cos she's going on vacation and she wanted to pass me over to Nourina, who's great and all, while she's away, but I said to Roxanne, only you can take care of my hair, I just can't trust anyone else but you, great as Nourina is—"

"Can you hear me okay, Gamay?"

"Perfectomento."

"You and your fellow DJ have twenty-four hours to deliver."

"Hey this is the Big M.I.A., we can do it any-ee way."

I'm so angry I have to lie down. True, they're not really being auditioned by a major multinational criminal organization, but they don't know that. When I look back on how much crawling I had to do to get a job interview, let alone a job, their waywardness cripples me with rage.

The next evening Gamay and Muscat report.

"Can we stop now?" Gamay enquires.

"What do you mean?"

"We've been waiting outside this shop for two hours."

Gamay and Muscat have failed to find Cosmo. They have failed to find the cat and are exhausted after a few hours' work. I'm angry with myself for taking on two DJs whose inspiration was a wine list. What did I expect?

"We ain't kennedying you, but we can't find him."

"You can stop anytime you like, but then you're out." I have to remind myself that I'm not paying them.

Furious, I take a walk along the beach. I have to make my way round a group of teens discovering illegal beer and going wild, and congratulating themselves on it. Unaware of how unoriginal, how prescribed, how prepaid this all is. It's so unoriginal it bores me and how, more than disappointment or sorrow at humanity's antics, it must bore God. All this stuff we find so important, absorbing, exciting and maddening.

The first kiss. The discovery of cheating. The acceleration of the Norton Commando. The struggle to get a decent passport photograph. Marrying your son. Getting your whites really white. Fury at the uselessness of doctors. Rage at unreturned borrowables. The impossibility of overcooking goose. The investigation of sodomy. The return of a long-lost friend. Having to throw out your favourite jacket because it's more holes than jacket. The pleasure of massacre. Squabbles about whether it's a beech marten or a pine marten. Kohlrabi or mangelwurzel. The right turning or the left turning. Old song, new throng. Same babble, different rabble.

Later that evening, sweetened by a session on the punchbag, as I make my way down Washington Avenue with the collecting tin, I spy Gamay and Muscat in a crowded café, not looking for Cosmo, but laying siege to an attractive but visibly underage girl and her fat friend.

I'm too tired to be severely disappointed, but... One: don't get caught. Two: if you're fifteen and doing a fifteen-year-old, that's nature; if you're forty and you're doing a fifteen-year-old, there's a decadent, sick grandeur going on; if you're twenty-one, you're a dud. Worse, Gamay and Muscat are getting nowhere.

They haven't seen me, and I back off. In any real criminal organization, they would be kneecapped, but all I could do would be to rant and, generally, ranting just makes you look ridiculous. I back off. Sometimes it's better to let others think they've had the better of you.

I'd given up on Gamay and Muscat. I hadn't heard from them for days when, reading the *Miami Herald*, I chanced upon a small item about a gunburst in the neighbourhood Mrs Garcia lived in. Two unknown assailants had opened fire on the house of Mr Dag Solomon, 76, a retired tollgate consultant and amateur gun collector. Mr Solomon was quoted: "I've had to wait fifty-four years to protect my family, but it was worth it." Mr Solomon went on to insist he had put thirty-four grouped rounds into the assailants' vehicle as it fled the scene. Mr Solomon was uninjured and so was his family, as they were visiting relatives in Vermont.

I phone Mrs Garcia. As I feared, Mr Solomon is her neighbour and owner of the offending cat. I offer Mrs Garcia my sympathy. I had envisioned a trap, a thirty-mile road trip for the cat, or at worst, some poisoned liver. I must learn to be more specific. The cat however is no longer a concern. Mrs Garcia has decided to move out.

Gamay and Muscat, I assume, must be dead or slipping away in an intensive-care unit or penal facility somewhere. I wait all day for the police to turn up and debate whether to mention to Sixto that I may have done a sterling job in attracting the forces of law and order into his multinational cocaine business.

This is the great dilemma about fucking up. Very often, an immediate and frank avowal of disaster will get you some credit and lessen the punishment. This is especially true of minor fuck-ups. Just say you're sorry about forgetting someone's birthday or an anniversary. Come clean. Be the big man.

However, with bigger fuck-ups, such as getting your wife's sister pregnant, there's always the temptation to keep quiet and hope you can euthanize the mishap without any wrath being spilt. It's a gamble, because if you botch the euthanasia, then the wrath gets wrathier. I don't sleep at all the next night, but I don't tell Sixto.

The next morning, as I head for the kitchen to make my cup of tea, a dark, broad-shouldered woman is there fixing herself a sandwich.

"Hi, I'm Gulin," she says with an accent I can't place and a smile that's both natural and a little forced. There are also, I notice, two piles of boxes that augur moving in.

Sixto explains to me that Gulin is a friend of his sister who lives in LA, but who had to leave. He is not thrilled by having another lodger. "My sister…" he fizzles, making strangling gestures.

"Does she know… about your business?" I ask.

"No," says Sixto. "My sister doesn't even know. But Gulin has more to worry about than I do. If she'd stayed in LA she'd be dead."

In the garden, we can see the builders reappearing with new windows. Even at a distance of thirty feet we can see that the new windows don't match. Sixto opens the window. "You're not thinking of putting those windows in?" The builders look at the windows as if for the first time and make an exhibition of surprise at the lack of match. They give exaggerated sighs and retreat.

Then I see the cat. It's black with white paws. I dislike cats. They scratch, smell and make me sneeze. But this cat is wise. It keeps its distance and makes no attempt to be pally. Sixto does some more strangling.

When I get to the Hierophant's office, the phone rings and to my surprise it's Gamay.

"We got him," he announces. I consider asking about the cat and the thirty-four grouped rounds, but then I realize I don't care.

"Eight," I say, referring to our prearranged interview spot. I get there early, excited by my fruitful machinations. At half-past eight, there's no sign of Gamay and Muscat. I restrain myself from phoning them. When you're kidnapping: time, traffic, whatever.

Just after nine they show up. "You're late," I say, not that bothered, but discipline for the disciples is important.

"We're early," says Gamay. "You said nine." I could explode, but maybe I did say nine, although I have more faith in my recollection than Gamay's. I will be taping my conversations from now on. The DJs have new transport; I assume the sharp-shooter trashed their barmonster.

"We ain't kennedying you, it's been hellacious these few days," continues Gamay. Naturally, I'm not in the least bit interested in Gamay's whingeing about how hard his existence is. I'm reworking my sermon to Cosmo, delivered in my position as the fear-driver who will inform Cosmo this is his last warning, that if he doesn't leave town he'll be fed to the gators. A brimstoning that will cut Cosmo out of the picture. One prayer answered, courtesy of Tyndale.

I strike a solemn pose and signal them to open up the trunk of the car where Cosmo has been stashed. They do my bidding.

A head rears up.

"Well," I say to Gamay. "Aren't you going to introduce me?"

"You want me to use your name, Tyndale?"

"Why not?"

"Tyndale – Cosmo. Uh, Cosmo – Tyndale."

"This is not Cosmo," I say.

"I'm not Cosmo," says the Head. The Head doesn't resemble Cosmo, but is remarkably composed for the victim of an abduction, more than composed in fact, quite mean. "I told them I'm not Cosmo."

Gamay and Muscat gawk at each other as if they've been swindled. Then each thinks about blaming the other, but they haven't got enough time to concoct a story.

"I've no idea how this happened," says Gamay. I have some idea, but explaining to Gamay and Muscat that if a goldfish could move the pieces, it would beat them at chess, won't improve anything.

"We really wanted to get Cosmo,' says Muscat.

"We wanted Cosmo bad," says Gamay. "I guess, I guess… we won't be joining the organization today. Muscat, man you're really disgracing us."

"Me?"

"You're just not good enough."

"Excuse us," I say to the Head as I close the trunk as courteously and gently as possible in the circumstances. I inform Gamay and Muscat, just in case they had any doubts, they are a long way from getting on the payroll.

"Tyndale, we're going to have a chilli-off," insists Gamay. "I'll show you who's the bad man here." He produces a small jar and then fishes out a long green chilli and swallows it. He flinches slightly, but is composed. Muscat takes a chilli and, imitating Gamay's gung-ho style, bites hard.

Without warning, Muscat collapses, and lies on the ground mewing faintly and crying. It's undeniable there is something undignified about a man crying, and it takes him ten minutes to pull himself together.

"Let me hear it," says Gamay. "Who's badder?"

"You're badder than me," hoarses Muscat.

Gamay may be badder than Muscat (not such an achievement), but I sense he's cheating. Although he's stupid, he has aspirations to slyness. Somehow he's picked out a milder chilli or one that's been treated to lose its edge. You can see things as you get older, although I can't say that being able to see that one dumbo is conning another dumbo about eating chillies is a wisdom that will get me anywhere.

I instruct them to turn out their pockets; I take their forty-two dollars and sixty cents and give them to the Head, and tell the DJs to drop the Head off somewhere out of the way, but where he'll have a good chance of getting a taxi.

Back home, I've just fallen asleep when Gamay phones me. "Tyndale, I just wanted to say... that Muscat... that Muscat... I told that 'tard it was the wrong guy. Tyndale?"

"Yes?"

"If you want to me to uh... you know... to solve the Muscat problem, solve it, you know, like solve it finally, just give me the word, man."

"Gamay, don't ever phone me again."

I've just got back to sleep when the phones rings again. It's Muscat.

"Tyndale, man, I just wanted to say... that 'tard Gamay... that fuckin 'tard, he's always holding me back. I just wanted to say I'm on board. I'm a hundred and fifty fuckin' per cent on board. I'm in this all the way… you know, if you want to make an example of Gamay, you can count on me a hundred and fifty per cent. Two hundred per cent."

"Three hundred per cent?"

"Three hundred and ten, man, I ain't kennedying you."

"Muscat, don't ever phone me again." This time I make sure my phone is off.

Two days later, I come down to the kitchen to make some holy breakfast when I find the builders gathered around the television watching a sitcom. They are drinking what looks very much like Sixto's beer.

I say nothing, but pick up a copy of the *Miami Herald* lying by the phone to read.

"Hey," shouts one of the builders, "I'm reading that." The impossibility of his reading a folded paper, two feet above and ten feet behind his eyes occurs to me. But in the mornings I prefer to be left alone, so I withdraw to my room.

When I leave at lunchtime, the builders are listening to some of Sixto's compas collection. An hour later when I return they're gone, and as I hydrate myself, I flick through the paper and notice a not-so-small item about the Mayor of Miami Beach's son being abducted. Unsportingly, the taxi fare isn't reported.

So, when Gamay phones up later and assures me they now have Cosmo ("we checked his ID") I'm very tempted to say forget it. But, barely visible, ahead of me, is the glimmer of success. Be unidirectional.

My car won't start. I call Gamay and Muscat repeatedly, but only get voicemail.

When the taxi drops me off at the new interview site ("Are you sure you want to be left here?") after a comically expensive ride, there is no sign of Gamay and Muscat. If I'd driven, I would have driven off by the time they roll in, an hour and a half late, claiming they couldn't find the turning. I'm very tired and dissatisfied.

To my great surprise, they extricate Cosmo from the trunk. He's even handcuffed. Something's wrong I think. We're in a dark, isolated, I don't know... *unused* part of Florida and Cosmo is on all fours in front of me, handcuffed. It's exactly how I wanted it. Cosmo is shaken, but seems emboldened by the sight of me.

"You," he says, "you can't do this." A little humiliation is in order. Recalling another anecdote of my Iraqi neighbour I order the DJs to urinate on Cosmo. Muscat can't go with everyone watching, and although Gamay manages a trickle, Cosmo keeps rolling out of range. If you fail, you always have the tactic of pretending you haven't, so I carry on with the admonition.

"Cosmo, you should go. You can go where you want, but you have to leave Florida." I then pull out the Hierophant's .22. The drawback with the .22 is that it's small and looks as if it came from a packet of cereal or a teenage girl's handbag. Professional killers apparently are very fond of the .22, but I doubt Cosmo knows that.

"This is a holy gun," I say, remixing the Hierophant's shtick. "The .22 is the choice of the godly, because it punishes the wrongdoer, but doesn't, like a .44, go through the wrongdoer, three walls, a gardener and then kill a child on a bike half a mile away."

Our eyes meet and Cosmo sneers: "You won't shoot me." This is the trouble with religion in the present day. Too many wishy-washy pencil-necked hand-clasping do-gooding over-forgiving softies have given the cloth a limp image. Nevertheless I'm astonished by Cosmo's front. If someone's gone to the trouble of threatening you, it's plain bad manners not to act threatened. In his position, even if I didn't take the threat seriously, I'd just say, sure whatever you want, and then, once de-handcuffed and de-waylaid, forget all about it.

"That was a rash thing to say Cosmo. You haven't thought this through. Even if I didn't want to shoot you before, now, to show you I'm not smoke, I really have to."

"No, you won't."

He was nearly right. I missed three times. I wanted to shoot him just at the base of his right toes, so that it would be painful, but there would be no danger of him bleeding to death. I get Gamay and Muscat to sit on him so he'll stop wriggling and I put one through his boot.

Surprisingly, Cosmo is surprised that I've shot him. On his face, incredulity tangles with pain. "Why did you shoot me?" he wails.

As we drive off, I'm partly pleased with myself that I've taken decisive action, partly unhappy at having to live in a world with guns. We leave Cosmo stranded in the middle of nowhere, which may well turn out to be more punitive than being shot. Will Cosmo skulk off or will he go berserk, get an automatic weapon and hose me down? He's not incapable of it. But you don't get anywhere without taking risks.

Five miles down the road we break down. The electrics are gone. Two hours later we're still stuck there with the breakdown people phoning us every fifteen minutes telling us they can't find us. There are one or two obvious things I know you can check for, and Muscat and Gamay have the same level of automotive knowledge as me. We stand there staring at the engine, because that's what you do with an engine or piece of equipment that's not working and you don't know how to repair. You stare at it manfully as if you are pondering all sorts of solutions, whereas in reality you're waiting for the breakdown people. It's a bitchslap for our masculinity, and we do our best to pretend that it isn't.

Far off in the distance I glimpse a bus. I just have the opportunity to see Cosmo being carried off towards Miami. It's a bad moment. If I had anything to go back to, I'd give it up and go back.

It's another two hours before we're recovered. I suffer a powerful temptation to shoot the breakdown people, but I realize that, gratifying though it would be, and invaluable as it might be as feedback on the quality of their service, it won't help my deification. Unidirectional, baby.

By the time I get back home it's very late and I'm surprised to see one of the builders, the carpenter, sitting watching television with a half-naked cutie, drinking what again bears a strong resemblance to Sixto's beer. The carpenter is angry at my entrance and, maintaining that he had forgotten a tool, leaves with the confused cutie. There are still two or three empty rooms in Sixto's place and the carpenter must have been doing the "come back to my palatial pad" routine. I find it outrageous that someone not even living in the house is pretending to be the owner. Leave that to me.

I contemplate miracles. Walking on water I dismiss as too tricky, and also a bit redundant. Great effect, but what good does it do anyone? Sighting the blind, raising the dead: those are the miracles that get you noticed, those are the services that the public wants.

I go down to have a holy breakfast. In the kitchen, Gulin is wobbling on a chair struggling to change a strip light. I step in because it seems courteous and because, with fifteen years in the lighting business, this is one thing I can handle.

As it turns out, I can't sort out the fitting which makes me glad I didn't mention that I had fifteen years in the lighting business.

Over tea, Gulin and I trade biographies (I sold electrical goods). She is Turkish, a former primary school teacher who decided one day ten years ago to fly into LA, with no work permit, no job, no contacts, no friends, three hundred dollars and maybe that many words of English. Anyone who knows LA, I think, will stand and salute. She has numerous anecdotes about the rich and famous whose children she looked after, and who were naturally, very unpleasant to work for. Then she got married, to a Turk.

"We went to Las Vegas for our honeymoon. The honeymoon was a good idea, the marriage wasn't."

Her husband is a security guard. There are lots of stories about security guards, none of them good.

"Are you divorced?"

"I can't divorce." She explains she had to disappear without warning and leave LA, because otherwise her husband would kill her. Some women telling you this would be unconvincing but a young lady who soldiers into LA on her own isn't one prone to panic or exaggeration.

"He's an unhappy man. He wouldn't accept me leaving." I understand.

He's me. I can see it. You go to America, work your balls off, eat macaroni cheese and tinned spinach for years, and instead of making it like your fellow villagers who went to America, your cousin Mehmet, for example, you are in a dead-end job earning just enough for burgers, a movie at the weekend and a trip back home every two years should you care to admit to not having made it. The only plus is your wife, whom you can't stand any more, but who is still your wife. When you realize that this life is over, that you haven't been nominated for anything worthwhile, there are three standard responses: you give up and erase yourself in television or booze, have a mad roll of the dice like me, or choose to make someone pay.

Not for the first time, I recognize that women are tougher. If their worldly progress doesn't progress the way they like, women can handle it. Men, in general, can't. Gulin's solution, pure disappearance, is the only practical one. Going to the police? Has he threatened you? No. Has he beaten you? No. Has he ever assaulted anyone? No. Why do you say he'll kill you? Because I know him. The notepads would come out only once her brains were on the wall.

Gulin's a very sturdy woman, so sturdily built that I can't help speculating that you could slap away with her, hard, doggy-style, and not end up fifteen yards from your starting point. But I consider this academically, theoretically, because this holy stuff truly grows on you. I'm getting quite above earthly matters and penile servitude.

Of course, this abstinence is abetted by age. When you're eighteen and male, all you want to do is eat fried chicken and copulate until you pass out, but now I can take it or leave it, which is ironic because the whole point of my scheme is to have bountiful supplies of pleasure and to trinket up.

Finally, I hear from the Hierophant.

"You have a servant heart," he tells me, as I assure him his parishioners are all in good order. He's calling from Cleveland and tells me that he won't be back for some time yet. His mother is still very ill. He sounds tired and mentions that the Evangelists have been singing his praises.

"They've got the sixty-seventh most happening church here. I always wanted to get on that list. Ah well, the Lord should be enough. It does no good to dwell on those most happening churches run by fornicators and coke fiends. The Lord should be enough for you and me, Tyndale. And you've proved to be a slowie rather than a showie."

"Is that good?"

"I've had showies before. They come along, talk big and then vanish without doing what they promised. Or I've had to boot them out. You're a tortoise slowie, reliable and you finish what you start."

I'm rather moved by his faith. Slowie isn't the praise I would have chosen for myself, but praise always gets through.

"We need to be doing more for the unchurched," the Hierophant muses. "Perhaps we should start a young Christian organization. That'd be a good way to get onto that most-happening church list. To move forward."

We? What he means is I can go out and bust a gut keeping kids away from all the things they're most interested in.

"That's a good idea, Gene. I was just saying to myself the other day that would be a good way forward."

"That's it, Tyndale, we've got to keep moving forward. Watch out for those giant midgets."

Why does everyone think going forward is such a great idea? What if there's a hundred-foot drop onto pointy rocks ahead of you? What if there's a very comfortable bed behind you? And what's the deal with the most happening church? Why not just say your church is happening? Surely if you're dealing with the churched, your word is good enough. Or if verification is obligatory, scare the congregation away for a few weeks, so it can rocket from four to forty-four. A thousand per cent increase. Beat that growth, growers of congregations.

Will the Hierophant ever return? Or will the Evangelists sign him up? He's a battler, but there comes that day when you get tired. It happens to athletes. One minute, they're world champions, the next they won't stir from bed. It's the same for preachers.

The Hierophant's sixty-six and, having been at the wheel in his absence, I can confirm his church is going nowhere. If the Evangelists in Ohio offer him a cushy post as drill sergeant, why not take it? It would suit me.

I ponder my failure back home, and how bizarre it is to be here, still penniless, but in the religion business. In the sunshine.

Why couldn't I make it back home? You'll say to me, Tyndale, my old china, why didn't you do something about being stuck in a dreary job? What did you *do* about it? And I'll say to you, I did do something. I did something a lot. I applied for all sorts of posts. I studied Arabic for three months in case I got a job in Dubai. I studied Czech for three months in case I got the job in the new office in Prague. I joined the right golf club, and bloody expensive it was. That's what makes it so annoying. I could have done nothing, saved the fees, and still had the failure.

The Reinholds arrive to congratulate me on Cosmo's departure. "How did you do it?" they ask. I modestly shrug my shoulders. They've brought some flowers for the church, big, bright and expensive. I wish they'd brought some of the folding stuff instead. I need some new, more Miamian threads. But I'm pleased that I've done something good, however small.

When I get back to Sixto's, a worried Gulin is patrolling outside.

Her cat, Orinoco, is nowhere to be found. Did a runner when the builders were changing a window. I've always disliked cats, but Orinoco is so well behaved and good-natured that I've been stroking him when no one is looking. Orinoco knows something. There's wisdom trapped inside that cat.

Despite not being a cat owner and having decades of cat contempt to my credit, I authoritatively assure Gulin there's nothing to worry about. I don't know why we all have this urge to talk confidently about subjects we have no knowledge of.

Gamay calls up on behalf of the DJs.

"Tyndale, listen man, I'm in the middle of sorting out my schedule. Should I leave a day aside for any joining ceremony?"

"You don't listen, do you?"

"No, all I'm saying is, compañero, I wouldn't want to make your life awkward by you arranging something and then me having arranged something."

"Don't phone me."

"Okay. I get it. I get it. Totalism. But before I go, I only wanted to say if it's an issue of space, like… there's only room for one person… but not enough room for two, you know, that's a problem that isn't a problem. Muscat's awful careless when he cleans his gun."

"I'm going to hang up now. I'm telling you this so you understand when you don't hear me any more that it's not a technical glitch, it's me hanging up on you."

He and Muscat are expecting a reward for having done something right? What do they expect? A badge? A uniform? A *Multinational Crime for Beginners* manual? I don't know what to do with the DJs. Momentarily they became a good solution for getting rid of Cosmo; only now does it occur to me that they may develop into a bigger problem than Cosmo. People, I've noticed, can get really angry when they feel they've been cheated, particularly when they actually have. Should Gamay and Muscat discover I'm just a chancer from another continent, the ugliness would flow freely.

Muscat phones up.

"Tyndale, this is Muscat. You know Gamay and I, we did that work for you?"

As if I would forget ordering a kidnapping. It's touching he views me so satanically.

"I just wanted to say we appreciate being given the chance. Thank you for thinking of us and you know, if you need anyone, you know, terrorized with some serious terror, bear us... I mean bear me in mind. I know we never discussed money, but I'm able to start real basic—"

I tell Muscat that he will have to wait. "It's easy to do something. Doing nothing's harder. You may not hear from me for six months. If you can't wait, if you can't take the discipline, you're out." Perhaps they'll get impatient or get arrested.

One of the few boons of having a job is that it gets you out of bed. If you have no obligation to get out of bed, it can sometimes be very hard to persuade yourself to rise. Most mornings I lie in bed praying as hard as I can, despite not believing in God. Praying that everyone will be happy.

I would like everyone to be happy, apart from a few mass murderers, my former employers, bankers. I'd really like everyone to be happy. Why can't happiness be granted to everyone or at least most of us? Why does everything have to be so hard? All the elements are there for a reasonable life. It's like loneliness. It's ridiculous that it exists, because however deformed or weird you are, there's someone out there like you; or, if you prefer, there's someone out there not like you.

I pray hard, because there's nothing else to do, but eventually I need a cup of tea. Downstairs Gulin is now despondent about Orinoco: "Four days he's been missing." Naturally, I assume that Orinoco has expired according to cat protocol: wheeled to death or eaten by some strange immigrant group. Gulin is touring the neighbourhood putting up posters and asking after Orinoco, to no avail.

"Whadya gonna do?" she sighs. She is so miserable and, precisely because she fights to hide it and doesn't ask for help, I volunteer to join in the hunt. I am provided with a snap of Orinoco and guided to some blocks north of Sixto's where she hasn't yet canvassed. As I start my investigation, I realize that my wandering around asking about a cat might look a little suspect.

The area I'm patrolling is markedly downmarket to Sixto's. It's not an area that would be the first choice for burglars or home-invaders, but I wonder if any of the residents would find my quest plausible. Having a dark thought was a mistake. It's curious that optimistic thoughts such as "I will win the lottery", "that promotion's mine", "I must find that antique armoire perfect for the corner", rarely bear fruit, but thoughts like "I'm going to get done" do.

A stubby man is watering a lawn. I explain my mission and get looks of puzzlement. The Waterer doesn't speak English, and I don't speak enough Spanish yet to spanglish a bridge. I show him the picture of Orinoco and, instead of shaking his head, he beckons me to follow him.

We walk round the back of the house, which is heavily vegetated, down a narrow path towards a shack. I'm now out of sight of the road, out of sight full stop. I'm uneasy about this, but I've asked about the cat, so it would be unreasonable to back out now.

I follow the Waterer into the shack. In a cardboard box are five ginger kittens. He picks up two of them and offers them to me in an all-yours gesture. The last thing I want are two kittens. I smile, shake my head and utter the word "no".

"No" is such a cosmopolitan word, at home up in Anchorage, or down in Cape Horn. A word understood by billions of earthlings. Understanding isn't always such a good thing. I add "thanks" to the "no", but the "no" has done its work.

The Waterer is angry. So angry he must have been steaming about something before I inquisitioned onto the scene. He shouts. Then he has another round of shouting that makes the previous shouting tame. I can't imagine he'd have been more furious or hate-contorted if I'd murdered his family. I am already backing off, smiling hard, when he produces a gun, grabs my hair and pushes the gun into my ear so forcefully it would have been painful if I hadn't been numbed by terror.

There are a number of questions here. Why is he so angry? Does he feel I have insulted his kittens and thus, by extension, him? That I have rummaged deep in my throat and spat the results on his generosity? Why exactly does he keep a gun in a shackful of kittens? Is he simply a far-sighted man who has firearms secreted all around his property in convenient, easy-to-grab locations?

I have never been so scared. I know I'm going to die and I shit myself, although I'm so busy with the terror I don't mind. The Waterer shouts for a long time, but eventually I figure out that the only reason he doesn't shoot me is not any regard for life or fear of any penalty, but because if he shoots me he'll have to spend time digging a hole or dragging me out to the Everglades. I can't say I knew him well, but I knew that's what he was thinking.

The walk home is unpleasant.

"What happened to you?" Gulin comments on my mashed ear the next day. I say nothing about my misadventure because I'm so shaken I don't want to relive it. I doubt if I'll live long enough to find it funny.

Sixto is quietly addressing the builders, "All I want are windows that look the same as the others. They don't have to be atomically similar, but let's say an averagely observant person couldn't tell they're different from twenty feet away." It's impossible to say whether his appeal is having any effect.

In addition to my sore ear, my underwear is moist because our tumble dryer has broken down. I am developing a new theory that no one enjoys life, that enjoyment is a unicorn, when Gamay and Muscat phone to provide me with more evidence.

"I said you'd have to wait.'

"Tyndale, this isn't business. This is not, not business. We want a drink, socio. A cafecito or something."

A career in lying clearly isn't lying in wait for Gamay. I'd anticipated they'd be off my back for at least a few weeks. Perhaps I should do something decisive to get rid of the DJs and not just trust they will wither away.

I agree to meet Gamay and Muscat at a fancy hot-dog diner of their choice, Dogma.

"Now for the dryer," announces Sixto seizing the phone. Making my coffee I hear a series of exclamations from Sixto: *how much, when, sorry, how much.* I feel for Sixto. I don't know how people our age or younger are running countries. Like Sixto, running a household is beyond me.

"I can't believe what they want to charge," Sixto says. "And they say the cocaine cowboys are destroying the country. The engineer's coming tomorrow at three. Anyone at home?"

"You don't need an engineer," says Gulin. "You probably just need a new circuit board. I can get that for you."

Sixto and I look at each other like kids whose homework has miraculously done itself.

"Well," says Sixto.

"I'll sort it out," Gulin says.

Unusually, Gamay and Muscat are at Dogma waiting for me. This is a bad sign. "I'm glad you called," I say, when there is no one in earshot. "I'm glad you called" is precisely what to say when the opposite is true. I learnt this from Bamford. It's a brilliant technique of wrong-footing. And you must avoid any hint of sarcasm or insincerity, otherwise it's worthless. Smile. Always smile and say thank you when someone hands you a basket of shit. They may doubt if they really gave you a basket of shit. You settle up later, when their backs are turned.

I look at Gamay and Muscat manfully and pausefully: "We may have to go to war."

Alarmingly, this prospect doesn't alarm them at all.

"Imperative," says Gamay.

"You know it," says Muscat.

"I need you to dig up... some tools." I give them a map purporting to show buried weapons in the Everglades. I debated long and hard about how vague to make the map. If it's really vague, then even Gamay and Muscat might guess that I'm duping them. If on the other hand I put in too much detail, they might come back to me and say there's no blasted oak three hundred yards past the alligator souvenir shop. What I want is for them to wade around in hazardous swamp for a few days until they get fed up or injured and give up.

Gamay and Muscat are excited. I suppose in all of us there is a desire to have secret knowledge, to lead a secret, outlaw life, particularly if it's well paid.

"This is the big test, so don't mess up," I warn them, getting up with no intention of paying for the drinks. I hear myself adding, "I ain't kennedying you."

Back at Sixto's, Gulin is in the garage, operating on the dryer. The operation isn't progressing smoothly – she is glaring at the new circuit board with disapproval – but you can tell that she will succeed. She's wearing a purple vest which reveals a tattoo of a stylized bird on her right shoulder. Some symbol I suppose. Living? Dead? You never ask about tattoos.

The tattoo surprises me; she struck me as someone who would regard tattoos as a frivolous expense. Her ears are unpierced and as far as my unexpert eye can tell cosmetics rarely reach her face.

"Here's a new career," I say as chatty encouragement. I am humbled by her endeavour. There are so many hurdles to clear before this stage. Knowing what a circuit board is. Finding a shop that sells circuit boards. Finding the circuit board in the shop that sells circuit boards. Buying the right one. Buying the right one at the right price. Buying the right one at the right price in working condition. Opening the dryer. And so on. I know I wouldn't make it. This would beat me. But there's a chance my divine project will work, because it doesn't involve any wiring or unscrewing anything.

I can't figure out what would be most helpful, to remain in a supportive role, or to leave her alone to fiddle it out with the dryer. I choose to allocate her a few smiling minutes as a nod to either option.

"It's not difficult,' she says. "Not that difficult."

"How's the job hunt going?"

"Slow. Contacts. Contacts.'

"What would you like to do?"

"What would I like to do?" Gulin consults the installation leaflet. "I'd like to be a journalist. But that's not gonna happen. Contacts. Contacts."

It's true. Of course, blaming and claiming is the refrain of the inert, the lazy, the dim, the moaner. I didn't get the break. I didn't have this. I didn't have that. But it's different with Gulin. I'm in the presence of someone very hard. Someone who delivers. How many times have you heard someone say I can sort that out and yet it remains unsorted? Four hours after her statement she's here wielding the screwdriver. When she says contacts, it's not a lament, it's a statement of fact. And true. What's the difference between standing in a dusty garage jousting with a circuit board (for no pay, to save someone else a few dollars) and sitting in an oak-lined office earning a car every hour, whether you do anything much or not? A school friend. An uncle. Someone you met on a train.

Naturally, in order to win the lottery, you have to buy a lottery ticket. And you can work hard to buy lots of tickets, you can buy lots of tickets if you put your mind to it. You can buy lots of tickets and win nothing.

Orinoco has returned, a little displeased. I'm not angry with the cat, because wherever it's been, it's definitely not the cat's fault. Orinoco's not that kind of cat. Gulin is cheered by Orinoco's return, but annoyed because she has been offered a childminding job, but she has no car, and it will take a three-hour combination of bus and foot to get there. She is tough enough to take it, but she can't arrive there early enough to satisfy her prospective employers, who aren't willing to offer her a live-in position.

She hasn't got enough money to get a closer place (Sixto's letting her live rent-free until she gets a job). She left her car behind in LA on the basis that cars can be traced, and flew into Orlando, hired a car, drove down to Miami, dumped her stuff, then drove to Tampa to drop off the car, confident that should bury her tracks.

This is the stuff that infuriates me. Here you have someone decent, that rarity, someone who wants to work, someone at ease with hard, menial, poorly paid work, but who can't get to the job, and until she gets there can't scrape together the money to get there. Gulin is the only one in this house with an interest in honourable employment, but can't reach it.

"You know, you can always borrow my car," I say. Sixto has two cars but his spare is on loan and he doesn't know when he'll get it back.

"No," she says. Politely, she manages to refuse twice, but is so desperate that's as far as she can go. Most of the places I need to get to I can reach by public transport, which isn't bad at all but, like public transport everywhere, is much favoured by the mentally ill, junkies and the generally nasty. It is noticeable that wherever you travel the stupid and ignorant are always the loudest. They can't talk, they have to shout, and are always to be found on public transport. Also, I have no hesitation in using my legs, unlike most Miamians, who would sooner drive half an hour to avoid a five-minute walk.

Gulin goes off to test the route to her job. Sixto then appears and studies the new windows. He strokes the paint.

"It's like they had to reinvent the concept of the window. It's taken them four months to change two windows. And these clowns came *recommended*."

I don't know why the thought comes to my mind, and as soon as I say it I regret it: "Have you checked if they open?"

Sixto's not good at rage, which is a novelty in someone of a Cuban background. He doesn't shout, swear, wave his hands or throw things. His mouth twitches a little and his breathing gets hard as the two of us are unable to get the windows to open even a fraction.

"You know, what's the worst part of this? I could have these guys killed. One phone call, a solution architect would fly in, bang, bang. That's what's so hard. One phone call. One phone call. I could really have them killed, no questions asked. It's so hard not to."

He circulates around the kitchen, nodding and breathing hard, I suppose having conversations of an imaginary, hostile nature with window-fitters.

On Collins Avenue, a bare-chested man who is a V of rocky pectorals and is wearing white naval bell-bottoms hands me a small plastic sachet. He is jigging around the sidewalk, handing out the sachets to passers-by. I usually accept proffered leaflets or items because if you've ever had to do a job like that, you will spend the rest of your life accepting proffered leaflets or items.

The sachet contains a clear substance which according to the packaging is personal lubricant. Since I have no immediate plans to bugger anyone, I'm not sure what to do with it.

Having enjoyed two lattes and an exceptionally good tuna Niçoise sandwich in the Loews Hotel I am about to leave without paying the bill, when I get a call from Gamay and Muscat. Not having heard from them for a week I had happily concluded that they had given up on joining an international criminal organization.

"We've got the tools," Gamay announces with the sort of pride a sixteen-year-old would have after bedding three beauty queens in one night.

I'm perplexed. Unwisely I tell them to meet me at the church. Gamay and Muscat struggle into the office carrying a large metal container they can barely carry. Then they go out and grunt back in with two more containers, dripping with sweat. They don't say a word but look at me grinning.

I have to do it. I open the latches on the uppermost container. Inside is an abundance of black sacking material, which contains a weighty object. I unfurl the material, and find myself holding an automatic weapon. If all the containers are full, there must be three dozen of them. I like to consider myself a man with a ready retort, but I'm unworded.

"It wasn't easy," beams Gamay. "Socio, your map wasn't that good. But hey, delivery is us."

I examine the gun. I don't like guns. They say people kill people, not guns. That's not right, people want to kill people, but the guns do it. I am quite tired of living, but this scares me. This is heaviness way beyond my abilities or interests. These containers contain illegality and danger out of all proportion to their volume.

"You boys really disappoint me," I say. The DJs are hesitant. Is this multinational criminal irony?

"These aren't ours. I don't know where you got these. But if I were you I'd take these back straight away, because the owners might be very angry. Buriers of guns aren't known for their sense of humour. Or for that matter, hesitation in shooting former DJs."

"Muscat, why are you disgracing us like this?" says Gamay.

"Me?" says Muscat. I, of course, have no interest in hearing the two of them volley the blame back and forth, but I hear it anyway.

"You shouldn't be here wasting Tyndale's time. You're just too soft." Gamay storms out and returns with a small box. "I thought we established who's Mr Bad," he continues, opening the box to reveal two scorpions. "Let's see who's hard." He takes one scorpion and dangles it above the back of his trousers.

"You're not doing that," exclaims Muscat. But Gamay drops the hapless scorpion into buttockville and then sits down, with considerable gusto and a crunching sound. My heart goes out to the scorpion. Gamay whoops as if downing a tequila and extracts some squished remains from his nether regions.

When I was growing up I had many dreams, but I never had one where I was sitting in an ailing church, vainly striving to be mistaken for God, surrounded by stacks of firearms, while an oxygen thief crushes a scorpion with his backside in an attempt to be recruited by an non-existent multinational criminal organization. A round of applause for the Unexpected.

Let's consider Gamay's show. Who carries around two live scorpions? You'd only do this if you're expecting to put on a show. Again, I can't divine how Gamay has cheated, but I'm convinced he hasn't exposed himself to any significant pain or toil – that's not his style. That he chose the larger scorpion is for me confirmation of a con.

Scorpions vary in their toxicity and, furthermore, like snakes you can milk them for their venom. I can talk about this with some authority, because one of my neighbours invested in a company making scorpion restrainers. Also, since their attack depends on penetrating skin, if you were to cut even a tiny amount off the very tip of the sting, it would no longer be hypodermic. We weren't given a chance to inspect the scorpion before it was arsed out of recognizability.

"You're harder than me," Muscat concedes, "harder and crazier." Gamay has the cheek to offer me the other scorpion.

I instruct Gamay and Muscat to take the guns away. I know they'll probably just stick them under their beds, but I want them gone. "This is on a need-to-know basis," I say, "and I don't need to know." They get sulky about having to lug the containers back out. For big, strong lads they are extraordinarily lazy.

"Don't phone me. I ain't kennedying you," I say, already picturing myself on flights out of the country; or, who knows, maybe my luck will change and I'll get a nice situation in the prison library to see out my declining years?

Sometimes a good night's sleep makes prospects look better, but not when you're strictly ruined. The misery is right there by the bedside table. I had to knock myself out by raiding Sixto's drinks cabinet, but the great thing about being abstinent is that when you have a drink, you get your money's worth.

I catch my reflection in the mirror. I look rather mad. I am probably going mad, but perhaps one of the consolations of going mad is that you don't mind too much.

In a mechanical, lifeless way I head off to the church and do some pastoral acts in a mechanical, lifeless way. I'm hoping I can escape our parishioners for surgery as there's no one around. Just as I'm locking up, the Reinholds greet me. Have they come to give me a present in gratitude? Because no matter how much punishment you take there's always a part of you that's hoping someone will walk in and hand you a fat cheque.

They don't look happy enough for my taste, and we have some pleasantries in the office before we get to the unzipping.

"We're grateful, we're very grateful for your help, Tyndale. We don't want you to think we're ungrateful. And I know you'll find this funny, but we need you to get Cosmo back."

I don't find it funny at all. I'm not that angry because if you're being burned at the stake, you don't get that upset if someone in the crowd throws on another bit of kindling, though you might be surprised to see who's throwing it.

The Reinhold's daughter has completely gone off the rails, her behaviour is even worse than before, so they want Cosmo back. There is only one question in life worth asking: is it written or not? Is there anything I can do to change my fortune or should I give up now? Are losers losers, or winners-in-waiting?

"I'll do my best," I say, because I want them gone. "But I can't promise anything."

Reinhold leaves his newspaper behind. Out of a desire to escape my life, I pick it up. On the front page of the *Miami Herald* is a bizarre abduction story involving the Dade County Police Commissioner's wife and teenage daughter. On a trip out to the Everglades, they were abducted by two powerfully built white males. Instead of being robbed or sexually assaulted as they feared, they were given spades and forced to dig holes for two days. Their abductors kept calling each other "Gammy" and "Musky". I don't bother reading the rest of the article.

Never, never work with people.

I'm on the verge of getting comfortable with complete despair, when something good happens.

While I'm handing out turkey subs to the homeless, the young guy, Fash, taps me on the shoulder and hands me my wallet, which must have fallen out of my pocket. It surprises and annoys me. It's so infuriating when you've settled into a doctrine of perfect misanthropy to have your philosophy challenged in this way, because you start asking the questions again: is there good? You waste so much time thinking. One of the great strengths of religion is that it gives you answers, you're ready with the thinking and saying. If nothing else it saves you so much time and energy. It's like shopping: if you don't know what you want you can spend the whole day looking at, say, trousers, whereas if you do you can buy them in ten minutes.

And it is pointless. One man exhibiting decency on the street in Miami isn't going to change anything. But you feel guilty, you feel wrong about throwing away that act of decency, as if it doesn't matter (although it doesn't – does it?).

Back at the church, before I can close the doors, a fifty-something woman slides in. This is the one of the dangers of offering help: the needy come and ask for it. The unneedy too. However, I feel better because it confirms my theory of swings and roundabouts. Someone hands me back my wallet, I get stuck with an irritating woman called Marysia.

I don't remember seeing her at any of our services, and let's face it, worshippers aren't hard to spot at the Church of the Heavily Armed Christ. My guess is she is here because all the other, better, proper churches have shown her the door. Everything about her is... irritating. She has a strange European accent, and emphasizes everything she says to underline how well she speaks English. Students of a language tend to fall into two main categories: the taxi-driver class where you have enough vocabulary to ask for the fare, and the show-off class.

"I was driving by when I saw your Church abutting on the..." Abutting? When was the last time you heard anyone use the word abutting? Have I led a very sheltered life? Is abutting making a comeback?

I check the clock when she arrives, because I intend to accord her ten minutes before claiming urgent prior commitments. When I repeatedly say things like "I must go" she ignores them so completely it's evident she's hardened to escape attempts. Displeasure tumbles from my face in vain.

Her woe is her two-year-old grandson who has digestive problems. You'd think it'd be difficult to talk about a kid's shit for fifty minutes. If you said to me, I'll give you a hundred grand if you could talk about it for fifty minutes, I'd certainly try, but I'd run out after ten or so. Marysia gabbles on about it for fifty minutes without pause or hesitation, though with a great deal of repetition. She has mastered some technique of breathing while simultaneously talking. I time her on the clock. Our bowels are a vital part of life, but even as a professional ear, I recoil at fifty minutes of a safari down the lower intestine of an infant so intricate I feel like an enzyme.

"The coprolith then proceeded…" I can guess what coprolith means, but I'm willing to bet the doctor that's treating the kid has never heard the word. Marysia's the sort of mother you'd move to the other side of the world to dodge.

She's really so, so irritating. And she didn't start out that way. She was probably a pleasant kid. She didn't set out to be irritating. She didn't volunteer, or take a course. She may have made some bad decisions, but who hasn't? Maybe she could have fought harder against the metamorphosis into a compulsive grouser, but who hasn't given up? And if there's no hope of redemption, there's no hope. For a second, I'm sorry for her. But only one.

Normally when I get a moaner in, I can drift off, abandon time, have a me moment, if for no other reason than that the true moaner doesn't notice you fleeing – the perpetual moaners really want to moan – but I can't shut her out. I seriously consider feigning a heart attack to shut her off when her phone goes and it's fortunately something significant requiring her presence elsewhere.

"Could you give me a prayer to help my grandson's stercoraceous fusillade?" she asks. I certainly can. I utter some words of respite for little Leon. Before she leaves Marysia gives me her card. I'm surprised. I expected her to be an assistant librarian in an outlying library, but she is Vice President of an oil company.

A number of thoughts go through my mind.

First: she knows nothing about oil. You might judge me a little peremptory, a little sweeping in making a statement like that having spent a single hour with her where the only subject of conversation was constipation. However I know I know as much about oil as Marysia. She knows nothing about oil.

Second: you don't want to tournamentize life, but there are victors and non-victors. Simple as that. She lucked out. Just because she knows nothing about oil, why shouldn't she be the Vice President of an oil company? That's the current style. There's so much movement in the job market, why should you be hampered by ignorance? I was almost a freak in staying at the same company for fifteen years. Of course, I tried to get out, but that's another story. You find complete ignorance everywhere: lawyers who know nothing about the law, doctors who know nothing about medicine.

One of my neighbours' daughters signed up to be a gofer in a public-relations company, one summer for two weeks. Within three months she was the boss, not because she was gifted or had a ruthless go-getting streak, but because there was a wave of resignations, accidents, pregnancies, stormings-out and, although she wasn't at all interested in public relations, she ran the company because she felt someone ought to.

Marysia leaves. Maybe it's the frequency of her voice.

Getting back home late one night, I notice across the road, framed by darkness, in a well-lit room, a couple getting fleshy. Either they were too eager to bother with the curtains or they're into the idea of an audience.

The house is rented out to tourists for short stints. I recognize the man first: it's my ex-wife's new partner. I have a good view of him as he thrusts away, and he has a very distinctive high forehead and hair like a shaving brush. On further observation, I realize the woman receiving his attentions is my ex-wife. It takes me time to recognize her because my angle of vision isn't good and because she's changed her hairstyle. Women are always altering their appearance and then get upset when you don't recognize them. The worst instance I know of this was Nelson picking up his wife's younger sister (whom he'd only met briefly a couple of times) and getting as far as the hotel-room key. "Of course, I knew it was you," he laughed when she revealed her identity, but his attempt to pass it off as a practical joke didn't minimize his punishment.

In the kitchen, I prepare myself that staple of lone males, toast. When I go up to my room and check, they're still at it. I could get very angry about this. I could rage about the near impossibility of my ex-wife renting the house opposite my abode from the billions of rentable homes on offer. I could fall prey to the suspicion that she's doing it deliberately, but for the knowledge that she'd be more horrified than me to discover our proximity. Somehow the total absurdity of the episode makes me feel this is a provocation, that this has been engineered by the universe to wind me up. Anything is better than chaos. And if bad luck doesn't upset you, it's not really such bad luck; naturally that's not such an easy trick to pull off, but there you are.

I have nothing against Dee's new man. He runs a business breeding ladybirds, which initially made me think he was mentally ill, until I learnt that gardeners buy them for pest control. He has a staff of twenty. He's never going to be rich in the having-your-own private-army way we dream of when we're young. But he has enough for a foreign holiday twice a year and a big house with a garden. Dee would prefer to have a senior banker to brag about, because the comic element to breeding ladybirds is unavoidable, but you can't have everything.

I'm not angry with Dee either. She wants to be happy. That's not unreasonable. I didn't appear like the path to happiness. I'm disappointed, and I feel sad because I have nothing to say to her and we can't even go out for a quick drink. There are few people I can relive the past with and there are going to be even fewer. I don't mind that they're happy. Because the happier the world is, the better off we all are.

The saddest thing is you can't even make someone like you, let alone love you.

Is the problem me? For years now, I've been pondering this.

Earlier on you think, when I leave school, it'll be all right. When I get that girlfriend, it'll be all right. When I get that job, it'll be all right. When I get married, it'll be all right, and of course it isn't. I've been trying to figure out what it is. Is it bad luck? A rule that no one told me about? That page of the existence manual you forgot to read? Some awkwardness or laziness in me? Will I ever find out?

All you can do: stay cool. Stay cool and wait for the opportunity. Action is only speeded-up waiting. All you can do is wait.

The Hierophant calls. His mother's worsening. There's nothing much he can do: in fact, apart from hand-holding there's nothing he can do. "She had an infection and they thought she was a goner."

He hasn't reached the stage of saying "it would have been better for her". What people generally mean is it would be better for them. Sometimes it would be better, but pretend, pretend. That's the problem with being decent. It ruins you. More than drugs. Walking away is the universal panacea.

The next call is from South Beach Police Station. Mrs Shepherd, our flower-gatherer, is in custody on theft charges. I'm really perplexed, but they won't go into details over the phone.

Before I leave, Mrs Blatt from next door arrives with a basket of marrows. She has some place out of town, apparently a secret marrow farm. It's very kind of her, but at Sixto's we've already been eating nothing but marrows for a week, and even though I'm fond of marrows, a man can only take so much marrow. Her charity hits the bin.

I phone Dishonest Dave for advice. "I'll meet you at the station," he insists.

Outside the police station, I wait for Dishonest Dave. From across the street I hear the rhythms of preaching. I approach the strains of damnation and brimstoning issued by a top spitfire:

"The burning never stops burning. God wants winners not sinners."

I make a note to steal the line, but it's only when I turn the corner and lock on to the source that I see it's not a flesh-and-blood preacher, but a tape coming from a boombox, with the impassive figure of the Prophet, gas-masked, standing next to it as custodian. Generally, the street-corner evangelists are either on the way up or down, either working up a routine or plain insane. It's rather lazy to hand a tape out.

"God wants to help. God wants to help you. With over four billions years of experience, God can give you everything you ever wanted right now, and God's dealers in Miami are the Fixico Sisters." Who are the Fixico sisters?

Dishonest Dave bounces up. I'm standing by an empty parked police car. "One second," says Dave. He takes out a mini-mill from a pocket, with which he grinds out some white powder onto the car's hood. A gold-plated razor blade hastens the powder into two lines; next, a metal snorter in the shape of a vacuum cleaner, with which he hoovers up the first line. He proffers the snorter and when I decline, he polishes off the remainder.

I can't actually see a police officer around, but it seems insanely insane. This reminds me of being with Nelson, magnified a thousand times. However, I have the courage of the dead.

"I needed that. Have you heard the 'Varying Latin American Nation Police-Station' story yet?" asks Dave. "There was this police station out in the countryside. Small police station. Closed at weekends. One Monday morning, the police come back and there's no police station. It's gone, there's only some foundations to show that there was once a building. The front door, the chairs, the windows, the bricks, the roof, the wiring, the nails, the sign saying police station, all gone. The whole police station has been stolen. That's a story you're going to hear in Miami. The location changes, but the story is the same. The Colombians tell it about the Ecuadorians. 'That's how thieving and poor the Ecuadorians are.' The Ecuadorians about the Colombians. The Uruguayans about the Paraguayans. You get the picture."

Across the street, I wonder why the preacher has lost his voice. Tape change? "And he will have no mercy, no mercy on that day," the voice rebooms. "But don't forget: carpenters charge... garages charge... dentists charge... the electric company charges... God works for free... God delivers right to your front

141

door for free. The Fixico Sisters are God's dealers." Great line. God works for free. That undercuts the Hierophant's affordable paradise. Basically there's the carrot-and-stick approach. You offer peace and happiness, but lob in some fear as well.

"I'm introducing myself as your counsel," says Dave as we enter.

"Have you studied law?" I ask. He looks offended. Inside we discover why Mrs Shepherd has been arrested.

There are some matey, good-natured policefolk. The police in Miami aren't like that. They frighten me. They're all huge, and they'll shoot you without any hesitation. I can't reproach them for this attitude. There are many evil, mad individuals with automatic weapons at large out there, not to mention the plain stupid ones.

They also have this "we know" look they give you. "We know all about it. We won't arrest you today, but we know all about it." And they're right, because who hasn't got some tax fraud or dope stashed away? Although, as far as I'm aware, I don't believe posing as the Supreme Being is an offence.

Mrs Shepherd is unrepentant, but pleased to see me. I introduce myself as the Sub-Hierophant of the Church of the Heavily Armed Christ. Dave introduces himself as counsel for the Sub-Hierophant of the Church of the Heavily Armed Christ. I'm wearing my suit, but I'm not casting holiness. I look, catching my reflection in the glass door, like a failed club owner, which, considering I'm an excessively failed club owner, is a step in the right direction. Dave looks like he should be in a cell for a gangland killing, twenty-five to life.

But the investigating officer is tolerant. He smiles the "we-know-all-about-it" smile to Dave. Mrs Shepherd has been caught in the Woodlawn cemetery.

We find out why Mrs Shepherd has been such a good source of flowers. She's been stealing them from the cemetery. She probably would have got away with it, but for the fact that, with Christmas coming up, she had been cutting down a small pine tree with a blunt, battery-operated turkey carver.

I can see Dave, even as a man who snorts coke off the back of police cars, is discomforted by this, as I am. This is bad juju. In capitals. I don't believe in God, not in the sense of a sentient force who's worried about whether you eat shellfish or which hand you wipe your arse with, but if there is anything on the other side, behind the scenes – ripping off the dead, shitting on the grieving? You are in big trouble. If I actually were God, I'd be making a note about this.

They can't, of course, prove that Mrs Shepherd has been the culprit lifting the flowers for the last two years, although the staff have been logging her and unfortunately she can't provide the name of even one grave she claims to be visiting in the cemetery. But like all police forces they're concerned about clearing up the thefts, so they suggest that if she fesses up to some others some community service can be arranged.

"But the Hierophant told me to do it," she maintains with a lack of loyalty that is truly remarkable. "You told me to do it, too," she adds in my direction. I admire the way she can turn on us without the slightest hesitation.

"This is a tragically... tragic case of tragic misunderstanding... tragically," sums up Dave. "Officer Blaine, do you like Miles Davis?"

We buy several tickets for Rescuers in the Ring, an annual charity event in which the police box the fire brigade, and we leave with Dishonest Dave promising unreleased Miles Davis out-takes from the period he was pimping his wife.

"You should listen to more Miles Davis. Yeah. I'll do you a compilation. Time for a drink, no?"

I list some excuses.

"No, no. It's my birthday and, as a present, you can come and have a drink with me."

We make for Dave's favourite hangout, Three Writers Losing Money. The drawback to not eating much and not drinking is that you become a pushover for alcohol when it makes its entrance. I want a mineral water, but Dave insists that on his birthday we have to drink Barbancourt. After three rums I'm just a Sub-Hierophant-shaped cushion. Dave fills me in on Haitian history from the period 1920 to 1935. He's quite animated on the subject, but I'm not listening closely. We chat to a friendly woman who has a business selling toe-separators, and Dave harries me into consuming two more rums.

You don't expect to be handcuffed to the fittings when you're out for a drink in a trendy club, so when Dave handcuffed me to some cast-iron latticework around our booth, I was slow to react. I waited to see if there would be a punchline or explanation.

"Admit it," says Dave. "You were thinking about going home."

I had been, although when you think of my bed, home is barely worth the effort of going home. I had been waiting for Dave to go to the toilet and then slumping out as fast as I could to get a taxi. I'm not quite sure why Dave needs to secure my company, since he's of a type that walks into a bar and ten minutes later is chatting to everyone.

"It's not your birthday, is it?"

"No."

"Why do you need to cuff me?"

"Generally, you're good company. Good company is hard to get, although, you are frankly disappointing me this evening."

A broad, sixty-something man with a weathered face studies Dave for a moment.

"You were a fighter, weren't you?"

Dave nods and we are joined by Mike, who has driven down to Miami from Savannah to see the plaque that commemorates the 5th Street gym, which, judging by the way the two of them go on about it, is a very big deal in the boxing world.

What intrigues me is how Mike, in poor lighting conditions, with a savage background din, could tell that Dave, sitting at a table, relating to me the history of trade tariffs in the Caribbean from 1880 to 1932, drinking Barbancourt rum, was a former pugilist. Dave isn't surprised at all. Dave and Mike discuss the history of heavyweight boxing from 1947 to 1974.

Boxing has this cultlike effect. Golfers can be tiresome about Scotland and the alloys used in their clubs, but it's different with boxing, perhaps because you have to pay some physical dues. Some of my neighbours boxed, and they all had the joy of being knocked out, broken noses, stitches. There's a whiff of human sacrifice about it.

Dave recaps Haitian history from 1780 to 1815, and also speaks knowledgeably about the political history of Colombia from 1920 to 1952. A skinny Chinese man coming in to sell some pirate DVDs moves us on to reflections about which biography of Bob Dylan is best and whether Mike would like a Frank Sinatra compilation. Dave has a brief row with a Jamaican. "While you were doing your sister in the sugar cane, we were reading Proust."

Mike works for a small company making putt returners. I wonder whether he's brought any samples with him, because I've never been able to find a putt returner that worked consistently. I hope to manoeuvre the topic of conversation around to this as we've now established some rapport, although there's an air of sourness about Mike which suggests gifts won't be forthcoming.

"You here for the pussy, Mike?" Dave asks after a short discourse on Russian absurdists in the 1930s.

"No."

"Married?"

"Yes. Well, was. My wife passed away."

"I'm sorry. Is this recent?"

"Yesterday."

A sufficient intimacy has now evolved for Mike to reveal to us that he's killed his wife and has her body stashed in his car parked outside.

Dave and I nod sympathetically. We've nearly been there. It's impossible to be married without at least once having considered killing your spouse. The trick, of course, is not to. Round about divorce time, you do hope your partner will walk under a truck, because it would be quicker and cheaper, tidier than a divorce, and because it would absolve you of failure.

Mike is taking a day or two of sunshine before handing himself in or killing himself. Our acquaintance with Mike has been brief, but we've taken a liking to him. He's a straightforward guy who snapped, hit his wife only once, after she broke an umbrella over his head; he is a tortured, remorse-seeping man whose misery has made him confess to utter strangers.

"What do you think Mike should do, Tyndale? Let's have the spiritual angle on this. Tyndale's the Sub-Hierophant of the Church of the Heavily Armed Christ," says Dave as if it's some hard-to-earn qualification, passing the buck, though he stressed the honorifics to give me a second more response time.

"Well," I say. Hoping some other words will sneak out in its wake. Very occasionally I've found myself saying something clever without it being me. I say "well" again and then I've run out.

This is the trouble with setting myself up as a spiritual pharmacist, I now have to unknot an unknottable knot. Mike has been courteous enough not to comment on the fact I'm handcuffed. I don't know what to say. I know fucked when I see it. Prison will not be kind to an office-warmer in his mid-sixties.

"Prison costs," Mike considers. "Why should I use up your hard-earned tax dollars?"

All in all, suicide probably is the tidiest solution. Dave counsels going on the run, since every day out of the joint will be a bonus. However, Mike wants the punishment. He wants the punishment especially if the punishment will destroy him. The only solution would be if I could resurrect his wife.

"Don't give up," I say, even though I don't believe it. If anyone is in the ideal position to give up, it's Mike, but you can't let someone go down the drain – well, not unless it's someone you hate. "Don't give up. You never know what's around the corner."

"Let me tell you a story about my uncle," says Dave. "He was a man with severe marital problems. He woke up one morning to find two dead men in his driveway."

I don't quite see why Dave tells us this story. The two dead men his uncle found had apparently stabbed each other to death. One he recognized as the contract killer he had hired to do his wife and, judging from his wife's expression when she saw the bodies, the other body was presumably the contract killer she had hired to do him. This cleared the air and last year they celebrated their fortieth wedding anniversary.

At two in the morning, Dave gets a call from a man with a freezer full of lamb chops, three tons of them. "This is the trouble with having a name like Dishonest Dave. I mean what can I do with three tons of lamb chops? Hang on." He disappears into the club's kitchen and on return announces with pleasure: "Our tab's clear."

As dawn manifests and I'm unshackled, Dave offers Mike to be his counsel and a compilation of Ornette Coleman. He also recommends South Beach police station as the best one to hand himself in at.

Dishonest Dave and I accompany Mike to his car as he has one putt returner with him. I had got round to mentioning my dissatisfaction with the putt returners I had encountered and embarrassingly Mike now insists I should take it off his hands as he won't be needing it. It's easier to agree and allow him this act of generosity as a start on the atonement, even though it's awkward accepting a gift from a man who's either going to be dead or locked up for good in a few hours – but nevertheless, a good putt returner…

I'm also concerned that the putt returner might be stuck in the back with his wife's corpse. Mike has a huge SUV which he has parked on some wasteland three blocks away. Get this. He parked out there to save the parking fee: old habits die hard. He takes a putt returner off the back seat.

"I'm not a bad person, but give me those keys," shouts a car-jacker with a gun. It's now that I digest that we're in a secluded stretch off the main strip, and while someone might take the trouble to report us getting shot, we can't count on any passing observers to note the robbery.

I'm very nervous that Mike will have a go at the jacker, death by criminal, and I think if he had been alone, he would have; I'm also nervous that Dave will have a go.

"It is you," I accuse Dave.

"I told you," says Dave, shrugging his shoulders.

"You don't want to take this car, son," Mike coaxes grandfatherly.

"You're an expert on what I want, are you? You've made a study of me for years?"

Now you can't really expect to like your car-jacker, but car-jacking is like everything else – it can be done professionally or it can be done imbecilely. Also, while some are driven to crime by desperation, he's enjoying it.

"I can give you a good reason not to take this car," says Mike.

"What's that?" says the jacker. "Crime doesn't pay? It looks pretty good from where I'm standing. Now, amuse me."

"Sorry?" says Mike.

"Amuse me. Entertain me. Sing me a song or something or I'll jink you good."

Is it really necessary to have this much humiliation in life? It occurs to me that, apart from not being in good voice, I don't know any songs, maybe a few first lines. Mike launches into something familiar – but which I can't name – with a confident, practised bass tone. You can see the jacker wants to fuss, but unfortunately he's got what he wanted.

"What's that?" asks the jacker pointing at the putt returner.

"A putt returner," I say. "It's for—"

"Does it work? I've never found one that works right."

"It's not very good..." But he's not falling for that. I hand it over. He gets in the car.

"Don't you want our wallets?" Dave asks.

"Are you calling me stupid? If I'd wanted your wallets, I would have asked for your wallets."

"Why don't you want our wallets? You're a joke. You forgot and now you're pretending that you didn't want them." I say nothing. Dave takes a clutch of dollar bills from his wallet and waves them. Mike moves forward to make another entreaty, but Dave restrains him. "Let him take the car."

The jacker has trouble with the ignition.

"That's piss-poor, not being able to start the car, for a jacker," Dave comments. Mike has to show him how to jiggle the key.

"I'm a wonderful human being," says the jacker as the engine revs. "But you have to do what you have to do. I have no problem with my self-esteem." We watch the car move down the road.

"You know," Dave says to Mike, "when you report this to the police, you don't have to mention that your wife wasn't alive when she left you."

"My husband used to cry all the time," says Gulin. She is making some pancakes, in good spirits. Her observation isn't spiteful, rather regretful.

I sympathize with her husband. You have to act tough outside, but the main merit of home is to be able to curl up and weep, and there is nowhere to hide in marriage: the soiled underwear, the buckling, the strange habits, the embarrassing and persistent medical condition. They all get repeated, thorough viewing.

Despair. What good is despair? Pain, now the utility of pain is indisputable. Pain teaches you to stay away from fire, indigestible foodstuffs and not to jump out of third-storey windows. Despair gets in the way, an emotional weed that entangles you and that makes things harder by throwing blackness everywhere. I can't see an upside to it.

Her marriage has gone down, her husband wants to kill her, and even if it was a doomed marriage it would be natural to be a little down about it, but if she's in distress, it's hidden. Most of us catch colds regularly, but there are hardy souls who don't. Gulin isn't one for brooding.

Gulin serves Napalm and me. Her good spirits are partly down to her new job, which requires her to live in. Her new employer is paralysed on one side, terminally ill and already has a rota of nurses but needs a round-the-clock helper for his business. I'd find it profoundly depressing caring for someone that ill, but Gulin is unfazed: "Hey we're all coming or going." Indeed, the prospect of non-stop, well-paid work pleases her.

I'm sure she does a good job too, but what will her efforts earn her? Her employer will be dead soon and she'll have to look for another position, something that takes time and effort even if you're good at it. That's the trouble with that line of work as an assistant, you can't move up, you can only move along and when the person providing the reference is dead it may not count for much. You want your job to be on a ladder, something where you can move up to be a senior something.

It's rare for her to cook, because she hardly ever seems to eat. She's wearing a pair of jeans and a white T-shirt which look good, but they will have been the cheapest jeans and T-shirt available on the continent. It is a little shaming to encounter someone just much tougher, more frugal, more joyful, more able than you; someone quite simply a better person.

"We'll miss you," says Napalm, reaching for his fourth pancake.

"I'll be back from time to time," says Gulin. She's keeping her room in case the arrangement doesn't work out. Napalm has already volunteered to take care of Orinoco. I take my fifth pancake. I'm too occupied stuffing my face to make much conversation.

"Why don't you ask me a question, Tyndale?" asks Gulin. "Tonight, but only tonight, you can ask me any question you like, and I won't be offended. I promise. Any question." This is definitely flirting.

What I want to ask is how can I be like you? How can I make myself like you? I know that there is no answer to that, or rather the answer is no.

"What's the meaning of life?" I ask.

She laughs.

"Well?" I insist.

"I said you could ask any question. I didn't say I'd answer it."

Her face and build are too solid to be considered by most as beautiful for a woman. I suppose pleasant to the eye is the most accurate way of describing her. Beauty, of course, is nothing, but it takes a long time to learn that.

"I need to talk to you," says Dishonest Dave. His tone alone communicates that something's badly amiss. "I… need to ask a favour. You do this feeding-the-homeless stuff now for the Hierophant. I want you to look out for someone."

"Sure." Considering all he's done for me, I'm delighted to do him a favour. He slides a photograph across my desk. "I want you to look out for him." It's a picture of a grinning man holding up a bottle of beer to the camera in a celebratory way.

"Who is it?"

"My brother."

Now he says it, the resemblance springs out. His brother is much heavier, fat indeed, but the arched eyebrows are the same.

"Yeah. My brother. He… he… well, he had a lot of problems. A lot of problems. I don't know where he is. I lost touch with him months ago. He may well be out there… so if you see him, I'd consider it a big favour if you'd let me know. A big favour. His name's Horace."

"Older brother?"

"Yeah. He… taught me how to box. We had no one else. He… he looked after me, you know?" On the words "looked after me", Dave's voice trembles and he sobs. I pass him a tissue (the Hierophant's office is always stocked with them). He takes a deep breath and pulls himself together.

"I can't believe I did that. It's unpardonable… absolutely unpardonable. What you must think of me."

He does suspect I think less of him. On the contrary, I know in the league table of hardness he is well above me. He was keen to get into the boxing ring to fight strong, well-trained athletes whose uppermost desire was to seriously injure or kill him. He's a survivor. I'm not. But these inconsistencies are interesting. Out there in some corner of Miami will be someone willing to take the life of a stranger for small change, but who would be too tongue-tied to ask a girl onto the dance floor. Of course, if you're worried about being hard you're not. The world's hardest man won't think himself hard.

"Everyone breaks. And remember, I am a pastor."

"No you're not."

"You'd be surprised."

"Horace was too generous. Most people who end up on the street have made a mistake. His was being too generous. He could have stayed with me, but he wouldn't."

Dave then offers to take me to a corrupt doctor, a Brazilian plastic surgeon. I don't have the heart to tell Dave that, mulling over my miracle, I've changed my mind and concluded that what I need is not a corrupt doctor, but an honest one.

"This guy is so crooked, whatever you want him for you'd better be quick, because he won't be out of jail long."

I don't see the dog until it's right next to us. If I said to you what would you do if you were attacked by a large, aggressive dog, you would probably come up with some sensible suggestions for self-defence, but when you are actually attacked by a large, aggressive dog you don't have those seconds of tranquillity in which to consider action.

The dog is four or five feet away from me, barking furiously. It's huge, a canine bodybuilder, stuffed with steak and steroids. I gingerly back off, because dogs don't like to attack from the front. As I move backwards, the dog matches me, maintaining the same distance. After a few yards of this retreat, I realize that the dog is not vicious or especially dangerous: it's doing what's expected of it. It's got loose by negotiating some gap in a fence or wobbly gate, and now the street is part of its territory.

Dave, meanwhile, I've registered out of the corner of my eye, has flown up a tree which I wouldn't be able to climb with the aid of a ladder.

"This, this is what happens when you leave your gun in the car." We had parked round the corner and were walking to the Brazilian's when the dog bounded up. The dog's barking diminishes and it observes me.

I observe the dog. Its muscles are astonishingly large and defined. It must have escaped from some garden nearby, and to some extent I'm glad that Dave doesn't have his gun, because this isn't the dog's fault. It's the owner's.

I like dogs. It's stupid to say that because dogs have their characters; there are nasty, jumpy, useless dogs. But generally I like dogs, and not for the most cited reason, loyalty. I like them because most are willing to work, unlike cats, but above all because they're willing to look stupid, unlike cats. Dogs don't mind making fools of themselves, because they know it gives the pack a laugh. It's what you want from your friends almost as much as their support: their folly. Got drunk and bedded someone incredibly ugly? Spent all your money on tatty sports memorabilia (which turns out to be counterfeit) without telling the wife? Rewired your home and set it on fire? We're grateful for the laugh. Everyone should do their share of jestering.

The dog licks its chops and we regard each other. The dog is bored and neither of us knows what to do. I won't attempt to go past this monster to get back to our car, and I can't spend the rest of my life walking backwards.

"When I find the owner..." Dave hisses from his branch. I see his expression and I understand that what I rated as anger in myself isn't. My wrath is only ambitious discontent: overgrown disappointment. A mountain range of rage is expanding behind Dave's features. It's rage you don't want to be around, because its extremity makes little distinction between its target and anything else in sight.

In the garden to my left, safely behind a fence, a poodle, attracted by the brouhaha, doggedly yelps and leaps against the mesh. Our monster doesn't even deign to look at it. After a while a woman emerges to lead the poodle away.

"Do you know whose dog this is?" I shout to her.

"No," she says, dragging her dog inside.

"Could you phone someone about this dog?" I indicate the monster.

"No. It's not my dog," she says. That's how it's going to end. It won't be some criminal mastermind or evil genius unleashing

155

the end of the world. It'll be someone lazy or stupid, someone not bothering to close a gate, and we'll all be finished. Because laziness always wins.

As I'm wondering how to deal with the impasse, a cyclist shoots past, having improperly assessed the scene as man with dog rather than man threatened by dog; the monster takes off after him barking, glad of purpose.

For several minutes Dave prowls around in the hope of locating the owner. Just as well for us all, there is no sign of dog or owner. The trip was wasted, since the Brazilian wasn't at home. Dave chews darkness all the way back.

What is it with the dogs and cats? Is this some code? I give it some thought. If it is a code, I can't figure it out. On a wall, I see a poster. Two white-haired grannies are peering out at me. They are bewildered, as if they are novices in the field of having their picture taken. The caption reads:

"The Fixico Sisters – God's Dealers."

"It's a small village in the East of Turkey," says Gulin of her birthplace. "It's the sort of place where you either spend your whole life, or you leave and never go back." She worked for a while as a teacher in a primary school, then left. "The winters are bad. It can get completely snowed in. I worry about my mother a lot. I'd like to bring her here, but, you know, the money and the visa…"

I'm making that dish that no one can mess up: spaghetti bolognese.

You may not make great spag bol, but you can't make it inedible (unless, perhaps, you're Napalm). As I watch the water boil and listen to Gulin, I keep on thinking about the odd memories I've been getting.

Really inconsequential memories, things I've never remembered once before (as far as I can remember), un-events: walking up stairs, waiting to get served in shops, making my way along deserted corridors, dull, non-essential scenes that have suddenly broken free from the depths of my mind and bobbed to the surface. Extraordinarily vivid dullness. Regurgitated boredom. Am I dying?

"Sixto says you like feeding people?"

"Me? I hardly ever cook."

"No, I meant you feed the homeless. You try to help people."

"It's rather pointless," I say with surprising bitterness.

"I know. That's why it's charming."

As we eat, I notice the paper is open at the entertainment page. It occurs to me that I haven't had a break since I arrived in Miami, an evening off, without plotting, without worrying about miracles: a holiday from myself.

"Why don't we go and see a film?"

"Sure."

"You choose," I say, pushing the paper over. Thankfully, Gulin picks the film I would have. There's nothing more irritating than spending an hour arguing over which film to see and then someone sulking about being forced to see something they didn't want. Getting the company right for a film is very important. One entire relationship I had went down over the choice of film – Carla had the best breasts I had ever got my hands on, but it ended after we went to see a French film. It was a long drive, expensive parking, and a film which I had suspected would be obscenely pretentious and which I found obscenely pretentious and she didn't – there's no way back from a disagreement like that.

As you get older, what you look for is less the film than the chance to forget yourself. It would be useful if there was just a switch at the back of your head you could flick to stop thinking for an afternoon… but there isn't.

We enjoy the film. "The beginning was a bit slow," Gulin comments, "but I loved the gag with the table." I was less enthusiastic about the table gag, but we're definitely close enough in our assessments for future trips.

As we saunter down Lincoln Road, I see a bearded panhandler. I recognize him as one of the doyens of the streets – so he is at least destitute, unlike many of the beggars who try it on. When you're with a woman, it's harder to ignore a request for a handout – you don't want to act callous or stingy. But I never give money. I hate beggars as much as bankers and lawyers, for the same reason – they take advantage of others.

"Drug money, please, I'm suffering from an overdose of reality," Beardy asks, in that isn't-it-funny-I'm-being-frank way.

We walk past, as I concentrate on our conversation about the funniest film ever made. Gulin turns to me and says: "I'm sorry. I never give. I just work too hard for the money. I'd better get back. My boss likes to start work very early."

Very often I have the conviction that my difficulties stem from my dislike of chocolate. You want to be like everyone else as much as possible. I've never met anyone who dislikes chocolate. I've come across several neutrals who can take it or leave it or who don't eat chocolate because they don't enjoy it; but no one like me who positively dislikes it. It's just that chocolate has that chocolate taste.

Am I the victim of a conspiracy of chocolate lovers? It'd be a subtle thing. No one would ever say: "We're not going to give you the job because we've never seen you eating chocolate." And it's not a subject I'd bring up, because I don't want to be set apart: but it does keep you at a distance.

It was particularly hard as a kid. As an adult you're allowed quirks. "I only listen to eighteenth-century opera", "I won't eat anything red", "Monday's the day I never wear underwear". But not liking chocolate when you're a kid is hard.

For Nelson's sixth birthday treat, a group of us went to the cinema to see a great film with hordes of extras getting blown up. As we went in, we were all given a chocolate ice cream. It was assumed we would all love one. I was sufficiently sensitive to know that this was considered a special gratification, so I couldn't dump my ice cream in a bin or give it to one of the other kids, because if the supervising adult saw me ditching it that would cause trouble, as the whole point of the exercise was for us to have that famous thing, the "good time".

Once in the darkness of the auditorium, I considered throwing the ice cream on the ground, but refrained from doing so in case it was spotted when the lights came back on. Even if I'd claimed I'd dropped it, I'd either look like an idiot or worse: I'd be bought another chocolate ice cream.

So I put the ice cream in my pocket.

Instead of enjoying the film, I spent the whole time puzzling how to cope with the melting ice cream. I was wearing my best jacket. This was a jacket that had involved a major shopping trip and a long lecture from my mother about how expensive it was and how carefully it should be treated. Thus I had a premonition of an ugly collision between the melting chocolate and my mother. But instead of being mature enough to act (get up, dump item in loo), I sat there hoping that the ice cream wouldn't melt and stain my jacket, in that way we do when, presented with difficult circumstances, we pretend they're not so difficult.

At the end of the evening I said thank you very much, as I had been taught, and was returned home. I could barely stand up with anxiety, but my mother took my jacket and hung it up without saying a word. Was this a ploy on her part to make me suffer? She made no mention of the ice cream and I welcomed the respite.

The next morning I woke up to an absence of ice-cream harangue, and eventually, unable to believe my luck, I examined my jacket which, to my astonishment, showed no sign of ice-cream seepage. I put my hand into the pocket: no stickiness. There was no ice cream. There was no wrapper. The whole treat had disappeared. The pocket was dry and snug, everything a superior pocket should be.

Mundaneness has a number of explanations. My neighbour in the cinema snaffled it. I hadn't put it in my pocket, I only thought I had and it fell onto the floor. My mother swiftly cleaned the pocket overnight and didn't scold me, as even the most rigorous of disciplinarians has a break every now and then. You could go on.

I, however, have to consider the possibility that it was a miracle which saved me from distress.

The useless miracle.

The small balm. Miracles are always presented as life-shaking events: the dead undeaded, surviving an unsurvivable crash. No one considers the possibility of the micro-miracle, or what I would term the useless miracle, the one that does you no good really. Let's say that ice cream had been miracled out of my pocket, but in reality I was no better off than if I had never been brainless enough to stuff the ice cream into my pocket in the first place.

I know of another one too.

Nelson had a useless miracle. One of the reasons he behaved so badly was his ridiculously indulgent father. Nelson's abuses were legion, and for years his father accepted Nelson's version of events. Nelson sold his father's collection of rare jazz records and claimed it as a burglary. Nelson, when demonstrating how easy it was to make a Molotov cocktail, had burnt out – unintentionally, because it was brand new and he liked it – the family car. The fire was pinned on a passing mysterious stranger.

Like many ridiculously indulgent people however, there came the moment when Nelson's father became ridiculously angry, when he realized that what everyone had been telling him was true and what Nelson was saying wasn't. A mighty backlog of chastisement rained down on Nelson, precisely when Nelson needed to borrow his father's top-of-the-range camera for a school project.

There was a gruelling lecture on the well-being of the camera. If it hadn't been a school project (an area where Nelson had been consistently undistinguished), his father would never have agreed. However, it was decreed that no yarn about muggings, bombings or alien abductions would be acceptable if the camera wasn't returned in perfect working order.

Nelson took his snaps in town, got off the underground to take the train home and as he did so felt strange.

He felt strange because the camera wasn't in his hand, and then came the burn of stupidity. He had put the camera down on the seat next to him and, engrossed in the blonde opposite, had got off at his stop automatically, habit-trained.

Nelson wasn't by nature timorous, but now he was terrified. He knew, compared with most of the fictions he had concocted,

"I left it on the train" had a gloriously simple and compelling honesty to it.

Compare this to his masterpiece: "Dad, I'm telling you it was a puma that trampled your daffodils", which even got Nelson his mugshot in the local paper. The article headed "Urban Puma?" was classic schlock use of the question mark. It made it clear the story was nonsense and that Nelson was a liar, but by then you've sold your paper.

Nelson's father wasn't a big man. The prospect of being assaulted by a skinny music teacher might not be so frightening, but when it becomes a certainty then it is daunting. Look how a lone wasp can cause havoc in a confined space or picnic, and a skinny music teacher is harder to stop.

While we all want to leave home, being kicked out onto the streets wasn't the way Nelson wanted to leave. Choking with terror, he spent hours zigzagging around, chasing the camera, going to lost property, plotting to get another camera through some desperate act of crime.

Finally he gave up and went home to collect his toothbrush and some clothes before his father returned. As he got off the underground, he glanced at the seat next to him and saw a camera. Not just the same model, but the same camera he had forgotten three hours earlier, with his pictures.

Nelson calmed down a lot after this.

I fret over the length of my sermon.

This is what makes your mark. You always make more of an impact if you keep it short, and if your congregation wants more they can come back next week. There were unmistakable signs of gratitude the first time when I released the worshippers after only ten minutes, as opposed to the Hierophant's customary half-hour. On the other hand, you don't want it too stunted: if you get dressed up and go to church you want something for your trouble. "You're good, Tyndale," Gert remarked, "but you're no Hierophant yet."

"Please give a sign of friendship," I urge.

Smiling, the congregation shake hands with each other. The faces are all pretty familiar, so this injunction is less for the purpose of ice-breaking: it's an injunction for injunction's sake. You have to get the congregation to stand up, sit down, say hallelujah, partly to keep them awake, but also to bond. Just as when a crowd responds to a nightclub comedian urging: "Please pinch the arse of the person on your left." Once you've responded, the hooks are in.

I keep my eyes on the rafters, so I don't take in too much of the congregation. It's not a good turnout. Nine, and it can't be said that they are the most affluent or influential citizens of our metropolis either. I get them to stand up and sit down a few more times, to work their cardiovascular systems, but despite my attempt to stir things up a little, Mrs Shepherd in the front row has her mouth so agape I fear an insect will fly in, and her countenance is so inscrutable I can't tell whether she's bored, bewildered or peeved by my words.

Behind her is a young guy, his hair gelled erect. I've never seen him before. A newcomer should make me pleased, but he is talking to the Reinholds. When I say talking, I do mean talking. Severe boredom during talks has often compelled me to make a hushed remark or witticism to my neighbour, but the Gel is actually talking louder than I am.

I halt my sermon.

The stoniness of the Reinholds makes the Gel switch his outburst to the grinny Luis. If smiling could get you anywhere, Luis would have his own country; you could chainsaw one of Luis's legs without removing his grin. You have to know Luis well (a junior archivist in a Cuban history project, although Chilean) to perceive that although he's grinning in a manner which would be overkill for most of us, he's very unhappy. The Gel blathers on, offering a pair of earbuds to Luis: "You see I'm in a band that's going places. You should listen to this demo."

This can't be true. If you are in a band that's going places you wouldn't be parking your arse in a church hall three-quarters empty, struggling to convince one junior archivist that you are. Most of us, when we're caught doing something embarrassing – dick hanging out of trousers, etc. – stop. Not the Gel. He eventually notices everyone is glaring at him and he takes advantage of the attention by reaching into his shoulder bag and unfolding some fanzine. "Here's a review I wrote about our band, which tells you why we are so good." He reads it out.

Why isn't he out on Ocean Drive expounding this to some teenage bunny from Des Moines who might fall for it? I persuade the Gel to leave the hall by promising to listen to his demo and to laud his music to the general populace.

"You're always welcome here, of course. But you know, the service isn't the proper time to promote your music," I say in a gentle, pastor-filled voice that surprises me by its mildness. He gets surprisingly nasty.

"What are you going to do about it, you miserable old man?"

This is the first time I've been called an old man.

I've long got used to not being a young man, but this is the first time I've been pronounced old. Doubtless to a seventeen-year-old like the Gel, I am decomposing. By many standards, over forty is old. It's also true that I'm not happy. Miserable is accurate, although not a fair comment, because I work hard to conceal my fundamental despair. This is the curious quality of insults: they can be insulting because they're not true ("you're a miserable old man") or because they are ("you're a miserable old man"), or even because they're half true. It's the contempt that the Gel invests in that description rather than its exactitude that makes it so offensive.

"It's best if you left," I say with admirable, pastor-like, calm and compassion. I'm getting good at this. But calm and compassion count for deplorably little on the street.

"Make me," he shouts, unimaginatively, and waves a fist under my nose. Someone does a bad job of raising a child and the rest of us have to foot the bill. It also astonishes me that teenagers think they invented violence. On top of that, the Gel is so skinny if I sat on him, he'd break into pieces.

I put the holiness on pause. Looking him in the eye, I punch him in the gut and he goes down like an obedient dog. My fist has been hurting since the incident with the corgi, and I've resisted the impulse to stick on a black eye. The face has too many bones.

The Gel has lost enough fights to know that it would be unwise to get up. He curls up on the ground, although my blow can't have been that painful. Giving him a kick in the ribs does occur to me, but that would be ungodly. We've clarified matters, and I trust it's been a teacher blow for him.

I'm a little ashamed of myself, but also a little pleased, which isn't much use to me. Shame or pleasure you can work with, but not the mix.

"Don't feel bad about failure," I add. "You're in good company."

Should you get up or stay down? It's an engrossing question, and one that you can never answer definitively. I reconsider my behaviour during the Japanese Oak Crisis.

"Think positive," my wife had told me. Wives tend to be very free with advice. Wives commonly believe they can do a better job of living their husbands' lives than the husbands. Maybe.

So I was thinking positive. I was so desperate I thought positive as I drove off to sort out the Japanese Oak Crisis. I was cheerful. I wasn't pretending to be cheerful. I was convinced I could go there and find a solution and everyone would be, if not happy, only slightly disgruntled. We could all go home, get a good night's sleep, and wake up next morning with the crisis out of our minds.

I hate bankers, and I've always hated bankers, but I'd done a deal with a bank who'd built an enormous new headquarters. I'd been delighted about the deal at first, the biggest I'd ever pulled off. Money had been splashed about because the bank wanted marblier marble than anyone else, and instead of getting some big rubber plants and some high-class goldfish for the building's atrium, they had imported three Japanese oaks.

The trees were, of course, a rare, outrageously expensive species, and after they had been planted in the atrium it turned out their acquisition and importation had contravened all sorts of laws and that agonizing fines and possibly jail was on the way (one of the drawbacks of oak trees is they are quite conspicuous).

The discomfiture over the oaks would have amused me, it would have amused me a lot, but for the fact they had died. Fried. Fried, it was maintained, by our lights. When I had done the specs no one had mentioned the oaks, and when they had bought the oaks I doubt they had asked enough searching questions about how to care for them.

It couldn't be proved that the lights were the killer, but someone had to be blamed, and the fingers favoured me. I had considered raising the argument that the oaks must be contemptibly weak to be frazzled by a few lights, but decided that wouldn't help matters.

I'd be positive and offer a discount on the bill (which, as they were a major financial institution, they hadn't yet paid).

My contact at the bank greeted me with a powerful uppercut and a yelp of outrage.

There are only two responses. Nelson and my crew would say never go down. Never go down on the street, because if you do, you're finished, they'll come in with the boot next and your skull will never be the same. But there is the alternative: if you're punched, lie down.

I did lie down, since, as I was thinking positively, I wasn't expecting an uppercut. Secondly, having grown up in a big city, I recognized someone whom I was incapable of knocking down. It would have been more embarrassing and awkward if there had been spectators, but it was just the two of us. Also getting up, even if only to get knocked down again, wouldn't improve matters or jolly the paying of our invoice.

It was more satisfying for all concerned that I stayed on the floor, while my attacker screamed at me about the ruin of his career, and as I was on the premises of a major financial institution I was optimistic about not being kicked to death.

It's disheartening to see how abruptly civilization goes. During prosperity, most of us are willing to give up a seat to a little old lady on a bus, but to avoid losing our job, the pension, the whole happiness pack, most of us would willingly do some murder.

Giving up a fight damages you, runs one argument, leaves you a little crippled. Did I stay down because of cowardice, common sense or laziness? Or a mix of all three? I haven't figured it out and it's unlikely I ever will.

I've been ill for two days now. I spent all day in bed yesterday, but despite the rest I'm worse. There's nothing like illness for making you give up completely. All my plans for making my centrality more central are gone. I care about nothing. I could be boxed up and buried without protest.

I'm making a cup of tea, when Gulin returns. When I want to say hello, a prolonged racking cough comes out, so prolonged and racking that I see stars.

"Are you okay?" she asks.

As I attempt to say yes, another bout of rasping, cruel coughing is unleashed.

"Have you got medicine?"

I nod.

"What?"

"Well… I took some paracetamol." Gulin regards me with dissatisfaction. I haven't seen her for weeks. She must be back to check up on Orinoco.

Another distasteful bout of coughing shakes me. Gulin is passing judgement on me. Too stupid to look after himself. She may have a point.

"I'll get you something."

"No, I'm fine."

But she's already on her way out. I'm too ill to protest any more. I'm too ill to care that much, but I am ashamed about someone who's been working a twelve-hour day for the last week driving out to get me some medicine.

Half an hour later I'm handed a packet of throat lozenges. Gulin refuses to reveal the price or to accept any payment. I know she won't have gone to the nearest drugstore; she'll have gone to the outlet in Miami where you can get this packet most cheaply. The first lozenge I take effects a dramatic improvement.

It's not just the kindness. Some individuals simply know how. They know where to shop and how to buy and when to do it. I don't.

I study the collection basket closely.

With the small flock we have at the Church of the Heavily Armed Christ, you can guess which bit of money came from which hand. There are a lot of coins (the Church is a convenient dump for pennies) and only one bill of a significant denomination, from Gert. Gert is the only regular who might be described as successful since, he has a business making parachutes for champagne corks, so that the corks float down to widespread delight after being popped. What I admire about Gert is that he doesn't allow his affluence to pressure him into making a large donation. His donation is often the largest, but never large.

What should you ask of your followers? It's a question of balance I suppose, like everything else. It wouldn't be any good demanding that they should collect aircraft engines as a path to enlightenment; expensive, and where would you store them? But you have to ask something, there has to be an admission fee, otherwise the customers can't see they're getting anything.

Would you tell everyone or indeed anyone if you had discovered something valuable or important? Why?

I love those stories about Europeans reaching America long before Columbus, and keeping quiet. It makes perfect sense: if you had found a continent rich in timber, game and fish why tell anyone outside your family? Why tell your family? Even if you had discovered something as minor as a technique for cooking the perfect burger, would you want to share it? As long as you have the technique, you have an edge; the second you share it, you're roadkill.

Dipping into some studies in the religion section at Books & Books in an attempt to steal some ideas, I read that the early religions were like that: velvet rope. Wanting to keep the riff-raff out, initiates only. Indeed in the famous Mysteries of Eleusis, you risked death if you revealed what was in the box (which leads me to surmise there was probably fuck-all).

That's why they were wiped out by the do-it-yourself religions. Inevitably, the priests and salesmen have hung on, but the genius of Christianity is that it basically involves a statement of faith: "I believe". It's a free gift. But the con of paying a lot of money to find out what's in the box will always be with us.

My guess would be that the best advice is never written down or shared. Those who knew how to get things done probably kept their mouths shut and pocketed the goodies.

"A cold shower is the first step towards paradise," I announce.

Cold showers are about right. I'm not asking too much or too little here. Sooner or later, we all have to wash. It's not as if you have to make a pilgrimage to find a shower head. Having a cold shower is quite an effort for me, so much so that I've only had one in my life, and that was because the boiler had gone, I had an urgent appointment and I was filthy. I couldn't believe how hard it was.

"Taking a cold shower is an act of faith," I continue. It is an act that sets you apart from those who don't follow the doctrines of the Church of the Heavily Armed Christ. It will make you feel you are part of the elect. And it's pocket-friendly.

Over the long term, your cold showers can save you money. And it does, and this is important, contain an agreeable vagueness. There is a huge difference between having a cold shower in the open, in a Swedish winter, and in a balmy condo in Miami, where the cold water would be called hot in many other parts of the world.

This admonition has an agreeable vagueness for the preacher too. If the preached whine about not getting the paradisiacal benefits promised, you can always insist that there aren't enough cold showers being taken or that the cold showers aren't cold enough. Moveable goalposts are a great invention.

Worshippers coming in late or leaving early are a nuisance you have to get used to.

It's irritating, but you can never expect to have everyone's full attention; you have to play the percentages. I'm elated that a group of three has entered the church, a little annoyed that they're doing so at the end of the service, after the collection basket has done its round.

I have just enough time to be perplexed about why two of them are carrying placards, when a booming voice bombasts:

"I am Dr Liberius Iyambo. I have come here on missionary work. You are vassals of the Devil."

The speaker is a plump African. Late thirties. Bright purple ecclesiastical garb. It's a church-jacking.

Dr Iyambo's two-person mob now elevate their placards and wave them up and down to make them more potent. One reads: "No Surrender, No Surrender, No Surrender to Satan." Poor preplanning in the painting means the repetition squashes the word "Satan" into much smaller letters and is almost impossible to read. The other: "You Are the Cloved Hoof of Evil".

Iyambo's mob is one grey-haired woman, a veteran of psychiatric institutions, and a bullet-headed Latino. They barely count as backup. They're going to stick with Iyambo, but they're merely stage dressing, froth. Iyambo, though, is a hard case who means business. That's the drawback to growing up in relative affluence, you can't compete with people who grew up without shoes and only ate every other day. Iyambo is fightsome in a way no amount of training or self-denial will make me.

"You are not doing the Lord's work," he shrieks, pointing his finger at me in an extremely pointing way, and then at the congregation. "This is not the Lord's work. This is an abomination. This is the work of the Devil."

It's flattering that he's attempting to take over my church. Suddenly, despite the pitiful flock and the light collection basket, it's desirable. I wait for my congregation to gasp in indignation, or to jeer Iyambo. A few frowns as a minimum? No, they actually look as if they're enjoying the floor show.

"I, Dr Liberius Iyambo, have come to show you the error of your ways. I have come to show you the true path and to save you from the pit."

It's more likely that my arse has a doctorate than Liberius. To be honest, I thought about titling up, but when you're going for the top you can't be bothered with worldly honorifics. Doctor this. Professor that. Field Marshal so-and-so.

"This man is a pawn of evil," he elaborates, megapointing me again. The congregation isn't buying into Iyambo yet, but they're listening. You really are on your own.

One thing I learnt from Bamford, though, was how to wrong-foot people. Smile. Say what the hearer wants to hear.

"I had no idea I was working for the wrong side," I say. "But thank you, thank you so much for coming here to help me. That's very noble of you. Why don't we discuss this over a drink?"

"Can't you smell the sulphuric emanations here?" Liberius can't just stop, of course. He has the gab and harangues the congregation some more, he has a victory crow, but they, disappointed there has been no liturgical punch-up, disperse.

Leaving his disciples outside, I usher Liberius into the Hierophant's office in a way he deems sufficiently submissive. The Hierophant keeps a couple of bottles of Israeli wine. I offer Liberius a slug of this and, rather like the Hierophant, he is tickled by the notion of holy wine "as drunk by our Lord". The wine is mouthwash in my opinion, which is rather useful.

"God does not love you," he smiles. "God does not like you one little bit."

"How can you be sure?"

"Because there is something of Sodom about you. God will punish you soon. Very soon." One doesn't expect extravagant thanks for a glass of bad wine, but ready abuse is a bit much. This is the thing about shouting and bullying: they work. They may require more effort, in terms of volume and front, than just saying hello, how are you – but they work. You have to find people who will respond to bullying and shouting, but whatever you're selling, you have to find those who will buy. Not everyone wants coke, a Porsche or bullying.

Liberius shows me a photo of a gormless twink as I refill his glass. "You see this. This is Robert Caradec. One thousand and three hundred and twenty-six days in hell. This disgusting abominator has been in hell one thousand three hundred and twenty-six days. In hell, burning every hour. Do you know what eternity is, with one thousand three hundred and twenty-six days deducted?"

"No."

"Eternity. God does not love everyone. He loves punishment." I have to say I'm impressed that even with an audience of one Liberius is giving it all he's got. Hardcore.

"Among the many great things I have achieved, and the many great things I have achieved are many and great, so many that even I cannot remember them all, perhaps the greatest of all will be bringing true religion to this city," Liberius says, high on his I, occasionally pausing to condemn me as a "reptile" or a "worthless reptile" or a "thrice worthless reptile", undeserving of redemption. He swigs the wine with the ease of a seasoned drinker and scoffs a packet of peanuts I had been saving for later.

"It's my pleasure to meet the shredder called Queen Mary," he mumbles only a few minutes later, slumping to his side. Liberius may well be able to hold his drink, but he certainly can't handle the drug I've slipped into the wine. It's a dangerous thing to do, but he's a robust figure, and frankly I don't give a toss. Living the law-abiding, non-drugging way has got me nowhere.

"Time consumers… are not all equal," continues Liberius face down on the floor, as I strip and handcuff him.

Providence had provided me with a wide selection of date-rape drugs and some magazines of astonishing sickness. Gert had come in the day before, bleating, "I'm horrified by what I'm becoming." Being horrified by what you're becoming is one of the most common human experiences. He had come to ditch his rufies and stash of filth in a bid for salvation. I gave him all the unction I could, but there's a problem with ditching your rufies and porn: you can always go out and buy some more tomorrow.

I'm worried about Gert, although he insists he hasn't done anything wrong. He just thinks about it all the time. I thought I'd seen it all, but even I was shocked by his stash. Some things are just plain bad for you. Cocaine. Absinthe. Images of torture. Decency.

I go through Liberius's pockets. He has a tragically small amount of money. There's a notebook with handwritten prayers composed by Liberius: "Prayer for someone disappointed by public transport". "Prayer when encountering difficulties with a can-opener". "Prayer on finding it harder to climb a glacier than you thought it would be". "Prayer for a poorly receiving television set". "Prayer on being provoked by your lawn-mower". "Prayer for when your pastor has been framed by his many enemies on completely spurious corruption charges".

I may crash here, but I won't go out a cipher ciphering, standing at the back quietly, hoping something will turn up. I phone Gamay.

"I've got a job."

"It's great to hear from you, Tyndale, it really is, but could we do this later? Someone must have spiked my drink last night because I'm really not up to speed—"

"Right now, and get Muscat."

"We don't need him. I can handle it. Imperative."

"Okay. And bring some female underwear."

Gamay will regret Muscat's absence when he finds out what the job is.

I assess Liberius as an evangelist who won't give up after one drugging and robbery. I don't want to be one of two dogs fighting over an almost shiny bone. Even if he achieved nothing else, Liberius could be very noisy and unpleasant.

Liberius's disciples are waiting for him outside. They're doormat folk, and would wait the whole day for Liberius. Poor-quality disciples, but disciples nevertheless. I'm envious.

"Liberius's making a call. He asked me to tell you that you can go."

The woman is perplexed. "But what about tomorrow?"

"He said to meet him at two."

"Where?"

"The usual place." They walk off reluctantly, constantly casting back glances in the hope that Liberius will appear and resummon them to his side. The rich get richer, the unhappy get unhappier.

As I predicted, when Gamay turns up, he's shy about taking his clothes off, although I don't know why since, whatever his spiritual and mental shortcomings, he's in good shape physically.

"No way," protests Gamay. "Imperative. This isn't right."

In order to remove Liberius from contention, I'm gambling on the one sin that is hard to dislodge from your halo. Whatever smorgasbord of evangelism Liberius is touting, buttock villainy is certainly out. Religions, while often being sniffy on the subject of ooohhh, are especially unforgiving on sodomy. You can stray in all sorts of ways and your flock will forgive you.

Spend the money earmarked for the needy on a sharp suit and you only have to look hangdog for a few weeks.

Verily, it could be argued that the traditional coke-n'-hookers fiasco that befalls nearly every preacher strengthens your position – having pulled yourself out of the mire of sin and fallibility, you can orate on it with more zest. You could rob an orphanage, shoot up a town, torch some churches, and even all that, after strenuous breast-beating, wouldn't necessarily bar you from the pulpit. But the road back from shirt-lifting is a tough one.

"Tyndale, man, you don't understand. I don't want to do this."

"Yes, I do understand. But consider this question. If you had a major, billion-dollar criminal organization would you make it easy or difficult for recruits to join? Easy or difficult?"

"Couldn't you, like, kill him instead?" suggests Gamay. This is how it starts. I can understand that Gamay is not eager to simulate sex with a ripe, unappealing African missionary, but I'm still a little shocked; although I have to confess there is a part of me that's receptive to the idea, if I could be sure Gamay could carry out the disposal without repercussions.

"You're thinking like an amateur," I reproach. "Why are you fussing? Your face won't be in the shots."

"But, Tyndale, I don't want to do this."

My phone rings.

"Why, hallo, Muscat, how are you?" I answer with exaggerated warmth. Gamay is now making frantic whatever-you-want gestures. "No, I haven't seen him. I haven't seen Gamay for a long time."

I've always enjoyed photography. A black man in a cheap pink bra is a great composition. Naturally, the only thing worse than sinning, is sinning ridiculously. I enjoy the session, working in bottles of rum, white powder, a teddy bear and anything I can think of to heighten the turpitude and humiliation. I order Gamay to drive the still-blurry Liberius to Daytona, and dump him there with some printouts of the pictures. Florida is a big place. I'm confident Liberius will get the message.

"When am I getting some money for this shit?" Gamay moans. "When I am going to get some disfrooting?"

"Easy or difficult?" I remind him.

That evening Muscat phones me again. "I haven't seen Gamay for a while. I don't want to say anything bad about him. I don't want to say anything too clear, Tyndale, that might be misleading, but I caught him looking at a website for the DEA. He could be ratting us out."

One of my neighbours who used to be a spy told me how to get information. You go to the nearest bar. Or restaurant. Whether you're targeting an office or a military base, there is always one relaxery where everyone gathers. Usually the nearest. There are a lot of things people don't need, but everyone needs a drink, everyone needs to eat.

You never approach anyone. You get them to approach you. You need a prop. According to my neighbour a small child or a dog is ideal for attracting people. "An infant-in-arms is the best tool a spy can have," he said. Failing that some object that has visual weight, a guitar or a chess set, something that invites comment. I hang around outside the crematorium a few lunchtimes and I finally spot a group of three heading off to a kebab joint.

I enter five minutes later, carrying the most bizarre item I could find at Dishonest Dave's, a stuffed gharial, an Indian crocodile that has a snout so preposterously thin that it looks like a pipe. It's a small one that fits comfortably under my arm.

The waitress refuses to acknowledge my gharial, and I order a classic shish. The three cremcrew are close by, unchatty in the way when you're having lunch with the colleagues you work with all day and with whom you've had lunch every day for the last month. Sideways, they take in the gharial, but say nothing.

"Is that thing real?" The gharial is working, but not in the right direction.

Some retiree with too much time on his hands interrogates me about the gharial. I outline something about its habitat and the problems the species is facing. I don't want to give away too much, because I want to save some gharial chat for the cremcrew and also because I don't know much about the gharial. Without any invitation the old guy sits down next to me and natters about the python epidemic in the Everglades, former pets on the run. "Those suckers are loving it in there. They're bigger than the alligators. They're eating up all the alligators." He rambles on for ten minutes without any encouragement from me.

I can see the cremcrew are finishing up. Patience, I think. No, too late for patience. "Could you pass me the ketchup?" I ask, pretending my bottle's caked.

It's enough. "You ain't going to eat your pet, are you?"

We chat. They're not in any rush to get back to work. Two of them leave. Man Three with a big beard is extremely relaxed about getting back to work. I explain I'm a salesman, laugh about fixing my expenses. "If I didn't have that extra on the side, I just wouldn't make it. Honesty just doesn't pay."

"It's hard to get by," he says. A skinny Chinese guy comes in proffering DVDs. My target frowns. "I know that guy isn't getting rich, but it's wrong." I explain I'm new to the city, and does he know where I can score some dope.

He ices up and leaves immediately. A law-abiding man. It's reassuring to learn they still exist. But it doesn't help me.

Dave calls me and says the Brazilian will meet us this evening. I have nothing to do tomorrow so I agree to meet since I know we'll end up burning the night right down.

We meet at an elegant bar, in a shitty area of North-Western Avenue. The waitress gives a squeal of pleasure as she recognizes Dave.

"You were right. You were right. How did you do that? Will you do it for my friend Amy?"

She returns with another waitress. Dave holds her hand, looks in her eyes and says "Jacques Higelin. Insane Clown Posse. Graham Central Station." The waitresses jump up and down in excitement.

We're joined by eurotrashy Eric, who works for his father's property-development business. Dave explains to Eric that vodou is nonsense. An hour later Dave is explaining to Avi and Macca, two stoners who work in a music store, that vodou is not to be trifled with, and that he once smoked so much dope he ate three light bulbs in a balsamic-vinegar dressing.

The bar looks more like a bar with Dave sitting in it. He should actually be paid for drinking in a bar. He's a true night-rider. He rides the night, and at the end of it, it's the night that's exhausted, not him. He just climbs off and looks for something else to do.

"The Brazilian's not coming, is he?" I remark after four hours.

"Shall we review the facts? He's a lying, cheating butcher: a lying cheating butcher several extended families would like to kill. He is what you requested: a corrupt, unscrupulous, unfeeling, money-grabbing scalpel fiend. So it may be that he is a man who does not feel bound by his word to attend this evening."

We have more drinks.

"So what do you want to do now?" asks Dave.

"It's about time to go home."

"To do what? Sit alone in your room?"

"A few hours' sleep a night never hurt anyone."

"What's your pecker up to these days?"

"Nothing."

"You need to get laid. No, you need to get married. Once you're married, you can get laid as much as you want. A wedding ring is the ultimate babe magnet. Don't get me wrong, I love my wife, but as soon as you get married they fall from the sky. But I won't misbehave. I did that a lot." He stares at a waitress. "And I'm certainly not going to misbehave with her – too skinny." A fuller waitress crosses our vision. "Now her – I could misbehave with her. But I won't. I did that a lot."

Undeniably, it's a tribute to the growth of our intimacy that Dave stands up and lowers his trousers to reveal his left buttock, which has odd word-shaped welts on it: PIC.

"Pic?"

"Pig. I thought I had the perfect system because I was sleeping with two girls called Stacey. No blurting out the wrong name, or if I did no one would mind. I'm asleep when I dream this incredible pain. I must have levitated three feet off the bed. I've got to hand it to Stacey. No clichéd stuff like ripping up my best suit or sugar in my gas tank. It couldn't have been easy to get a brand made, to heat it up till it's red hot."

"What went wrong?"

"I don't know. They wouldn't tell me. That was unfair. I mean they had their fun. They could have told me where I slipped up."

I want to go home. Dave persuades me to go to a charity event at a golf club. "It's for kids," he says handing me a flyer with a picture of a baby with kidney problems. Even I can't say no to seriously ill kids. You just can't. I realize it's going to be an all-nighter and that I seem incapable of learning from experience. You swear you won't make the same mistake again, but you do.

Outside, there's another homeless guy guarding a boombox.

The voice is saying: "We have to choose. We have been put here to choose. You must choose the right path. You must avoid the wrong path." The homeless guy is wearing a T-shirt with the slogan "Avoid the Wrong Path". It makes me angry. Who the hell would choose the wrong path? No one, apart from a few headcases maybe, would choose the wrong path. If a path were clearly marked "the wrong path" who would choose it? The problems with paths is that they are rarely marked, and certainly never clearly, reliably marked.

"The Fixico Sisters have helped many to find the right path and saved many from the wrong path," the voice continues.

"Who are the Fixico Sisters?" asks Dave.

"Never heard of them."

"They must be new to town. They sound like some mean competition."

At the charity function, I wonder why it is, when you go out drinking, you go to different places to do exactly the same thing. A waitress comes up to Dave and gives him a big hug. "You were so right," she says.

"Too skinny, too skinny," comments Dave, as we settle into a corner; this is the main purpose of waitresses and barmaids it seems, not just to serve beverages and repasts, but to provide debate for the male clientele, as to whether they'd like to mount them or not, and why. Dave produces his mill and starts grinding out the white powder. I can't believe he's doing this in public. "Is that a good idea?"

"I know we don't go back that far, but do you think I'm stupid?" This is one of the least question-like of questions.

"No, but…"

"Do you think I'm stupid?"

"Well…" I indicate the mill.

"I'll let you into a secret. It's aspirin. I get bad migraines sometimes and I find it works best this way."

"Ah."

"I may be dishonest, but what I'm dishonest about is being dishonest."

"And the stolen stuff?"

"A lot of the stuff in my shop's stolen. But *I* didn't steal it. It's stuff recovered by the police, and when they can't trace the owners it gets auctioned off. I know quite a few criminals, it's true, but I also know quite a few museum curators. I do business with some criminals, that's true, but anyone who does business is doing business with some criminals. I pay my taxes and at the end of the night, I go home to my wife. You're disappointed in me, aren't you?"

"Ah."

"It may well be that out of the two of us, you are the more dishonest."

We drink and observe the charity. Why do we do it? Is it to feel better about ourselves, in the way we drink fruit juice after a debauch? Is it to appear better to others? I look at the revellers and suspect that in a few hours they'll be back to normal: shafting colleagues and customers, failing friends and relatives. And what about the charity? What happens to the money if you really want to spend it charitably? How do you find seriously ill kids? Do you advertise? How do you decide whether one kid is more seriously ill than another? If I could change this world, I would.

"You know what we really want, life-wise?" Dave asks.

"No, I don't."

"Fun you can have easy. You can have fun easily with one of the friendly waitresses of Miami. That you can get anywhere. What we want is… nagging."

"Nagging?"

"Nagging. Yes, you can have too much nagging, like you can have too much rum. When your wife goes on about why haven't you fixed the tap or why haven't you thrown out your favourite red shirt, even though it's full of holes. But imagine this: you go out on a three-day bender, you spend all the money and you come home and your wife just says, 'Never mind, dear. You must have had a good time.' Imagine how terrible that would be. Nagging is where home is."

Dave then drags me to an illegal drinking club. "You should see this place. It's an illegal drinking club."

"I've been to an illegal drinking club before."

"Not this one."

I give up. The only difference I've ever noticed between legal and illegal drinking establishments is that the illegal ones are much, much worse. You go for the illegality. The decor is Albanian bunker and the other customers are very fat, depressed old men who don't speak English. Much later I detect some daylight pushing through the shutters over the one window. What I think is dawn is in fact noon.

We leave and Dave insists on buying me lunch. I have a cramp in my neck and I have to hold my head at an odd angle which makes me want to be out of the public gaze. There is a restaurant opposite.

"It's a shithole," I protest.

"Shitholes are good," says Dave, skirting two junkies to enter the Miami Restaurant.

I was amused to discover that the quintessential Cuban restaurant in Miami is called Versailles, as opposed to the names you'd think more likely such as Habana, the Well-Lynched Comandante or the Old Country.

One of my neighbours, a chef, told me that the first restaurant in Paris was called the Tavern of London. In London the clubs and restaurants tend to be called Paris this, Bombay that, something Cairo or any word from the Spanish, French or Arabic languages. For some reason, any establishment in London calling itself London, or in Paris calling itself Paris or in Miami calling itself Miami is best avoided.

If nothing else calling yourself the Miami Restaurant is just so lazy. It's a Vietnamese restaurant. I've had some good meals in Vietnamese restaurants, but I've never had good service or a trace of a smile. The unhappy history of the country, or the unhappy history of those running the restaurants may have something to do with it, but I've always had the sense that the staff were figuring out whether they could get away with killing me.

To my surprise, the soup we order is quite good, and its spicy tang invigorates me.

"You know what my secret is?" asks Dave.

"Which secret is this?"

"To keep the marriage hot, hot, hot."

"So what's the secret?"

"Hypnosis."

"Hypnosis?"

"Every two weeks or so I have a session." This is rather sweet. "I went to see this hypnotist to help me give up smoking. It worked like a charm. I was forty a day, and then, wham. No more. So one day it occurred to me, it might work, you know, dick-wise too."

Does it work because it works or because he wants it to? Does it matter? On the street, I see one of the junkies getting ready to inject herself between her toes. Having grown up in a big city, I've seen plenty of junkies, but not like these. The junkies here aren't dirty, degraded, they're no longer human.

We ask for the bill and discover neither of us has enough cash left. The old woman is very reluctant to take Dave's credit card.

"Is this really your card?" she says coming back.

Dave reaches into his pocket for his ID.

"Is this your name really?" she says. I see the card is in the name of Soleil D. Magny. I suppose Dave has to have a real name.

"My father liked the idea of an unusual name."

"What does the D stand for?" she asks.

"Dave."

"This is so weird," says the old woman. "We have a man upstairs with the same name."

"Can't be."

"We rent out room upstairs. Man has same name as you. Same middle name too. Looks like you."

"You don't meet many Magnys let alone Soleil D.s," says Dave. "You're not clintoning us?"

"So strange. Come upstairs and meet him."

This is very odd. We are the only customers. Even without the junkie signpost, this is obviously not a good neighbourhood. I don't like the old woman. She doesn't seem like a friendly person who wants to engineer introductions.

She leads us into the back and goes up a narrow staircase. There's a bad, hard-to-determine smell. Dave falls back, and as the old woman shouts "Where are you?" Dave coughs loud and long, to cover the sound of him racking his gun which he sticks in the back of his trousers. I'm very unhappy about this. Dave looks scared, and when people who are tougher than you are scared, it's really time to be scared. Infuriatingly, he's also excited.

"You know the stories, don't you?" he whispers.

"Stories?"

"Stories about meeting yourself."

"No. They all end badly, do they?"

"Very badly."

I only follow him because I don't want to be left behind on my own. We move into a dark, narrow corridor where the carpet has been rotting for years.

"Down there," says the old woman, indicating a weathered door, backing off in a very backing-off manner. All my alarm bells are ringing and I'm faint. If anyone fires a gun in this corridor, it's going to hit someone.

Dave composes himself for a moment. Then knocks with a force between polite and firm on the door. We wait. The floorboards creak underneath us. No sounds of stirring come from the room. Dave turns.

"He didn't hear you," says the old woman. "Knock again."

"I knocked once. That's enough."

Outside, as we look for a taxi, Dave stoops down to throw up in the gutter.

"I had to knock once."

"What was going on there?"

"Something."

As a coward and a weakling I admire courage, although it could be argued that being brave doesn't benefit you much and being a coward can be advantageous. Being a coward and a weakling can be a nuisance on occasion, but owning a yacht with a helicopter on it can doubtless be a nuisance from time to time. Where do you want the yacht moored? Do you need a third maid? The coward dies running away from the battle, the brave man dies running towards it.

"Does anything really frighten you?'

"There are people in this city who terrify me. I sleep with a Mac-10 under the bed."

What hope is there for me? I've seen better men than me broken. Braver men than me are scared.

"You looked stressed," says Dave. "Have you listened to the early Sun Ra? It's much underrated. I'll do you a compilation."

Two days later he calls me to tell that he went back to the restaurant. It was closed down. He knocked, rang, shouted, but there was no response.

"Freeze!" is what I hear first.

I've just opened my car door. "Don't move, Tyndale," comes a shout. But of course, I do move. I turn around to see two policemen advancing to me, guns brandished.

I can't say I'm surprised. There is a flash of burning fear and rage, but there is also calm, because now it's over, I can give up.

One handcuffs me. I say nothing, because what is there to say? They have so many reasons to arrest me, I'm guilty of so much.

"You're under arrest, Tyndale," the policeman says as if it weren't perfectly obvious. I'm not surprised they use my first name; it's probably some psychological thing that it's harder to shoot at someone who uses your first name.

"You're under arrest, Tyndale," says the other policeman. I say nothing. There will probably be a few years of my life left once I'm released from prison; I consider how I feel about that.

"Don't you want to know what you're being arrested for?"

It's only polite to ask. "What?"

"Tyndale, you're being arrested for being a miserable bastard."

I gaze at him blankly.

"You face three charges. Firstly, being a miserable bastard. Secondly, being a tightwad. Thirdly, and most importantly, you are charged with failing to recognize the genius of DJs Gamay and Muscat."

I now spot Gamay and Muscat walking up, Gamay grinning like the oxygen thief, the passer of water that he is, Muscat very uncertain about how he should be behaving. I also now notice that the policemen's uniforms are not quite right: they are stripogram police officers, actors making a few bucks.

"We wanted to give you a laugh, bro," says Gamay.

I've never had a frightening quality, physically, but I can honestly say that I've never been so angry in my life. My face makes the DJs quail.

"Tyndale, you needed to loosen up man," continues Gamay. "Don't lose your sense of humour, man. It's all over when you lose your sense of humour." I emit such hatred that Gamay turns to Muscat: "I told you this was a bad idea."

"Me?"

I'm uncuffed, the counterfeit officers give me their card, and Gamay and Muscat scoot. They just run. Fast. I'm so angry I can barely stand up and it doesn't seem wise to drive anywhere in my present state, when a courier appears in the driveway. He has a parcel for Napalm, so I sign for it (with difficulty as my hand is shaking so much) and take it inside.

I go upstairs and knock on Napalm's door – it swings open slightly. I catch a glimpse in the wardrobe of a woman, hiding. "Sorry," I say, embarrassed, closing the door. "Sorry, I've got a parcel for Napalm," I announce. There is no acknowledgement or sound. This strikes me as odd. "Is everything okay?" I ask.

Finally, I knock again ostentatiously and peer in. The wardrobe is almost closed, but I realize that the woman is a doll. One of those high-end life-size dolls, with perfect hair, eyelashes and lovingly made openings.

I have to save Napalm.

It's easy to say that it's his fault, that he has selected this diversion; but that overlooks his looks and bad luck. We've all had dates where, with the best will, we've smothered the cupid. Everything's going nicely and then you say: "You have athletic legs." You mean shapely legs that you'd like to spend time licking. Your remark is interpreted as suggesting your date's legs are those of a hairy weightlifter. It's no use explaining.

Similarly, the momentum can go by trying to sleep with her on a first date. Or not trying to sleep with her on a first date. Failure can stow away anywhere.

We've all had the bungle: unwittingly eating garlic, wearing a purple shirt for a purple-hater, supporting the wrong political party. What if every time you had bad luck? And Napalm is starting with considerable disadvantages.

The basic blow-up dolls are a joke. No one sane could imagine using them. But these custom-built dolls are unsettling, because you can just about imagine being desperate enough to... of course, in nearly every way it's unhealthy to have an imaginary relationship, but if you think it over, most relationships have an imaginary element to them, sometimes a very substantial one.

We've probably all hugged a pillow, and how many women are half-silicone anyway?

The danger of these creations is that they can give you something. It's like drugs; the problem is not the drugs, but the world, which often is rarely as satisfying. A life-size doll could give you enough, if you were beaten enough, to give up. Because the only law is: laziness always wins.

I leave the parcel by the door.

"How are you?" asks Dr Greer.

This is the social convention, but I always find it odd doctors ask this. "Fucking ill, or I wouldn't be here, would I?" is the reply I normally have to stifle. But this time, as far as I'm aware, I'm perfectly healthy. Apart, of course, from my persistent and embarrassing medical condition, but I've worn out seven doctors on that with no result, so I'm not wasting my time raising that.

"I've been having these pains in my arms," I say going on to list many of the other classic precursors of a heart attack. Dr Greer is immediately alarmed. Doctors as a group have their deadbeats, chancers, and many of them are in it for the money, but you get quite a few like Greer who actually like their patients and want to help them. I admire him for that; it's not so difficult to be warm-hearted in your student days, but to make the decency last... for someone in his fifties to still care about the generality is an achievement.

"My doctor back home kept telling me I was going to drop dead," I continue. I don't like lying to Greer, he really is one of those genuinely cheerful individuals.

"Do you smoke?" he asks.

"Yes," I lie. "Not that much. Twenty a day." I'm sure like all doctors he'll multiply that by two. Ironically, with all the holiness, I've lost a lot of weight and I look good. But I've done my research and I'm ready to fake the tests. And if you say you have the pains, they can't say you haven't.

I take off my shirt for stethoscope access and so that Dr Greer can see the tattoo I've had done on my chest. It's large, it's memorable and above all, it's easy to copy, even for someone like me with no artistic talent: it's a fish, the ichthys.

Dr Greer prescribes me all sorts of drugs and tests. I'll take the tests, but not the drugs.

I'll see him a couple more times until I'm known as the man bound to have a heart attack.

It occurs to me that I can simply walk into their office and declare that the Church of the Heavily Armed Christ has an interest in burial rites and could we get a group discount. What worries me is that I'd be put on to someone at the top. I don't need someone at the top. Someone at the top wouldn't be willing to take a risk for what I can offer. I need someone near the bottom...

I'm approaching the funeral home when, although it seems too early for lunch, I spot a quartet of undertakers sauntering out to the diner across the road. On impulse, I follow them in.

They wait for the waitress with a subdued manner, not on account of any professional lugubriousness, but with a countenance I can remember from my days of employment: *it's only twelve o'clock and it's thirty years to retirement.*

A girl with tennis-ball breasts and a blue top to demonstrate them, sits down at the table next to the undertakers. Out of the four of them, the one who I'd put my money on leans over and says politely:

"Excuse me. You know that costs are rising all the time?"

"Sorry?"

"Funerals are getting more expensive, year on year. Well above inflation. Buy now, die later." He hands the girl a card. "We put the fun into funerals."

The girl walks out.

Two of his companions are too weary to be moved by his antics, but one, who has some authority, snaps: "Didsbury!"

"Aren't we supposed to drum up trade?"

"Yeah, that worked."

"She'll be back," Didsbury insists. I doubt it. Women are very inflexible in many ways. Once they've filed you away under "arsehole", there's nothing, but nothing you can do about it. You can save the world, but you'll still be an arsehole who saved the world.

At another table, there's a young mother facing the burger problem. Her kid is six or seven. She's a stir-crazy single mother who's meeting a friend for lunch. She's tired, not merely in the drained-parent sense, but tired of having made the wrong choice.

The kid was asked if he was hungry, because there are no children's portions. After a lengthy discussion of the menu, the kid ordered the special burger. The burger is spectacular and comes with a fancy salad.

The kid isn't eating the burger and burgers don't get better as they cool. He fiddles with the cutlery. He fiddles with the straw of his drink. He fiddles with some electronic toy. The mother is chatting with her friend and is pretending not to notice the burger problem. She wants a laugh with her friend. She has been a good mother, providing her child with what he wanted. Now if she challenges her son on why he isn't eating the burger, there will be conflict, spoiling the lunch. She should enforce the law, because the burger is the most expensive item on the menu, and in about two hours the kid will be bleating for food. This is the hard thing, you do the right thing and it's not enough – you're always asked for more.

My feeling is she will let it slide, because laziness always wins.

"Didsbury, go and check up on the hearse," says the ranking undertaker.

"I went last time, Jerry. Why don't you go and see if the bodrod is still there?"

"I told you if you call the Cadillac that again, you're fired."

"Okay. Okay. Stevie, go check up on the deadsled." Stevie stares at the chilli sauce, decommissioned, preoccupied with the hopelessness of his existence.

"You can't call it that either, Didsbury."

"Okay, I guess I'll have to check out the woewheels myself."

Didsbury mooches out. He's what I want. The square wheel. I wait a moment then tail him out, round the corner to where the hearse is parked in the shade. Didsbury is approachable, but how to approach him on this subject?

Didsbury, despite my efforts to be inconspicuous, has scoped me. As I stealth towards him, he lights a cigarette and beckons me over.

"It's a fine machine, huh?" he says, patting the hearse. I agree. "We have to keep a close eye on it. Betcha didn't know that hearses are the most stolen cars?"

"Really?"

"Kids love 'em. Goths are turned on by these things like flies n' shit. We have every anti-theft device on the market, but we still lose a couple every year. But if you want a ride, you don't necessarily have to die or steal one. Every other weekend I get to look after the heavenly taxi. If someone wants to hire it for a big entrance at a party or some very private excursion, it's no problem." He has me down as a ghoul.

"Here's my number," he hands me a card. I smile and take it.

"Thanks, Didsbury," I say. "I'll definitely be in touch."

Never help anyone. There are a number of reasons. One, the ten minutes you spend helping the little old lady across the road or taking the strain on a neighbour's grand piano is ten minutes you could have spent furthering your career. Those ten minutes here and there add up. Loyalty is a vice: if a friend is in trouble, drop him. Don't waste time offering advice, solace or lending money. Find a friend who is going somewhere. Friends in need impede.

If they sort out their troubles you'll probably see them down the line and if not… there's nothing more tedious and time-consuming than struggling to cheer someone up because their spouse has died or because they want to kill themselves. A television is more use to you than miserable friends. The time you squander listening to their woes could be spent ingratiating yourself with your superiors.

Honesty? Honesty: a con invented and promoted by the dishonest. Anyone's who tried honesty knows that it's painful and unprofitable. The crooks praise it and nurture it, naturally, because if everyone were dishonest there would be too much competition. There have to be mugs to be gimplied, they are an essential part of the economic cycle.

As for being public-spirited, it's fine as long as you're being paid for it. It's like charity, if you're working for a charity (holidays, pension, expenses form), charity is a good idea, otherwise: no.

My proof. How many toppers can you think of who are likeable? Not every big boss is loathsome, but most are. The few who aren't can be regarded as a statistical aberration. The admirable are usually found wandering around without power or prestige.

I hate the rich. The rich who were always rich I dislike because they have no idea; when you tell them about how hard things are they are as mystified as if you've said something in a long-dead language.

The rich who've made themselves rich I dislike because they, typically, think it's something to do with them. It's like the guy with the winning lottery ticket thinking he controls the lottery.

We're all trapped by our lives. "Anyone can make money," said my one rich neighbour; he was clever and hard-working, he'd made his money doing up houses in an age when property prices had boggled everyone. "Money is nothing," said my mother, although she had grown up in poverty. She was right in a way.

But it's different for men. Making money is part of it. For women making children. For men making money.

I hate the poor. No money? No job? No prospects? No drive? Have four, five, six kids that someone else's taxes can raise. Throw more souls into misery. The middle folks aren't much better; they can be ridiculously pleased about owning a house with a garden.

No calls from the Hierophant for over a week now. Something must be wrong. He was phoning every other day.

You always wonder when you don't hear from acquaintances, when they fade away. Were they too busy? Too happy? Too broken? Dead? I'm of a generation where we had little death in the early years. One or two lost to motorbikes. We seemed pretty unmortal. Now the cardiac arrests and cancers will be clocking in.

I go round to the Hierophant's house to check it's still in good order. I jump a good six inches in the air when I discover the Hierophant sitting there.

For a moment I wonder if he's dead, because my entrance (and it's a small place where you can't miss the sounds of entry) hasn't registered. Motionless. He stares into space. It's not the focusless gaze of shock or exhaustion. It's pure emptiness – everything used up.

"Gene?" I ask. He turns to me. He emits a low, but rank odour.

"There's nothing you can say," he says finally.

"I'm sorry," I say because you can't say anything else.

"'There can't be a God,' she said to me. 'Because otherwise I wouldn't suffer this much.'"

This frightens me. It's terrifying when you see someone you know for a fact is tougher than you, a lot tougher, smashed to bits.

Our earthly time is mostly a battle to conceal. To conceal our odours, our disappointing features. There's the physical and then there's the spiritual, striving to hide the greed, the hate, the weakness. Civilization is spiritual clothing. It's a pretence that we are better than we are, spiritual garb, spiritual aftershave.

"Is there anything I can do?"

"Go away." Misery has this quality: there's almost always a part of you that doesn't want to be cheered up. And there is sometimes a certain arrogance in thinking you can help others.

I go out and buy some food and leave it for the Hierophant. I have the feeling it won't get eaten, but I have to try. I know also that I want to help him somehow. I hate myself for wanting to help him. I'm a millimetre away from sinking into the shit and I want to do the hardest thing in the world: to give faith to someone.

It's true that I'm plotting to gimpli the public at large, but my plan is to fool the dim and unpleasant, or at least people I don't know, and I'm not seeking to divest them of their lifetime savings. I'm just asking for a large number of people to reach into their wallets and take out one bill for me. One modest donation for Tyndale, and I believe I'll be offering something in exchange: a jolt of hope.

One of my neighbours was a guitarist. I'd say he was the best guitarist in the world. You could spend a week arguing about what best is, and whether I'm qualified to judge what's the best, which, of course, I'm not. But he probably was one of the ten best guitarists in the world. His father had been a guitar teacher and he'd started at the age of four. I'll tell you how good he was. Several professional guitarists stopped playing after seeing him: his superiority despaired them so completely they couldn't go on.

They gave up because they could see how good he was, and how, despite this, he was playing in small clubs to small audiences. It wasn't that he was unrecognized, he was recognized, but not enough. He had record deals, he went on tours abroad, he had some of the trappings of success, but not the success. He climbed on the ladder, but couldn't get off the bottom rung. Being good isn't enough: the world has to know you're good, it has to be explained.

"Looks like we're out of business," says Sixto showing me a newspaper article about a huge drug swoop in Colombia. Thirty-five arrests, four shot dead.

"Us?" I ask.

"Us."

"Maybe they'll get lawyered up and get off," I suggest.

"No," says Sixto. "It's a business where you might not get arrested, but once you're arrested and once you're on the front page, you're finished."

Should I mention to him my suspicion that my bad luck has brought down a ruthless, long-established, major multinational criminal organization? There are certain things about yourself you don't like to admit, but I think I have to admit it: I am bad news. I was in denial for too long. I do a few odd jobs on the peripheries for this cartel and, suddenly, they're behind bars. Would Sixto be upset if I told him? I worked for the old lighting company in the country. True they fired me, but a year afterwards, they were liquidated. The rot had gone too deep.

Sixto isn't bothered. "I'd had enough anyway. And this means we get a very nice bonus."

Sixto thinks that, with the head decapitated, the whole network will simply dissolve. And that the money that should have gone up the pipeline will stay with us.

"We'll do nothing for a while. See if anyone turns up asking about the accounts. If they do, we pay up like good boys. If not, keepers keepers. I'll make sure you get a cut. But I'm selling this place soon, whatever happens. Time to move on."

Some money would be nice. It could help me help someone.

The only good thing about misfortune is that it can provide an opportunity for kindness. Without trouble there would be fewer opportunities for kindness.

"Look, I've got to warn you, about Napalm," I say to Dave as we draw up. "He really does look very funny."

"Belongs in a circus does he?"

"I'm just warning you. So you don't react when you meet him."

"Tyndale. You're a good friend, but I've got tell you, you do talk garbage sometimes. What do you think I'll do, shout out 'You're the ugliest fucker I've ever seen'? What you must think of me."

We get out of the car. Napalm comes down the driveway. Dave doubles up with laughter. He's laughing so hard, tears brim.

"The baby-in-the-blender joke," I say to Napalm, referring to a joke he told me a day earlier. Dave's still laughing so hard he can't shake hands with Napalm. "Sorry," he gasps. "Sorry."

We go to two places I don't even notice the names of. Dave is very charming to Napalm, introduces him to several women, but I can see my idea of taking Napalm out on the town is a non-starter. A barmaid brings her friend over for Dave to pronounce on. "It's amazing. He just knows what you'll like." Dave holds her hand and pronounces: "Mose Allison. King

Pleasure. Rammstein." The two women regard Napalm as if he were our pet monkey.

When Napalm goes off to the toilet Dave turns to me:

"No one's ever going to believe me. And it's hard to describe. I mean, it's not classic fright-night ugly."

"No."

"It's more weird. Somewhere between weird and funny. There's not much he can do is there?"

"No."

"Plastic surgery? Worth a try."

Dave promises to stock some of Napalm's waterskis. We go outside.

"What's next?" Dave muses. "Tyndale and I usually like to round off the evening by getting mugged."

As Dave says this, a hooded figure walks up behind him and pulls a gun. This time we aren't in a dark parking lot, but in a brightly lit street.

"Gentlemen, I'm offering you an investment opportunity. I only need two hundred dollars."

"Wait a minute, are you mugging us?" asks Dave.

"No, this is an exciting investment opportunity."

"So what are we investing in?"

"Me."

"And what do you do?"

"I sing."

"And what do we get for our money?"'

"Double."

"How do we collect?"

"When I'm famous you can write me and I'll send you your money. My name's Slow Joe."

"Why can't you admit you're mugging us?"

"Because this is a unique, once-in-a-lifetime investment opportunity, nothing else."

"I warn you," interjects Napalm. "I have a photographic memory. I'm making a detailed description of you and I'm willing to use it in a court of law."

"If it's not a mugging, why the gun?"

"I only carry it for protection. You won't believe the jealousy my talent stirs up." I watch a police car drive by, quite slowly.

"Look," says Dave. "I'll give you fifty if you fess up that it's a mugging."

"It's fifty each, minimum. Investment. That's the best I can do."

To my amazement, Dave reaches into his pocket and counts out three fifties. Slow Joe leaves us with a disc of his songs.

"What happened there?" I ask.

"I'm tired," says Dave. "I don't suppose you wanted to disarm him? I used to get trouble every six months or so. Now it's every week. This city is getting safer, statistics prove it. Everyone says so. You may be unlucky with lines, but I'm the mugger magnet."

I'm beginning to think he's right.

"I'm willing to testify," says Napalm.

"Here," says Dave, giving him Slow Joe's music. "Take it. I'm afraid I might like it."

It makes me angry.

The injustice of Napalm's lot makes me angry. My being angry about it makes me angry. Being angry about Napalm being Napalm doesn't advance my mission one inch. Anger, like most emotions, is a waste of time.

My getting this worked up about it is probably another sign of my cracking up. One of my neighbours who went mad spent the weeks before the padded cell obsessing about squirrels eating the nuts in his bird-feeder instead of doing something about his business going bust. Getting concerned about the problems of your fellow man is one way of fleeing your own. There are so many strictly legal, free ways of disregarding your doom; preventing squirrels getting at the nuts, watching television, sleeping, marathon-running, playing the harp, being concerned about others.

Sixto gives me some cash.

"All quiet on the where's-our-money front," he grins.

I resolve to make a gift to Napalm. To give him something that will last his lifetime: a great memory.

I decide to consult Dave, but as I drive along Biscayne Boulevard I see an obviously street-walking streetwalker. I had been considering an escort agency, because anyone working a street corner isn't at the successful, sophisticated end of the market, but the girl has a cute air about her, and indeed her average looks make her more plausible... and laziness always wins.

Our eyes lock as I lower the window.

"How you doing?" I ask, because it seems like an uncontroversial gambit.

"How am I doing? I'm out on the street letting creeps fuck my butt for small change so I can buy smack. How the fuck do you think I am?"

I raise the window and drive off.

Stopping off for a coffee on Lincoln Road, I find a paper which carries an ad for Gold Starr Girlz:

"We only work with the most beautiful and high-class girls, the champagne-minded elite who have glamorous and chic lives, at ease in luxury hotels or exclusive nightclubs. Our beautiful escorts, whether models or distinguished scholars, are waiting for high-class gentlemen to take them to superior, internationally known, celebrity-flooded restaurants."

With a powerful feeling of futility, I enter the premises of Gold Starr Girlz. I sense my mission to enhappy Napalm will fail. I strive to shake off the doom, but it remains.

They are extraordinarily friendly at Gold Starr. They show no disappointment or amazement as I ask for a one-hour outing. I doubt they would ever show disappointment or amazement whatever I asked for. When I see their prices, I swoon. I came ready to be fleeced – this is a top agency in a city awash with money, but I can't believe even the rich would pay these prices. With these prices they have no choice but to be extraordinarily friendly.

As I flip through their catalogue, despite the glossiness and the thoughtfully lit curves, there's something sad about it. Do what you want, earn your money however you want, but there's a sorrow lurking here. I really wonder whether the clients are that eager for friction, or whether it's the company. Who would pay these prices for an emission, when you can have a historical re-enactment in your fist for free? I know many of my colleagues ended up paying not because of the ooohhh, but because they were bored in a strange city.

But not with these prices. There's only one way to deal with sharks asking ludicrous prices.

"Don't you have anyone more expensive?" I ask.

"We could double our charges if you prefer?"

"Nothing personal, but I need someone higher-class."

Trying to fix Napalm's life has wasted half my day and I have got nowhere. Should I quit? Everything is a gamble, and generally when I gamble I lose.

"Why are you asking me?" snaps Dave when I call him for advice. "Any form of depravity is my province? I'm the spawn of Satan, am I?"

Nevertheless, he recommends the Dreamery and, when he hears that I'm on the case for Napalm's benefit, offers to make a contribution.

The Dreamery's brochure: "We welcome you to an unhurried uniting of nations. Ideal for any event, high-school reunions or the opera, our well-interviewed, good-looking beauties can confidently and confidentially flesh your dreams. Our watch-word: anything to anyone."

I can't believe the prices. I'm in the wrong business. The beaches here are littered with single women whose first thought is fun. This agency can't be about emission either. I've often suspected that paying a high price is more to do with the sheer pleasure of paying rather than what is purchased.

My goggle eyes betray me.

"We do have a girl *du jour*."

I've gone too far to back out now. I book an hour with Shy. Shy is petite, wiry and wears an admiral's cap which is too large and almost hides her face. Her clothes, however, would function nicely on a six-year-old in a hot climate, so most of her severely tanned body demands inspection. "I've got other outfits; if you want I can change?"

We sit down at the News Café.

"I've got a special job, if you're interested," I say.

"Everyone's job is special."

I haven't met many pros. They've tended to be vinegary or victimy. Shy, apart from her clothes, is more like a banker or an engineer. I'm looking into the eyes of someone calm, invincible.

"It's a job which perhaps your employers don't need to know about."

"OTB, huh?"

"OTB?"

"Off the books. We can talk about that."

I study her shoes. I know nothing about shoes, but they are so perfect, the leather so lush, they must cost more than my car. Shy's twenty-one and I have no doubt by the time she's thirty she'll be rich. Her heart has been discarded or maybe was never installed. Not caring about anyone really frees you up.

It's interesting sitting with Shy. The other customers look at me like I'm something, because I'm sitting with Shy: she's so unmistakably one of the elect. Whether she's my daughter, my friend or my purchase, my status is raised. The admiration of idiots isn't worth much, but it's pleasant, like a warm breeze.

"I have this friend," I begin. I outline Napalm's barriers to progress, and the scenario I want her to act out for me.

"Okay, the GFE."

"GFE?"

"The girlfriend experience." Of course: you believe you've come up with something new but it's long been someone's acronym.

I stare at Shy's breasts as we construct the plot, because they insist. There is such beauty about young flesh. Is my staring an old habit, or the return of an ageless folly? Mind you, if I want to hide myself in women again I won't be starting with Shy, who has the warmth of a chopping board.

Some of the successful people I've known have struck me like that: intelligent individuals who at a young age assessed life as awful, and never wasted time on happiness. They weren't unpleasant, indeed they were good company, but you couldn't imagine them being greatly upset about anything: one of their family dying or their wife leaving them. They were emotional amputees. Shut-downs. Unexpecters.

I can't imagine Shy caring about anyone, not even a cat. Unfortunately, deep within me the desire to be happy still skulks. Who's the mistaker here? Are decency and love simply masks for arrogance and selfishness? Is rectitude a pledge that eventually we will get something in return?

We construct a plot. Napalm meets Shy, a meek librarian from Iowa on her last-but-one day of holiday. Shy falls for Napalm, spends night with him, but before leaving explains that her fiancé, with whom she split up just before her holiday, has got in touch and begged her to come back and, although Napalm has taken her to undreamt ecstatics, Shy has been through so much with her fiancé that she has to give him another chance, blah, blah, blah. So dumped, but dumped lovingly, wistfully.

Napalm gets a memory of astonishing wriggling and gasping that he can cherish and build on.

"Do you have the right gear?"

"You'd be surprised how often I play the librarian. Everyone wants to do a librarian. CIM."

I don't ask. I produce a picture of Napalm.

"You weren't exaggerating," she comments. As we renegotiate the price, I observe her breasts and it occurs to me that the appeal of youth isn't entirely the tenacity of flesh, it's its unsoiled quality (not in Shy's case obviously); when we hit the forties it's hard not to be a sack of poison, ears dripping disillusion.

We agree a price, a price I wouldn't have agreed to if I hadn't already invested so much time in the project. Shy takes the down payment with a minimum of courtesy.

Back home, I fall to my knees and pray hard. I see no hope. Is that because there is no hope, or it's just out of sight?

I arrange to meet Napalm in an internet café that afternoon. Shy can engineer contact when I fail to show up.

"You can pretend to be having trouble with your computer, or—" I suggest.

"Hey. I have it under control," Shy assures. I am worried however. I'm worried that even a toned-down Shy will be too good to be true. That like all of us Napalm'll miss the opportunity of a lifetime. He won't believe he can board.

It's a grim morning. I've been asked to conduct a memorial service for one of the congregation's brother. Heavy traffic caused by a suicide made me late. A guy jumped off the tenth floor of a hotel with his four-year-old son: a lawyer in good health. That's what makes it especially sad: someone healthy, well-off. If you're old and ill, why not check out at your convenience? But otherwise it's probably lack of someone to back you, to listen to you, to say to you with sincerity "fuck 'em" and give you a hearty slap on the back. It often is that simple. Just as the right drug can stop an ailment dead, so a few words from the right person at the right time can save a life.

You can't understand it when you're younger. But as you age you do understand how you get tired: your existence might not be that awful, but you just get tired. And you understand how you might get so disillusioned that you'd want to protect your child from that.

The memorial service is for Wilson's brother. I was reluctant to accept the commission because I wasn't sure Wilson had ever attended the Church of the Heavily Armed Christ. I didn't remember ever seeing Wilson at the services, but he claims he was. He probably, like most of us, is a crisis worshipper. I agreed, probably because it was easier to say yes than no.

According to Wilson, his brother didn't drink, smoke or do drugs. He was a keen swimmer, mostly vegetarian and he helped out at a shelter for stray dogs once a week. He was twenty-three and he collapsed changing television channels. Just like that. It's the sort of incident that makes you feel you should be out raping, robbing, stubbing out cigarettes on kids, because patently there's no benefit in living sensibly.

The burial that's finishing as I arrive is another youngster.

A frat boy who let off a fire extinguisher. He was unlucky too, when you consider that at any given moment there are hundreds of thousands of drunken youths letting off fire extinguishers all over the globe, and yet you never hear of a fatality. Of course, he made the mistake of letting off the fire extinguisher into his mouth, so unlike Wilson's brother he did do something reckless, even if the penalty was unduly harsh. Would Wilson's family feel better if he had been involved with tomfoolery, say juggling chainsaws as he changed television channel?

"This is a bitter moment for us," I say, giving a eulogy of someone I don't know to people I don't know. "What sort of man was Harvey? A young man."

I notice two enormous insects on one of the wreaths; they are either wrestling or getting it on, buzzily. Should I shoo them off? Have the others not noticed? The insects are very large and very noisy. Is this a message from nature – it all continues? "All we can do is lean on each other for solace." I'm surprised at how emotional I am becoming and how eloquent I sound at my first funeral service.

"I don't understand," Wilson says afterwards. "My brother lived right. There's this guy who lives opposite us, he does drugs, he doesn't wash. He's got to be over sixty. He sits on the porch smashing beer bottles over his head. For hours. He's here. My brother's gone."

There's no answer. "I don't understand either, Wilson," I say, because I don't, and because I can't attempt a clever answer to balm his pain. I wonder why I am here consoling someone I don't know for no money. "But you must make the most of life. Your brother would want you to do that." I sound quite convincing. I'm getting the voice.

"I don't understand," says Wilson.

He'll be saying this all day so I depart. Then, discreetly using the Burger King opposite as cover, I go to observe Napalm and Shy.

I reflect on the many ways the encounter could go wrong. Shy might have run off with the money. Napalm might have failed to turn up. The café might have burnt down overnight. To my relief, I see across the street, Napalm and Shy engaged in conversation. I wouldn't have recognized Shy at all. Women have this ability to transform themselves, by a new dress and doing their hair. Gone is the hyper-whore of yesterday, replaced by a close-to-frumpy bookworm.

This is what's so infuriating about life: it occasionally works. Every so often, you need a loan, you ask a girl out, apply for a job, and you get a yes. There's just enough compliance to keep you in the game, like the odds in casinos, carefully honed to yield enough to keep punters on the premises.

I buy a burger.

The girl behind the counter is chatting to the server on her right and gives me change for a twenty-dollar bill, whereas I gave her a ten. I suppose it's your reflex that tells you about yourself. I hand the money back. She looks at me confused. Tired? It takes her a while to comprehend I'm giving back money I could have walked off with. She doesn't thank me.

I can't win. If I'd gone off with the money, I would have felt bad, because she probably would have been given a hard time over the missing bucks. One checkout girl I knew was reduced to tears over a few absent coins. On the other hand, although the sum of money is tiny and, even multiplied a thousand times, would make no difference in the level of my happiness, I'm a little displeased with myself for refusing free money.

Goodness and decency should be punished. What sort of world would it be if good acts were rewarded? Imagine if you spent an hour at the hospital cheering up a lonely, dying patient, and then got your promotion? You give five dollars for famine victims and then you win five thousand on the lottery? Kindness would be a career move, generosity selfishness.

Goodness should be loved for itself, and perhaps the tribulations of the righteous are the proof of a just God. Goodness should cost. Goodness should hurt. Although, personally, I'd prefer a universe where five bucks gets you five thousand and where the lonely and dying would have a throng of well-wishers.

I withdraw and as I spot a florist's across the road it occurs to me that no one is buying flowers for Gulin. Flowers aren't that important; they don't last long. And, of course, Gulin could always buy them for herself, but that won't do. It makes me angry that she isn't getting bought any flowers. She's working her guts out, is the most honest and cheerful of us – she deserves a small gesture like that.

"Hi," says the florist warmly, but I'm not letting her good nature induce me into spending big. Buying flowers is also one of the great wastes of money. Buy someone a candle, a box of chocolates or a poster and they get something out of it, but flowers are a blink, and in my experience usually more expensive than the aforementioned items.

"What sort of thing are you looking for?" the florist asks. I don't want to say the cheapest ones you have, but that's precisely what I want. It's the purchasing of flowers that's important, not the price.

The florist is very friendly (and you always have this question with a very friendly woman: is she merely very friendly, because occasionally you do meet very friendly women and men, or is she being very friendly to you?).

The florist gives me a discount on two sprays of carnations. While she's wrapping up my selection, a girl of about sixteen comes in with a squat, older man. The girl carries an elaborate cone of flowers (of a type unknown to me), woven with lengthy fronds.

"I just passed my course," she says. "I just wanted to show you."

"That's fantastic. Isn't it?" the florist remarks, seeking my agreement.

"Yes," I say, because it's easy to say and the bouquet's not bad.

"I just wanted to show you," the girl says. "Only three of us on the course passed." How can you fail a flower-arranging course if you, say, actually turn up? I couldn't arrange a bouquet as well as the one the girl's brandishing, but then, if I had the basic principles explained, I don't think I'd have any trouble passing.

"Only three of them passed," says the older man, with the pride only a father could muster. He and his daughter are not overloaded with brains or money. It's hard to know how to react.

It's good that she's passed a course. It's good she has something approaching a skill. It's good that she's close to her father, it's good that he has pride in his daughter's achievements, but it's also somewhat depressing that someone can get quite so worked up about bunching some flowers together.

"I just wanted to show you," the girl says. Many conversations are, essentially, repetition.

"That's really fantastic," the florist says, no longer wrapping up my flowers. I'm all for encouragement and being benign, but not when it's hampering my purchase. I want to buy the flowers and go. Another day I might have wanted to wallow in the general good cheer, but now I really want to pay and leave.

It's odd how some of us have no ambition. I went to school with kids like that – kids whose dearest wish was to become a window-cleaner like their dads. I never understood that, because the best thing about ambition is that it costs nothing. Why not aspire to be an astronaut, a wadologist, an idol, why opt for window-cleaner?

On the other hand, there is an advantage to not having a masterplan: if you don't have a masterplan, by definition you can't fail in your masterplan, although I doubt if my contemporaries were far-sighted enough to see that.

It's true I never dreamt in a concrete way, but I had entertained a conviction that my greatness would be acknowledged or that I would have accumulated vast wealth through some vague but inevitable process by the time I was twenty or so.

But then so many of us are passengers. Many of the poor are poor because they've not been given a chance, but some because they're feckless. I realize I'm annoyed with the father and daughter because they're only an exaggerated version of me. I've been unquestioning and rut-hugging most of my life.

What am I doing here? I'm angry at finding myself stuck in a florist's. Stuck in a florist's instead of working on my divinity. Stuck in a florist's spending the last of my money on cheap flowers for someone I hardly know, in between arranging for a cripplingly expensive call girl for someone else I hardly know. And on top of it all, I still have a persistent and embarrassing medical complaint. My lungs are so full of futility I can barely breathe.

"She just wanted to show you," says the father.

I still have some slim chance of turning it around. I don't believe that, but I have to. There is such evil within us, waiting to be called upon. If you said to me, "Your happiness can be arranged but your happiness depends on everyone else in this shop dying now," I wouldn't agree to it, but I wouldn't agree to it because, while a part of me would welcome the happiness, another part wouldn't – in other words I wouldn't really be happy. Because a part of me still would hope I could reach happiness without a horror like that.

But if you said to me, "You will be in extreme pain until these three die," I wonder how long I would hold out. Ten seconds? Ten hours? Ten days?

"Thank you for showing it to me," says the florist with a smile, still not wrapping up my flowers. I can't detect any signs of insincerity. She has a business to run and it's impressive she can stop and be so kind to someone who's not going to be any use to her. She's a very decent soul and that's why she'll always run a small shop.

On my way back, it occurs to me that I should have checked to see if Gulin will be home that evening. She only comes back sporadically. I fear the flowers will go to waste, but I had to buy them while I had the strength. Gulin doesn't return that night.

I pray hard. I pray for everyone. Just in case.

The most wearing aspect of being a pastor is that your flock expects you to talk a lot. Being a deity or a sage entitles you to continental silences, but, more than anything else, your audience expects you to talk, to enthuse. Saying goodbye to each and every member of the congregation after the service, fondly and with accurate knowledge of their occupations, dwellings and doings, is expected.

"Acts 11:14," says Ben.

Is there anything more irritating than quoters of scripture? He waits for a response. I pretend I know what he is talking about by saying nothing and smiling.

At first I decided that as I was running a Church, I should take a look at the Bible, but then I came to the conclusion it wasn't worth the effort, since there would always be hordes of pedants like Ben who've been at it for years and who could outscripture me. I've memorized one or two phrases so general they could be a response to any question from "Would you like a radish?" to "Is there a hell?" But I save them for ecclesiastical emergencies.

"I'm a pastor as well," says Ben, thus revealing that he's irked about a confirmed space-waster like me having charge of a church, however ramshackle, and at the same time seeking to establish consanguinity – we both hover between the deity and the masses.

His complaint is about Georgia, the one attractive member of the congregation, who hardly ever appears, but who has saucer-sized areolae and a fondness for see-through tops. This is one question I have never been able to resolve: are there women who are honestly unaware that see-through tops are actually see-through and that they are a universal invitation to wanking?

I nod sympathetically, but as far as I'm concerned we need more, not fewer see-through tops in this church. I restrain myself from counselling Ben to go home and ease one out. Self-service is, after all, quite possibly God's greatest favour to us.

When I shake the hand of Mrs Barrodale, her young daughter comments: "God is boring." Her mother is embarrassed. She could be embarrassed because her daughter might have said something untrue. But she is embarrassed because her daughter is quite right. Religion, regrettably, like our existence, is mostly dull. Until it isn't. And then you start begging for it to be dull again.

I shouldn't be here gossiping with my flock. I should be making miracles. While I'm locking up the church, Gert runs up.

"It's a miracle," he pants. He is holding a mug.

"What?"

"I was driving along the Palmetto, drinking my coffee when this truck changed lanes. If I hadn't have been driving more slowly because of the coffee…"

He's very shaken.

"What happened?"

"Most mornings I see this homeless guy, and I was always thinking I should buy him some food. I was in a rush, but I said to myself, you're always in a rush, you're always thinking you're going to buy him a sandwich, but you never do. So I say today, today I will. I stop and say, 'You want some food?' 'No man,' he says, 'what I need is a latte'. Okay, I buy him a latte, if he wants a latte, give him a latte, I'm already late now. But I buy myself a latte too, and I have it in my own mug, because I hate that styrofoam stuff. I'm not irresponsible. I'm driving real slowly and carefully because I'm drinking a coffee, because I don't have proper control. Then this truck changes lanes and smashes into two cars. I slam on the brakes and stop inches from the burning wrecks. The coffee's spilt, but this face forms on the side of the mug and I understand it's a miracle – the coffee saved me."

He shows me the mug. The foam has shaped itself into the face of a bearded, long-haired man. It does look like a work of art. It's not one of those stains that might be something if you look at it from the right angle and a distance – it's very much the traditional image of Christ; it's curious that he's portrayed that way. He's never a short, paunchy, bald guy.

"You should tell the papers," I say.

Gert nods enthusiastically. "Yeah, yeah." I was joking, but I can see he will. It occurs to me that we could contact the sour chronicler of religious affairs, Virginia. A bit of publicity for the Church can't do any harm, and if some decoration on a mug was not the sort of miracle I was contemplating, well, we all have to start somewhere.

I let Gert make the call, because I can't bring myself to recount the incident of the foam Jesus. To my surprise, Virginia comes round immediately. It must be a slow news day.

"So you think it's divine intervention?" she asks. She looks sceptical and superior, but that's her default setting. Gert doesn't notice, or doesn't mind. He's a mixture of shock and mania. He regales her with his near miss which killed three people.

Virginia doesn't want to be here. She wants to be on a big paper working on a big story, covering it a big distance from Miami. Fair enough. She's smart and she's ruthless, but even that's not enough. Doubtless, she's as smart and determined as most of the reporters who are covering wars, famines or the activities of presidential penises. Hard work just isn't enough.

She thinks she's better than this, because she probably is. Not everyone who graduates from journalism school can make it: there are only so many chocolate bars to go round. That's one of the problems, there aren't enough chocolate bars, so people either have to accept something other than chocolate bars or they are going to be unhappy.

Close to distaste, she shakes my hand farewell.

Driving home later, I'm surprised to hear Gert on the radio, now claiming to be a habitual feeder and succourer of the down-and-out.

Napalm is watching the television when I get back home and again I hear a snatch of Gert's voice as the miraculous mug is picked up by the local television. Napalm is watching television the way he watched television the week before.

I observe Napalm closely. I expect some posturese to signal that he has been transformed. A straighter gait. A bounce. A whistle. He goes to the fridge and takes out some pineapple juice and pours it as if he hasn't just spent the weekend with one of Miami's most accomplished prostitutes.

"How are things?" I ask.

"Fine," he says shuffling off upstairs. Has something gone wrong? But even if something has gone wrong, there should be some debris of despair, some glinting shards of ecstasy, not this flatness. I want to probe further, but I don't want to act suspiciously.

Everyone, whether they're a fourteen-year-old living in a dreary provincial town where the greatest danger is aggressive gnats or a world-famous starlet with a stable of bodyguards, has the same weaknesses and challenges: meeting people, and meeting people they like. It's just scale. We all have our ruts, some smaller, some larger. It just depends which league we play in. Everyone has done something bad, whether it's drinking the last of the pineapple juice or murdering their spouse.

I don't understand myself, so it's no surprise I can't understand others.

I call to arrange a meeting with Shy in a diner. I want a debrief. I'm in bed when Sixto taps on my door to inform me that Gert has made the national channels.

That a simple stunt like this can generate so much hoo-ha surprises me and makes me quite angry. Why am I investing so much time in a major miracle when some spilt coffee can grab everyone's attention? But I'm not entirely displeased. I repeat to myself that it's all useful publicity for the church, and thus me. Gert is merely the warm-up act.

I consider how much of my life has been spent waiting, standing outside cinemas, twiddling my thumbs in restaurants, waiting for women. They owe me months, if not years of my life. If you're punctual what it boils down to is that you're going to spend much of your life waiting. Similarly, if you behave generously, you're exposing yourself to ingratitude; but if you don't help others, you can't be disappointed, if you don't lend money, they can't fail to pay it back. In olden days, I suppose, if you lived in a small village, there was a chance people would remember, or not want to be seen as ungrateful or debtors, but not now.

But I can't work myself up into a real state, as Shy arrives after ten minutes.

"What happened?"

"With the lights off, it's never so bad."

"And you told him it couldn't work out?"

"No."

I get angry. Why can't people carry out their orders? I paid a fortune for this.

"But we agreed."

"I didn't use the sob story, because he dumped me."

"How?"

"He said, sorry, it couldn't work out, no hard feelings."

"And you said?"

"I said I was sorry, but I wished him well."

This stumps me.

"Now," she says. "You can do me a favour. Give me a good write-up on my website. Use your imagination."

She leaves as a large man with a shaved head is chatting with the boss. I now tune into their conversation.

"Come on, give me a chance," he says. He wants a job.

"Sorry," says the boss.

"You'd be foolish not to give me a job," says the man, "and you don't look like a fool to me." This line could have been delivered with charm, but it isn't, and there's nothing worse than failed wit or fumbled camaraderie. In the right place, at the right time, with the right delivery it could have worked. He's an arsehole, but is it his fault? If you're born with big ears is that your fault?

"Sorry," says the boss. The boss is good. He's not giving a reason, because if you give a reason, you give someone something to refute.

"Hey, look, this is how keen I am to work in your kitchen: I'll work for free just to show you what a dynamite cook I am."

"Sorry," says the boss, not embarrassed about walking off.

Compassion is a disease. I want to help him. You see lots of people asking for handouts, you rarely see people fighting for a job. Compassion may also be another form of arrogance. Christ knows I can't even help myself, why do I think I can help someone else? He's me. Another forty-something sinker, going down.

It occurs to me that one area where the Church of the Heavily Armed Christ hasn't made any effort is good, straight, unreligious fun. Why not have a purely social evening? A barbecue? A lunch? Some tasty food to lure pilgrims in?

"I hear you're looking for work," I say.

"I'm the original man looking for work. Everyone calls me Saffron." He shakes my hand and writes down his number for me.

"You're a man who uses his own judgement," he says to me. "That's a very rare thing." This is intended as a compliment, but it sounds to me like a flaw.

"Oh, and it's not true that I've attacked every one of my employers," he assures me.

On the way home, I spot a body lying next to the road. Its posture is odd. The raggedy clothes suggest it's some wino sleeping it off. But what if it's not? I drive on for a while. I want to drive on very badly, but I can't. I turn round, stop and get out. I search for the old man's pulse and can't find any. The skin is cold and waxy.

Three black kids lope past. "He's dead isn't he?" they laugh. I can comprehend the lack of interest in offering help, but is there any need to laugh about it? I call for an ambulance.

The crew arrive after fifteen minutes and walk up suspiciously. "You called it in?" They ask accusingly. They look around constantly as if they're expecting to be ambushed. Reluctantly, as if under duress, they circle the body. I feel obliged to stay. They fiddle with him, and after a few minutes his eyes blink into life. He's not some heart-attack victim but a wino sleeping it off.

"This gentleman was worried about you," the medic indicates me. The wino's face is gratitude-free, and will remain so. The boys were right. They were right and I was wrong. Walk on and laugh. That's the way.

I've arranged for Gert to come in on Sunday to talk about his mug. Late Saturday night, minutes before I close up the Church, he phones me to tell me he can't make it.

"Nothing personal, Tyndale. But with a miracle like this, I need a bigger church. I'll be working with the Fixico Sisters."

"Who are the Fixico Sisters?"

There's no answer, Gert's hung up.

I walk out and I see that, outside the huge building next to the church, despite it being so late, there are still workmen fiddling around.

The building's of such a size and style it must have been a theatre back in the Twenties, and was last an unsuccessful camping-goods shop. Until recently it was derelict, and I had considered the possibility that when my act took off, it could be turned into a new, larger home for the Church of the Heavily Armed Christ. But then dozens of men in hard hats turned up to renovate with an astonishing, round-the-clock will. That's Miami, blocks go from stone-dead to swinging in months. I'm curious who our new neighbours will be.

A foreman gives an order and a giant neon sign lights up. The sign says in blue, "The Temple of Extreme Abundance". Underneath, now made legible by the dropped light is a large poster on a noticeboard: "Wish large. The Fixico Sisters are God's dealers".

This time I invite Dave for a drink.

"I'm not lucky."

"Everyone thinks that," counters Dave. "Everyone thinks they're dynamite in bed and that they haven't had enough luck."

"But I am. I'm not unlucky in the sense that I break a leg every six months, or that I come home and find the house burnt down and my family eaten by wild animals. The really ugly stuff stays away. I'm just not allowed any luck."

"Don't moan. Your lack of dignity is starting to pain me."

"Okay. I can prove it you."

We go to Publix where I pick up two cabbages. I tell Dave to choose a checkout for me and for him to go to another one. We both have two carts in front of us. Dave goes through the checkout with his cabbage in three minutes, while I haven't moved an inch, and the lady at my checkout is arguing determinedly about the validity of the discount coupon she's hoping to use. Dave beckons me to another checkout where there's only one cart. The cash register goes down and the assistant looks in vain for a supervisor to sort out the malfunction. On the other side I study a mother and daughter: the daughter's around eighteen, the mother forty. How your tastes change. I choose the mother for erotic speculation to while away the time. Fifteen minutes later I manage to pay for the cabbage.

"What does that prove?" sneers Dave.

"We can do it again."

At McDonalds Dave is served in two minutes thirty seconds. The server at my counter disappears for a full five minutes and it's ten minutes before I get my burger. At the Sears in the Dadeland Mall it takes Dave thirty-five seconds to purchase a canary-yellow T-shirt. It takes me twenty-two minutes. I get Dave to choose numbers and buy two lottery tickets. Dave doesn't win anything, but he has two numbers. The ticket he gave me has no hits.

"You're sure you're not doing it deliberately?" he asks. "This is very interesting."

The next day we take a trip out on the gambling boat. I've always found gambling boring (unless you're losing or winning huge sums of money, stakes I'm not prepared to play for). For most of us it's about losing small sums of money steadily, in not very interesting circumstances.

We sit at the roulette table. I bet on black. Dave bets on red. I put down dollar chips to stretch my loss. Dave plays five dollar chips. I win twice, because as Dave says, no one can be unlucky all the time, and because it's not just about my luck, but the luck of the others at the table. Dave wins sixteen times.

"We have to be careful with this," he says. "We need an either-or bet. Basketball. The Miami Heat – we can have a bet on them when they play. But we can't go too wild, because then your bad luck wouldn't be bad luck any more, it would change to good luck so we wouldn't win, if we had a massive bet."

I think I understand him. We start betting on the matches. I choose the good odds, Dave takes the long shot. I lose, and Dave wins – modest amounts. He wants to give me half, but I tell him that will jinx our betting. Slipping me ten per cent seems to allow the system to work. I have an income.

"Okay, yes, so I have a history of uncontrollable violence. Let's talk about that. I'm not going to hide that. But it's a history, you know what I'm saying, a history, like in the past, when I was young, and I only did it for recognition and respect. It's not like I did it for laughs or I enjoyed it. That uncontrollable-violence shit is draining. And people talk, people talk, they blow it up like a great big Zep balloon, know what I'm saying? What you've heard, you've got to divide by ten," Saffron assures me.

I've decided we need more fun at the Church of the Heavily Armed Christ. You can go overboard on the holiness. What we need is an evening of fun, good food, barbecues. Barbecues with see-through tops. Now that I have some money in my pocket, I can hire someone to knock up food for the homeless, and entertain the congregation in style.

"I haven't heard anything. Honestly," I assure Saffron. He has an amazing number of tats.

"You must have heard about the blancmange?"

"No."

"You must have heard about it. But remember, divide by ten. At least. As a minimum."

"When can you start?"

"I'm ready to go-go. This old ex-armed robber loves to work."

"Tomorrow, say eight?"

"Man, I'd love to but it's my anger-management group. And it's important to manage that anger. It's controllable anger, but you know, it needs to be controlled."

"Friday?"

"Man, I've got this hospital appointment. I've got this funny feeling in my ankle, kinda hard to say what it is exactly and I've been waiting months to see a doctor. My ankle's never been the same since that time, well, this is another thing you've got to divide by ten, cos even if I tell you it's going to sound worse than it is."

"Saturday?"

"Normally, most weeks, no problem, but I'm waiting for a delivery of a new fridge and those delivery guys they lie worse than politicians, you never know when they're going to turn up. And you need a fridge in Miami."

"You need a fridge in Miami. Sunday?"

"Well, I could do Sunday, but that's the day I normally have my kids. Now, I don't have to see them, but it's the only chance I get to see them, and those young boys, they need a father to make sure they stay away from uncontrollable violence and armed robbery and shit. But if you want to insist, for you—"

"Monday?"

"Okay. Monday. Monday's cool. I can't wait to get started. No, fuck. Wait. You're not going to believe this. The electricity company's coming Monday to reconnect the supply. There was a misunderstanding about the payments, and that company remembers what happened years ago. They never forget. It's no use telling them that I'm reformed. Those utility guys, man, they're worse than the delivery guys. There's just no telling when they'll turn up. Oh, wait, don't give me that look. I know that look."

"Look?"

"I can see that look in your eyes. I've seen that look before. It's that this reformed armed robber, he's talking, he's talking but he's not serious about being a chef. See, something like that, when I was younger, man, that would have been like a demand, like a plea for uncontrollable violence. But I'm not that young man. I'm forty-four, I love my freedom, I love being out on the streets, so that's why I'm not going to smash your face into the desk until the look is well and truly gone. Because that ain't me."

"Saffron—"

"No. No, I can see you have doubts. No, I don't want a man of God to tell a lie, I can see you have doubts. So here's what I'm going do. Next Tuesday, I'm going to turn up, as long as my Mom's feeling okay, and she hasn't been feeling too good lately, you know, she hasn't had an easy life. What with my history and all, but, but next Tuesday I'm going to cook you some dynamite food, and I'm going to volunteer. I'm volunteering my services, that means you don't have to pay me, you're just going to thank me."

"See you Tuesday."

"See you Tuesday."

Saffron doesn't turn up on Tuesday, or any other day. I was quite sure he wouldn't. I'm pleased to be right, but as usual it doesn't do me any good.

I buy Didsbury a beer.

We're down in Coconut Grove, in an undistinguished bar. I don't want Didsbury to think I'm made of money, but he should be able to help me pull off a miracle. What I need is one big stunt. Just one. Coming back from the dead should get me noticed. If that doesn't get me some respect, I'm giving up.

"So when do you want the woewagon?" he asks.

"The woewagon's not what I want. I have another business proposition to put to you. There's something else I want you to help me with."

"You're not a body-jumper are you?" Didsbury gets up to leave.

"No. I'm not. All I need is to borrow a fresh corpse, one careful owner, for a few hours."

"What do you want the body for?"

"So I look dead."

"Couldn't you hold your breath or something?"

"I need a death certificate. There's no rush with this. I'm willing to wait until you have a client who looks like me, more or less. Then it's just a question of getting a doctor to examine him."

"Man, do you know the trouble I could get in for that?"

I name a price. It tells him I'm serious. His expression tells me that he'll dither about it, but that he's going to say yes.

He names another price. It's not much higher than my figure, but negotiation isn't just about the money – it's about feeling you have the power to change things.

"I wouldn't even think about this, but my mother's ill, and those doctors." This may be true or it may not. It makes no difference to me. Didsbury has huge hands – and he has the longest thumbs I've ever seen. His thumbs look as if they've had another pair of thumbs grafted onto them, long thumbs to boot. He'd make a great monkey, never falling out of the trees.

"And you promise you're not into any sick stuff? I'm dextrous on the morals, but I ain't going that far."

"I promise; and you can be around to chaperone me." Didsbury's straining to convince himself, but he'll succeed.

"I don't know," he says. "You sure I can't interest you in the choking chariot for an evening?"

"No."

"How about some solar-powered gravestones? I've got a load of those."

"Not for me," I say. "But I know a man who could take them off your hands."

When I walk through the sombre entrance of the funeral home, I ask myself how I will remember this moment. Will I remember walking through this entrance as the prelude to an exciting chapter of my life or as the descent to an even greater misery? Why couldn't I like chocolate?

"Relax," says Didsbury. My trepidation must be dangling. "No one's coming round. It's total quiet. People don't die during holidays."

I'm going through with this although I've now reached the stage where I don't want to, where I no longer see how it can help; I'm doing it because I feel I should. I've never taken a really big risk with a long, painful fall to the ground, and maybe this is why I've never got on. Plus chocolate.

I meet Mr Yates. Geologist new to Miami. New to death. Don to his friends and embalmer. I can't say he looks like me, but he definitely doesn't *not* look like me, and he admirably does the job of being my height and short on hair.

We load him into a lightweight wardrobe, and I succumb to a momentary guilt about what we're doing. Don can't mind, but his family members might. Really, taking the body for a tour isn't immoral or indeed illegal (it occurred to me if we were caught, there's nothing they could actually charge me with since Don is being treated with respect).

Then we place the wardrobe in the van. The wardrobe is there to dispel notions that we're carrying a body. I've always been a little disgruntled about being average: average height, average build and, for a while, average income (how I miss that). I always wished there was something outstanding about me, just one thing: able to put up straight shelves, cooking a great rack of lamb, knowing all the capitals of the world, having a fine tenor voice.

Now as Didsbury and I struggle with Don, I'm very glad I'm not six foot two. We wheel the wardrobe most of the way on one of those wheely things, but some good old-fashioned shunting is required – Didsbury is beefy and is used to carrying heavy loads, but I'm not. I'm positively faint from the strain. It passes through my mind how comic it would be if I dropped dead in the middle of a bodysnatch.

"How do you like your job?" I ask as we drive off, to pass the crime cordially.

Didsbury shifts gear. "It's okay, I guess. It's pretty much like anywhere else. We all pretend to get on, but really we hate each other."

I expect to be challenged, but we aren't. That's it. One of Didsbury's colleagues could have come back to pick up a book he'd forgotten, but it didn't happen. We might have been stopped by the police who might have insisted on searching the van, but it didn't happen. You either get away with it or you don't, and it doesn't have anything to do with you.

We carry the wardrobe in as Didsbury whistles and I gasp and moan. He's perfectly calm, although he's the one who stands to lose something substantial. We lay Don out and I make a note to do something nice for him, send flowers or donate to his favourite charity.

"Remember," says Didsbury. "Don doesn't leave my sight." Didsbury's a farmer's boy – I don't know why farmers are cast as simpletons or fools, because they're not. To make it as a farmer you've got to be switched on: you're dealing with nature, a very unforgiving employer.

Some adjustments have to be made. Don has bushy chest hair, so that has to go. He also gets a severe haircut. After I've hennaed a tattoo of a fish on his chest, and fitted Don with a pair of Miami Dolphins shorts, I leave in different clothes, with a baseball cap, dark glasses. Who was that you saw?

"You got six hours," Didsbury reminds me, checking that the air conditioning is on full. Now Sixto, as a concerned friend, phones for an ambulance and the doctor. I've spent a fair amount of time cultivating Dr Greer, who has a reputation as the only doctor who makes house calls in Miami. Will he come? Or will it be some uninterested locum?

I go round the block to a bar and sit down. The portering and the nerves have made me desperate for a drink. The bar is empty and the barman is fussing with something round the back. I let out a couple of "hallos".

"Have a bourbon," urges a voice behind me.

"A water's fine, thanks."

"I didn't say I was buying. I said have a bourbon. I can't stand drinking alone, and Stan here's barely human."

The speaker is a wizened boozehound, and Stan is an even more wizened boozehound, who lets off a snotty snort of a laugh, revealing a mouth with two teeth. Stan slaps his thigh, in that well-known gesture, to confirm to any casual onlookers that he is suffering from hilarity.

Their pastiness suggests they belong in some chilly northern city, they look like third-generation lushes whom fresh air would kill: utterly out of place, like trouts in an armchair.

"A mineral water, please," I say to the barman who has come within hailing distance. He is confused by this and stands in a contemplative pose.

"Stan. Stan! Stan! What we have here is a coward. What we have here is someone who wants to live... for ever."

"No, I'm someone who wants to have a glass of water."

Stan, if it weren't for the dehydrating effects of alcohol,

would be wetting himself by now. Another lengthy foghorn laugh rips out.

"No, I know your type," continues the alpha boozehound. "You want to live for ever, you want to temple your body. You're a weaselly little wanter of immortality. You drink water and you nibble celery like the rabbit you are."

The barman is taking an incredibly long time to manage the task of opening what I am sure will turn out to be an expensive bottle of mineral water, and finding a glass to pour the water into. I have a powerful urge to leave, but I badly need a drink.

"You don't have the cojones for bourbon. You're not man enough to raise a glass to the grim reaper. Stan and me, we just don't care. We're booze braves. Our balls are bigger than watermelons." The force of his mirth tosses Stan around: he needs a seat belt to prevent himself from injury.

The barman has now wandered off, very slowly, presumably to look for a glass. All I want is a glass of water, for which I am prepared to pay, promptly. I'm here, the water is here: why can't we be united? To be a good barman requires more ability than the wages suggest.

"I bet you're thinking here's some miserable old drunk, who has fucked up doozily and is crawling into a bottle. Here's a bozo, unhappy in love, no money. He's drinking because he has no future, no friends, no one who'll listen to him but a worthless leech like Stan."

"Well," I say, not in the mood for charity.

"But you're wrong. I'm happy. I bet I'm happier than you. I'm not drinking because I'm unhappy; I'm not drinking because I want to forget. I am drinking because I love it. I love boozing, and if I drop dead today I don't care. I'll go out grinning because I'm happy, and you, you mineral-lapping rabbit, you,

you're miserable. I can tell it. You've got boo-hoo-hoo plastered all over you."

The barman, having absconded in his quest for a bit of lemon, finally achieves the union of water and glass. I seek the point furthest from the blotto brothers and turn my back, to signal that conversation is not desired.

"You think I'm some delusion-prone delusion-lover... off on a delusion masterclass, sitting here, saying I'm happy when I'm not, unliving my life, but I am happy, pal. Let me tell you why: I own the bar."

Stan falls off his seat and can't make it back.

"That's right: this is mine, all mine. It's a fascinating story. You'll want to hear a fascinating story, right? I had this cousin, Barry. Barry was never very happy. He didn't drink and he hated me, mostly because I was happy. I didn't really care because I was happy, but I did notice how he made comments about my drinking and doing nothing and letting my women pay for everything, because he did it very loudly and very often."

Here Stan high-fives him from the floor.

"Barry didn't drink, and he worked hard. He worked hard though it didn't do much to make him happy. He started poor like me, but had all sorts of crappy jobs, busboy and junior dishwasher to get through school; he got two degrees, one in electrical engineering and one in computing, I think it was computing, although I can't remember exactly, because I didn't really care. Then he started up a business, some computing shit, doing I don't know what because I don't give a shit. He explained it to me once but I wasn't listening and he made a pile. Not rich enough to get his face in the magazines, or not in magazines worth reading, but you know, nice. Now Cousin Barry never had a wife or any children, whether that's because he was too busy, or wasn't into it or was simply too stingy to have any offspring, who knows? I don't give a shit. But he didn't have any other family but me.

"Now the idea that I might end up with his money terrified him, cos although he was sure the drinking would take me first, he was worried one day, you know, his plane might nosedive, he might munch on a sickly shellfish and through a terrible twist of fate the old booze filter here would be left with the cash. 'The otters,' he'd say to me, very loudly and very often, 'the otters will get everything.' He wanted to set up some ottery or whatever you call a home for, you know, otters with sad stories. He'd tell me that very often, although he hated me. He kept in touch, mostly so he could tell me about the distressed otters. He was waiting for me to get angry about the otters. Did the old booze filter here give a shit? No, I was happy. Suddenly, Cousin Barry gets a rare parasite, probably from his otters, is a sensation in the medical journals and drops dead. I was sad, family's family, and actually I enjoyed the calls about the otters, those graduates of the school of hard knocks with paw ailments. But, but it turns out that there's a tiny problem with Barry's will. The problem is that Barry did it himself. As I said he started poor and he hated spending money. Barry would have picked a nickel out of a dungheap with his teeth. I'd guess even at the end he was boosting toilet paper from hotels. So he saved himself a few hundred bucks. The end result: the otters get dick. The otters go boo-hoo and I get a bar where I'm my own best customer. But I don't want you to conclude I have such a sunny disposition because of the money. Ask me what I'd be doing if I didn't have the money, if Barry had made some otters very happy?"

"What would you be doing?"

"I'd be drinking. Just more slowly."

Stan foghorns again although I'm sure he's heard this one before. I make for the door.

"Hey, you're not going to live for ever. Have a bourbon and show cirrhosis who's the boss."

I wonder how to kill the time while I'm dead. I considered making an appearance at the church or somewhere where I'm known, as bilocation is always an impressive trick, but I feel somehow it could be used against me. He couldn't have been dead because he's on camera at Publix.

I sit on a bench and take in the sunshine. It truly is one of the great pleasures in life; it's very hard to be worried or unhappy. My phone rings. It's Didsbury.

"Man, you're deader than a doornail. You've joined the great unbreathing, the motionless majority. You're ready for the soil nap."

It's a very strange business getting what you want. First of all it's a very unfamiliar sensation. You have doubts that you've got it. Then you're not so pleased to have it; it doesn't look quite as great as it did.

Don is relieved of his duties as a part-time me and returned to bereavement central (with the accompanying desperate grunts from me). Then I wait a few hours and have the resurrection. I felt very bad about calling Dr Greer.

"Look, sorry to bother you, but I don't think I'm dead."

"This I have to see." I sit there in my Miami Dolphins shorts (not the ones Don was wearing), with my tattoo on display.

"You look... very much different than earlier." Is there a trace of suspicion in his eyes? Nothing he can do about it if there is. "How do you feel?"

"A bit tired, but otherwise okay." I'm uneasy about wasting the time of someone so decent and professional.

"You remember anything?"

"No. Went to bed last night and just woke up."

"That's what I call sleep. Remember you need to lose weight. Man, I've never got it so wrong, but everyone gets a resurrector once. Sure someone didn't slip you some zombie juice?"

It's no use doing something remarkable if word doesn't spread. Well, some remarkable things are rewarding in themselves. Sleeping with the hundred most beautiful women in the world in a month for example, though most of us would still like the news trumpeted. But what if you can hold your breath for nine minutes? Or really speak a dozen languages fluently? You'd want others to know, you'd want some whoops for your talent and dedication.

Virginia has a scowl of mild disgust. I remind myself the scowl is all-purpose, so I don't take it personally. She'd rather not be here, interviewing a loser spat out by death, and who can blame her?

"So, all sorts of exciting stuff happening around your church. You died?"

"That's what I'm told."

"And how long for?"

"No one's sure, but a day or so, earth time."

"So Mr Corbett, tell us all about it?"

I've considered this carefully of course.

"It's hard to describe,' I start. "It's very hard to describe. You're trying to put something unearthly into earthly terms, it's like…" I hesitate as if I'm thinking, but I'm merely holding back the line, "trying to turn mayonnaise into music. What I experienced was too… wide to be fitted into words."

"Did you see light?"

"No. You see, light is a physical term, something we know physically. It was *like* light, but not light."

"Hmm. Is there anything you can tell me about that time?"

"Well," and here I'm willing to dispense free hope. Hope is the one drug that does nothing but good. "As I say, I can't describe it in physical terms, but it was… comforting."

"What brought you back?"

"Me. I decided that my work here wasn't finished."

"Uh-huh. What is your work exactly?"

"I have some teaching to do, and many people to help."

"Hmm. What is your teaching?"

"Don't expect any reward." For some reason this now sounds stupid, and my honed wisdom falls to the ground like a dead, repellent insect. Virginia keeps writing for a long time without any more questions. A photographer takes my picture with a loud yawn. He only takes one picture and leaves.

"When do you expect your article to run?" I ask.

"Soon. But it isn't my decision."

The Hierophant isn't in a coma, but he doesn't move and he doesn't say anything. The doctors are getting bored with him. They like to make a judgement and issue a prescription, and there isn't a medication to combat capitulation, when you have decided that the game just isn't worth it any more. Also, doctors aren't much interested in the elderly: it doesn't seem worth the effort. When you're in your twenties and you go to the doctor with anything less obvious than a broken leg, they tell you you have a virus: go to bed, take a pill. When you hit forty they blame everything on your age (what do you expect? You're on the way out).

237

The Hierophant hasn't eaten anything and he hasn't washed. He doesn't smell good. He has to my knowledge been wearing the same blue shirt for three days, and I can assume the same goes for the other articles of clothing.

"Can I get you something to eat?" I ask. The eyes register my request, but there is no response.

"Are you feeling okay?" I ask. Obviously he's not, but I hope this might provoke an utterance.

"Would you like a drink?" No response. I left a glass of water yesterday and it's been emptied, but he must be in danger of dehydrating, which won't help putting him in a more dynamic frame of mind.

When my marriage collapsed I went to a party with a neighbour I barely knew. After a trip to the loo, I found my companion had vanished and I was in a room full of people I didn't know. They were jabbering away and it was as if everyone there was a couple holding an intense conversation in a language I didn't understand. I had no way of breaking in. I'd been in situations before where I was awkward, or didn't have much to say, but this was different: I didn't belong. No one was unfriendly, but just as blue isn't orange, there was a gulf between us. As if I was wrapped in inch-thick cellophane. I wonder if this, the chocolate aside, is something everyone feels sometime. You're in the wrong room, on the wrong planet.

But I understand the Hierophant. I've been close to this as well. Not speaking because you don't see any value in communication.

"Okay," I say. The Hierophant is barefoot. I place a couple of matches between his toes, and I light them. The Hierophant watches them burn for a few moments. He fidgets slightly. I snuff out the matches.

Five minutes later. "Hell, Tyndale, that really hurt," he says. But then nothing more.

I resolve to shake the Hierophant out of this. He wanted the Church of the Heavily Armed Christ to be on the list of the most happening churches. It will be. With a resurrection to boot.

What the hell has happened to my miracle?

I chase Virginia with no result.

However, one of the few benefits of having a small con-gregation is that it's easier to make it larger and more happening. Just getting Gamay and Muscat in the hall is about a ten-per-cent increase, and their bulk really eats up the space. They have brought four "friends" with them who look like scared skateboarders forced off the street, because they are; but bodies count, not audience enjoyment, and a morning in church won't do anyone any lasting harm.

"Tyndale, man, you mustn't think we're afraid of getting our hands dirty. Couldn't we off some vatos for you?" whines Gamay.

"That's not the job. You have to do the job given. The job given is to get ten more worshippers next Sunday." I explain again the importance of discipline, and how failure to deliver will mean failure to join.

"How about torching some competitors?" continues Gamay. It's more and more evident that Gamay isn't just primed to commit violence, he's itching to do it.

"Get more people for next Sunday."

"You know, Tyndale, we've spent a lot of time at your bidding and we have nothing to show for it. If I'd worked at Publix packing bags, I'd have been better off; even a dollar an hour would be better than this, because we're getting zippo an hour."

Gamay stares at me and the hatred is unmistakable. It's like that when you have a pet alligator or python, one day it's too big to be flushed down the toilet. One day you see it's big enough to harm you, one day you're aware it doesn't like you very much.

"Do you have a problem? Because I'd like to make it clear if you do have a problem that's too bad." I really should be afraid of Gamay because he could pulp me, but if he hit me it would be the perfect excuse for disqualifying him from membership. There's going to be ugliness, but I don't see why I shouldn't use that old technique of putting off finding a solution. Only now that Sixto's employers have gone kaput, does it occur to me I could have got rid of the DJs by putting them on a plane and sending them to a real multinational criminal organization.

"No, there are no problems at all, Tyndale, how could there be problems? There are just, you know... things we could be happier about."

"Welcome to life."

The next Saturday afternoon I'm in the office wondering why nothing has appeared in the paper about my miracle, and to which restaurant I will take the chief head-counter. The most-happening-church assessors have secret visitors who come and go mysteriously, but this is an official, preannounced check.

Bribery is like flattery. It works. Even if you know the flattery is totally insincere and ulterior, the mere act of someone taking the trouble to flatter you is flattering. Similarly, bribery always works – it might not work as well as you would like, it may not get anywhere near what you want, but it always gets through. However, there has to be a discretion and a decorum to greasing palms. The head-counter should have a memorable meal, he should be pampered; but, but you don't want to go somewhere where his conscience might be niggled by an absurdly priced bottle of wine.

Muscat bursts in and pulls out a gun from the back of his jeans.

I'm going to die.

I don't have much time for regret or fear. Tears start to poke at my eyes and I notice that Gamay is wearing a T-shirt emblazoned with the slogan "Hotties Expertly Fucked Here", a slogan that will doubtless preclude that remote possibility of him becoming acquainted with a member of the opposite sex.

Despite the hurdle of his monumental stupidity, Muscat has figured out that I'm taking him for a ride, that I've been using him as slave labour (even though the results have been unsatisfactory in the extreme, and frankly if he had been my slave I would have sold him or traded him for any espresso machine). He is too dim and angry to foresee the consequences of murder and he's going to kill me. I thought it would be Gamay, but wrong again. Muscat is going to shoot me, it's in his eyes. Fair enough.

Then it isn't. He's lost his murder.

"I'm a bona-fide person, Tyndale," he announces. I try to say something, but my voice is absent.

"I'm a bona-fide person, Tyndale," he repeats. I welcome the repetition since I am unable to contribute anything to the conversation. "I have rights. You've got to let me go."

"Whatever," I croak, probably too faintly to be heard. I'd always hoped that I could confront danger without embarrassment, but my voice is really letting me down.

"You've got to let me go. I don't want you coming after me. It's over, okay, you've got to understand that, you've got to promise that you won't come after me. Don't try and drag me back. I promise I won't squeal about your organization. Watch, my lips are sealed, I'll never say a word. I just want to be happy, I'm going anyway, and I'm never coming back, so don't try and stop me. Okay, just don't stop me or I'll have to hurt you."

"Muscat, I've always liked you," I say, as my voice has reassembled. This is a line that always works a little even if both parties suspect it's not true. "If you can give me your word that you'll leave, and that you'll never, never come back, I should be able to square it with the powers up top. After all, you were never formally signed up. If you had been in on our secrets, well, that would be different."

"Thanks, Tyndale, man, thanks, you're a hero. I owe you big, I ain't kennedying you," he says, lowering the gun. He looks tearful. "Maybe we should stay in touch somehow, we have a very special relationship."

"I'd like nothing more than to stay in touch, but that would be dangerous for you."

"Okay. Cool. Cool. I'm sorry, Tyndale, I know you're losing a unique soldier and you must be disappointed, but I've found something much better than ass-kicking wealth and respect on the streets. Wait." He vanishes.

I'm hoping he might not come back, but he does, with a short, dark-haired girl. Young, but, actually, legal.

"This is Maria." She shakes my hand with a genuine smile. She seems perfectly pleasant – why she's adopting Muscat is beyond me, but that's her affair.

"I'm moving to Idaho to be with Maria. It's the chicken business for us. It's really interesting. The public doesn't appreciate how interesting chickens are—"

"Muscat, it's not a good idea for you to hang around."

"Sure. Have you ever tasted an egg from an old-school chicken that's eaten plenty of nature?"

"It was nice meeting you, Maria." As he ushers her out, I wonder if I should ask about Gamay, but I don't want to delay him for a second on his trip to Idaho. It's a rare occurrence, but sometimes your problems evaporate.

However, two minutes later Muscat returns:

"Tyndale, man, I just wanted to explain that this is the real thing."

"No. I understand. I really do," I say giving him a gentle push towards his new future.

"She's just everything. I mean your cleaner, Trixi. Man, I had the hots for her. I was spanking the monkey like... like a monkey. But this is different. She's changed me, she's in charge, and it feels great. She chooses my clothes, she made me understand about chicken-farming. I wish my mother was still here to meet her, but I'm sure she'll be looking down on us from a pearly seat when we get married."

It's remarkable how the deceased are supposed to be hovering around when there is a happy event: a wedding, a birth, a football match won, but no one ever contemplates the ancestors hanging around when you're beating up someone much weaker than you, stealing a bottle of vodka from a supermarket, or rimming your best friend's wife.

I'm now steering Muscat out the door, but he pushes back in.

"Tyndale, there's one other thing, you might as well know." He gazes at his shoes. "Gamay, he won't be joining your organization."

"Farming chickens too?"

"No. He's definitely in a real no-chicken-farming situation."

"Which is?"

"He's kinda dead."

"What happened?"

"That's a reasonable question, Tyndale. It all depends on how you look at it. It's funny you mentioned chickens. Basically, he won a game of chicken. You know, like nothing to do with chickens, the feathery things, but being chicken. He was jawing on about being badder than me etcetera. I was in the SUV and he was in the road. You know, I just wanted to see him jump, jump out the way, cos I thought he would. I mean if you had an SUV powering towards you, what would you do?"

"Get out of the way."

"Yeah, but he didn't. He'd driven first and I'd jumped. I jumped out of the way cos I could see for sure he wasn't stopping. So I said to myself, I ain't stopping either. He stood there. Looking sure I'd stop, real confident. Went right under the wheels looking real confident. Real confident to the end. Looked real confident after the end. Man, I was so furious with him. I had to spend the whole day with the police, explaining what happened. If he hadn't been in the middle of the fucking road, where he had no business being, pumped full of coke n' acid, I'd be in jail, for real. It could have been goodbye to my Idaho disfrooting."

"That's... unfortunate." I choose my word carefully, because I find it hard to express any real regret. It's dishonest to lie any more than is absolutely necessary. How much truth is Muscat telling me about Gamay's accident?

"Yeah, he may have been tougher than me, but he wasn't tougher than General Motors."

I shake hands manfully with Muscat in a have-a-good-life way and he leaves. Cherishing that strange feeling of things going your way, I settle back in my chair.

Incredibly, five minutes later, Muscat's back again, clutching a picture of a chicken:

"Rhode Island Red. Seriously, you should try it." Then he's really gone.

There are huge lights. It looks more like a concert or some gala, red-carpet award ceremony than a church service. I am astonished by the numbers of the crowd streaming in, many of them openly affluent as well as the no-hopers and doormats who are the staple of any religion. I check out the sound system and the lighting, which alone cost more than the entire worth of the Church of the Heavily Armed Christ.

There's something outrageous about this, especially as it's only twelve yards from our front door: it would be impossible for it to be closer or more in our face. It would be worth throwing open our church, I reflect, since some of their worshippers would certainly spill into our place by accident.

I squeeze through parked cars and join the flow inside. "Luxury for free", says one sign. This isn't the hard sell, this is the hard giveaway. As I enter I see the Locketts seated at the front, with their daughter, Esther.

I have to admit I thought of getting in touch with them, but was too afraid of bad news. Esther looks well, but the darkness cut into her parents' face suggests that the problem is still there. There are four wheelchair-bound invalids placed up front next to the Locketts, and several others who manifestly aren't full of the life force. The Fixico sisters have gathered a couple of hospital wards of the infirm.

You can't lose really. If they peg out, you've been a big-hearted wheelchair-lover, a comfort to the afflicted, and ill faces are quickly forgotten. If, on the other hand, someone overcomes their paralysis or terminal cancer, you've got an earner. It works on a percentage basis, the way you used to ask as many girls to parties as possible because at least one would get drunk, bored or stranded and decide on you.

As far as I'm concerned there's nothing wrong with misleading healthy, employed individuals and taking their money in exchange for illusions, because a good illusion is a beautiful thing, but it's wrong to feed off the sick.

I wave to the Reinholds. They return my greeting with that artificial naturality of those caught with their pants down. Virginia scowls there with her notepad. She hasn't returned my calls. I waited a day or two for her article to appear. Nothing. Did I give up? No. I phoned. I caught her once, she said she didn't know when it would run. Her editor wouldn't give her an answer, she said. Surely a stock fuck-off.

I left three more messages for her. One message can easily get waylaid or forgotten about. In stressful times so can two. Four messages: you're desperate or a nuisance. So I left three. Nothing.

Did I give up? No. I introduced myself to local radio and television. I talked to a couple of people who sounded interested in the story, but nothing. I had a leaflet printed up about my resurrection, which I distributed to the handful of parishioners at the Church of the Heavily Armed Christ: nothing.

It's as if the Fixico sisters are giving away free money. I now catch a glimpse of Georgia a few rows ahead. The Temple of Extreme Abundance has no problem with see-through tops. Luis is next to her.

I've lost. My miracle has had less coverage and impact than a missing dog. My flock has deserted en masse. I've lost, I'm finished, but I don't mind. I don't mind, because I have enough character and backbone to be manful for a few hours. Tomorrow, I'll be sobbing and suicidal.

Very often when you look at things with hindsight you can see where you went wrong, but sometimes you look at things and you can't see where you went wrong. Why couldn't I achieve even a fifth of a congregation like this?

Which is worse? To lose badly or to lose by a whisker? Even as a connoisseur of failure I can't make up my mind. Being thrashed is especially humiliating and painful at the time, but you can put that out of your mind by consigning the whole episode to oblivion, but losing by just one point can give you the twinges of if-onlys in perpetuity.

Some guy beckons me over. I recognize Fash, the homeless guy who didn't look homeless, because he had a self-awareness instead of the out-to-lunch sign the others displayed.

His hand, I notice as we shake, is immaculately clean. I sit next to him because it's the holy thing to frequent the unfortunate. Although he's not doing unfortunate tonight. He's very smart, looking distinctly unstreet. His shirt, on closer inspection, looks like silk and a distinct, appealing aroma of soap or moisturizer wafts around him.

I sit next to Fash although I can't help thinking that who you hang with tells you who you are. Look at who sits opposite you at your dinner party and you'll have a good idea of who you are. One of my neighbours was really successful and I kept on inviting him over for supper but, while never actually refusing, he never made it.

Fash is definitely too groomed, and his shirt has shop-newness

– he can't be out on the street any more. I'm about to ask about his change of fortune when the show starts.

As the music swirls around us, I concede that there's no way we can even attempt to compete with this; the Hierophant and I are not outclassed: we're not even good enough to be outclassed.

The preacher comes out and starts his stuff. Great diction, great teeth, great suit. The two Fixico sisters, Margi and Argi, are enthroned behind, watching him. I suspected that the two old dears might have been recruited by a more unscrupulous version of myself to act as a white-haired-granny, crochet-knitting, tea-pouring, everything's-fine front, but I can see I was wrong and it's the other way around.

The preacher is the froth, and the ladies are the power. However rarely, there are those individuals you come across, even if you only exchange a hello, whom you immediately sense are decent, they seep goodness (and it is heartening that you will get to encounter some decent people who, nevertheless, being decent, will be unprosperous and unpowerful). The reverse of this warming phenomenon is that, equally, there are souls who simply sprout evil.

The Fixico sisters scare me.

Clichéd little old ladies, complete with horn-rimmed glasses, their eyes have an insect glint. They would eat you alive, and they wouldn't even show any pleasure. They aren't just here to bamboozle the invertebrates, there is something not merely dishonest, but very unwholesome here. What's also interesting is that no one else but me is aware of this.

Rapture and respect are all I witness around me, and I begin to question my judgement as you always do when the herd goes against you.

"God spoke to Margi and Argi," says the preacher.

248

This is a good one. God spoke. The ultimate name-dropping. The supreme being, a close personal friend of mine, always dropping round for a chat. The supreme being giving me tips. Telling me to tell you what to do. Of course, the most beautiful thing about a sound bite from God is, while you can't prove he did, no one can prove he didn't. It's like bumping into a celebrity at your deli. Always possible.

"God told the sisters they had a special gift. God told them they had the gift of helping others." I am tempted to get up and shout, "No. I didn't." But I don't think this will be a fruitful tactic and then my career as a deity is over.

"The Fixico sisters had neighbours like many of you once," the preacher continues. "Worried about bills, worried about their family, worried about their health. They began helping their neighbours by using their faith. Now their neighbours have everything and they want to share their secret with you."

Having explained that the Fixico sisters are aching to share their secret, as is very often the case with those who claim they have an important secret to share, the secret doesn't actually get shared, just advertised. The preacher sits down and we get some music: live choir, five musicians. They're very good and my foot taps along.

Then Gert waltzes up to talk about his coffee mug. He evinces no guilt at having switched churches. He's very happy. "Because of the Fixico sisters my business is thriving and my heart is full of joy. I can't thank them enough."

Fash leans to my ear: "They're evil," he whispers. Fash is now my friend. My close friend. I admire the judgement. I admire the confident, succinct way he transmits his verdict. We stay another half an hour, and as we walk out Fash says:

"I'd like to have a talk. Why don't you come back to my

place?" I agree because I have nothing else to do. Fash has clearly changed fortunes big time – we get into a car (a dull, old car, but still a car), and drive down to one of those little man-made islands off the beach. A guard in a little box raises a barrier to allow us in. What's going on?

We pull up outside a fancy house. Fash must have some job house-sitting or toadying for some moneybags, either that or he's taking it in the arse for a living. I wouldn't say it's the most opulent house I've ever been in, but well to the top of the list. Three bedrooms, but cavernous ones, large, expensive, flashy art on the walls, a garden with a jetty at the end and a boat. If I had this, I'd lock the door and chuckle for the rest of my life.

"So whose place is this?"

"Mine," he says, as a maid offers us drinks. "I hope dishonesty doesn't bother you too much."

"Not too much."

"In my defence, from a technical point of view, when I was homeless, I was genuinely homeless, I only bought this place last month."

"Lottery?"

"No, I was born loaded, I had money even when I was out on the streets, I just didn't have it… on me. I cut myself off. I've always been more than well-off, rather painfully rich. You'll find this ridiculous, but I was curious how I'd be treated if I didn't have any money."

"Like shit?"

"You know it. But it was… educational to get away from my life."

"You actually lived out on the streets?"

"Oh yeah. For two months," Fash sips on what I'm sure is a very well-made cocktail. Mine certainly is. "It could have been worse, you ain't going to freeze here, and I had a Kevlar jacket, but it was very tough at first. One night I woke up, someone was pissing on me. Another homeless guy. The whole of Miami to relieve himself in, he had to straddle me. That's what you had to deal with. A couple of times I cracked, if I'd had a credit card or any money on me I'd have walked into a hotel. I cried after I gave you back your wallet. But I tell you what was enlightening."

"What?"

"How fast you get used to it. You get used to it fast. Not washing. The dirt. When I had my first proper bath, there was a crust on the water, I turned the tub into a swamp, there was *vegetation*. All in all, I prefer to be liked for my money. But what I wanted to talk to you about is this: to offer you a job. I hope the offer of a well-paid job won't offend you?"

"What's that?"

"I want you to, how shall I phrase this? From a compassion and helpfulness point of view, it might jar against your position on compassion and helpfulness, all that forgiving stuff. I want you to… what's the right word? I want you to destroy the Fixico sisters."

"Driving a car," says Dave. "Most of us don't think about what driving a car means. For most of us, a car is a necessity, not a luxury. Without a car, most of us would be finished, but no one really considers how a car is as deadly as a pearl-handled Colt .45. No I take that back, as deadly as the M16. A Colt can't cut someone in half. The deaths and the maimings. Take the Vietnam War. Five-star war, tanks, planes. A decade of war, fifty thousand dead Americans, all the hoopla, razzmatazz about it. The roads of America have that many fatalities every year. Where are the sit-ins about the automobile?"

We are walking down a quiet stretch of Collins Avenue towards an art exhibition put on by Dave's second cousin's girlfriend when a solitary figure comes around the corner. There's no one but us on the street for three or four blocks, and I fear that we're in line for another mugging, but I see that the figure is tiny, a hunched old man with a walking stick.

When we get closer I see that he is wearing a singlet. Fashion is, of course, a personal statement, but when you get to eighty you shouldn't be choosing clothing that highlights your roasted, wizened arms. Put it away, pops. We're about to pass him, when he snaps:

"I'll be taking your money, wimps."

Dave looks at me.

The he-hag is having trouble standing up, his right eye looks blind. He's toothless. He can't be far from ninety, and he was a small, thin man before he shrivelled up. We go round him, when he shouts:

"Give me your money, pussies. If you don't give me your money I'll tell the police you mugged me." He produces a pair of dentures from his pocket, cracked as if by force, falls to the ground and shouts for help.

Dave reaches into his jacket, pulls out a wallet and hands it over.

"Tell me, what is it about me?' he asks.

"You're bitches. You're not men enough to laugh about beating up an old fart."

We walk on.

"What?" says Dave. "You were expecting me to beat him up? Thanks. My wife she says I'm asking for it. 'What do you mean,

I'm asking for it?' I say. 'You're always getting mugged you must be doing something to attract it,' she says. 'How?' I say. 'What exactly am I doing to attract it, dear wife,' I say. 'Please tell me.' 'I don't know,' she says, 'but you must be doing something. Or it wouldn't happen would it? Stop it before you get hurt.'"

"Acceptance is important. But it's also dangerous because it's very close to surrender. It's standing right next to surrender. You have to look carefully. You have to accept certain things though. I have to accept that I couldn't save my brother. I have to accept my face makes me muggee of the month. Yeah."

Dave explains that from now on he will carry a dupe wallet, which contains out-of-date credit cards and some Haitian banknotes, street value, two cents top. "I thought about getting one of those booby-trapped attaché cases, give the thief an electric shock or blowing off his fingers. I liked that idea a lot. I really did. Those fingers just flying away. But I'm putting this in the wallet instead."

He hands me a card.

"You're on the wrong path. You think you've got ahead just now. You're not stealing from others but yourself. You're stealing your future. Go to the Church of the Heavily Armed Christ for true help."

"Finding a card like that would be freaky."

"Hey, you wanted a higher body count." Dave stares out at the waves. One or two big ships are on the horizon, almost erased by distance. "Survival. Survival is overrated."

He gives me my cut of our latest winnings.

My first job for the Fixico sisters is standing in front of the Omni, playing their tape and handing out leaflets. I keep wishing some policeman or authority figure would stop me or move me along, but, unfortunately, when you're religious you tend to be ignored.

"Do you believe this stuff?" says one recipient.

I restrain myself from replying, "Of course not. You're quite right, it's the most outrageous rubbish and the paper's too hard to wipe your arse with." I reply:

"Have a good and profitable day, sir." I mean it too. I'm in a good mood. I like the idea of most people having a good and profitable day. Just not the Fixico sisters.

It's very tempting to openly sabotage the Fixicos at grass roots, but you never know who's around.

Calvin, my team leader, for instance. Calvin's a born crawler and a natural number four or five. Anything higher up the chain of command would be too much, but he likes belonging and mild responsibility. He'd be happy working in a bank or shooting captives in the back of the head in some ethnic dispute, but somehow circumstances have brought him to work as one of the Fixicos' enforcers, checking up on us, the rabble, the street soldiers.

"You're not standing right," was one of the things Calvin carpeted me for. I straightened up, assuming I was being accused of slouching. "You're not standing right," he continued. I'm now so unslouched I am bending over backwards.

This is one of the golden rules of management, of course: you have to make it clear what you want. "You're not standing right," he shouts in my face again. Getting louder is often seen as a means of being clearer. I long to hit him – but this is the most important skill you have to have in life, working with people you hate.

He points at my left leg. "Straighten that leg." I'm standing on my leg, so by implication it's straight. I will my leg straighter, but nothing happens, because it's physically impossible to make the leg straighter. "Will you straighten that leg?" he screams again. I can't make my left leg any straighter, and as far as I can tell – and I should know – it's no more crooked than my right leg.

I smile. Always smile. I don't understand why Calvin is screaming at me. The homeless who worked for the Fixicos at the beginning not only had very poor deportment, they flopped on the sidewalk, they fiddled with their balls and were encrusted in vomit. Is this a new order in the Fixico regime or is it directed at me? Are they trying to get rid of me? The sudden fussiness is ridiculous. No army would be this bothered about straight legs. It would be very easy to get angry about some failed lawyer called Calvin, a wimpy failed lawyer ten years younger than me, a wimpy failed lawyer ten years younger than me who is stupid enough to take the Fixico sisters seriously, shouting in my face: very easy indeed.

But I don't hit Calvin. I don't protest. I smile. The smile is a genuine smile because I'm promising myself when this is all over, I'll take the time and trouble to find Calvin, and kick the crap out of him, vicious-style. It's important to reward yourself. I really don't want another person to hate, I'm quite full-up, but sometimes you have to rise to the challenge. As Calvin tells me I'm not using my hands properly, I soothe myself by imagining his cries for mercy.

Calvin, though hard work, is easy to spot: very tall and he's addicted to dark suits even in this heat. There's no sign of him so I'm content for the moment.

I'm standing there watching the buzzards circle, some spread out to sun themselves on the roofs, being relaxed by them, when a black limo pulls up opposite. A window slides down and I can make out one of the Fixico sisters scrutinizing me.

I think it's Margi, who's the older one, although even close up it's almost impossible to tell them apart as they dress and style themselves identically. Margi's just that bit fatter and looser round the jowl.

Am I imagining it, or is she suspicious of me? Is she wondering why I've agreed to be one of her minions? She's right to wonder, why has this sub-hierophant gone renegade and joined her ranks? But I'm doing the job to the letter. I must be the least-mad, most qualified leaflet-distributor in her empire. Her cunning is alerted, and she might want to find fault with me, but she can't. I've always been a good employee. Maybe not a great employee, but a good one, and this time I'm making a special effort.

The limo drives off. She smells danger, but can't see it. The Fixico sisters can't know that if I have one talent, it's for destroying the organization I work for. But happily, this talent is well hidden.

I can't prove this, of course, but the results speak for themselves. Emptying the pews of the Church of the Heavily Armed Christ isn't much of an achievement, but pulling down a long-established, major multinational criminal organization in the space of a few months isn't bad. Those felons in their cells in Bogotá will be wondering where it went wrong. Were they weak in their bribing of politicos? Did someone grass? Did they tread on someone's toes? They'll never be thinking that one of their unknown, part-time delivery boys in Miami was the cause of their downfall. Of course, the lighting company took several years, but I was probably struggling against the good fortune of others.

I'm in no rush. I really have nothing much else to do.

So now I'm giving up. Giving up can be quite enjoyable. I have to accept I'm not going to make it as God. What exactly I will do I don't know, but I'm putting off acting by acting (action is often only speeded-up waiting). My preoccupation now is to deal with the Fixico sisters. Hatred can be as sustaining as love, even if there can be unpleasant side effects.

Los Angeles was where the Fixico sisters started. Then they moved east, through New Mexico, Texas, Louisiana, Tampa and now Miami, mysteriously acquiring money and influence along the way. Fash was appalled by how he saw them treating the homeless, and their philosophy of "give to receive" which concentrated, for the subordinates anyway, on the giving and not the receiving. Fash, who had worked for a few days as a boombox escort, was asked to leave. "They claimed I was asking difficult questions," said Fash. "I only asked one: where's the money going?" A vagrant, he added, who failed to return a boombox (they're very basic so the resell value would only be almost nothing) was found dead. Of course, if you live out on the street your life expectancy's not great.

"And, I trust I don't need to mention that if you help me in this, as they say, I'll make it very much worth your while..." Fash said.

"I have no idea what they say, because I've never been urged to accept a well-paid job."

"So you'll take it?"

"No."

I explained to Fash that he shouldn't involve me directly in his plans to block the Fixico sisters. I would go solo, as the jinxer, and web myself into the Fixicos.

"I don't understand," he said.

"Doesn't matter. We pride ourselves on being unorthodox

257

at the Church of the Heavily Armed Christ. But I've got some good ideas for your money," I continued. His money would be better used to build up the Hierophant, buy some advertising and above all to remove the Locketts and Esther from the orbit of the Fixicos. Fash found a leukaemia specialist in New York who's supposed to be the best in the country, who might help, and in any case New York is a long way from here.

I make a point of standing in the sun. I really like it.

"Do you want to talk about it?" asks Sixto.

"No," I reply.

"Sure?"

"Yes."

"Maybe I can offer some suggestions." Sixto has now qualified as a psychotherapist, whatever that means. He is packing his best crockery away, meticulously, into boxes and is eager to practise.

"I don't need suggestions. What I need is a new life."

"Maybe I could make you see your life in a new way."

"Sixto, I appreciate the offer. I have a problem – I'm not stupid enough to believe in nonsense."

Sixto considers the empty boxes and his remaining bric-a-brac. We rarely go home. What we do is return to a collection of furniture to sleep with. A selection of objects to dust. That's what centres most of us – our favourite dust-gatherers. Of course, I'd like my own collection of objects to come back to; it's more comforting than one would like to admit.

Failure gets a bad press. Naturally, you have to fight the laziness for a while before you give up, but failure is the norm.

It's a big club. Most attempts end in failure. And all success ends in failure, eventually. Success can make you forget that. One of my neighbours had a mail-order business. I can't remember the exact figure but I think she said as long as they got a 0.1% response from their mailshots, that was fine.

Napalm comes in. I study him. Nothing.

"Hey, Napalm," says Sixto. "We were just discussing the human race. There's no hope." Anyone who says this usually doesn't mean it. Who says, "Have you noticed my nose is in the middle of my face?"

Napalm checks the fridge. He pours himself a large pineapple juice and goes upstairs. Nothing.

"Tell me about your mad love?" asks Sixto. I don't know why I reply. Perhaps Sixto does have a skill.

"It was mad."

"Who was she? What did she look like? Why and how did it end?"

"She was beautiful. Clever. Great nose. A great nose."

"And?"

"She moved. I wrote a long letter, detailing the madness of my love. On very expensive paper. I wrote, and this was the killer line, I had chosen her out of the billions of people on this planet."

"What happened?"

"The letter didn't reach her – her mother was forwarding her mail. It ended up in the glove compartment of her mother's car. A year later her mother discovered it and passed it on. The recipient of my madness got in touch and said how moved she was by the letter."

"And?"

"I was married by then. I got married two days before she called."

259

"You gave up too easily."

"No, I didn't. I talked to her mother. 'Has my letter arrived?' 'Yes.' 'Have you given it to her?' 'Yes.' I thought she had received it, but wasn't interested."

"That's infuriating."

"I used to get angry. You always wonder about those roads you didn't take. How it would have turned out? But now I console myself with the thought that the roads untravelled would probably have been just as disaster-strewn as the ones I took."

"That's consolation?"

"Works for me."

Sixto pulls out some long steel device from a drawer, some costly culinary tool. "You know what's frightening? Not only do I not remember buying this, I don't know what it's for." He tosses it into a box. I'm glad I travel light.

"So what important truth have you learnt that you would be willing to share with others?" I ask.

"You mean, if I had to distil the wisdom of my thirty-two years on this planet into one sentence? If I had ten seconds to transmit only one important universal truth, as my message to mankind?"

"Yes."

Sixto pauses. After deliberation, "Most cats don't like to be microwaved."

"Inexpensive perversions. You have inexpensive perversions, you're laughing," says a passing woman, who looks like the last woman to make that remark. Perhaps her husband's are expensive.

"We all need a moral code to ignore," her companion agrees.

As I have succeeded in collecting more in donations than any of the Fixicos' other street representatives, I've been promoted to South Beach.

Calvin is unhappy about this, but cash is cash – and he doesn't know that I rarely collect any money from the public, I simply hand in a few bills from my pocket. I'm not up against any serious competition: many of the others are so disturbed they would be as likely to eat a dollar bill as spend it.

And the money I am feeding into the Fixicos will do damage – it's been Tyndaled. Will I be lucky in being unlucky? Or will I be unlucky in not being unlucky? How should I look at it?

Calvin is desperate to find fault with me, but can't. Doing your job is often one of the subtlest but most satisfying ways of needling your employer. It can drive them mad when you do exactly what you're told.

I haven't been wasting my time completely. My tan is bone-deep and, in my shirt pocket, on a folded piece of paper, is Calvin's home address. That I know where to find him is very comforting.

If you have to spend hours hanging around a street corner, Lincoln Road is definitely the place to do it. Intriguing pedestrians and good restaurants. An elderly man wearing only a white dressing gown and white slippers comes up to me. I doubt his outfit is a fashion statement.

He is brandishing two huge cigars and a box of matches. He cheerily offers me one of the cigars, saying something in Spanish I don't understand... I refuse. He persists in a good-natured but firm manner. I accept.

We smoke the cigars while he yacks vivaciously, in Spanish, about the past, I assume. I can't work out whether he knows

I don't understand a word or whether he has me down as a listening addict… My guess is he's some Cuban who's climbed out of a window at his daughter's house or a hospital where he's not allowed to light up. He maintains the gestureful monologue (although I can see he's ill) for half an hour. Then he shakes my hand, thanks me and shuffles off.

I continue to watch the style warriors trooping by and mentally munch another grouper sandwich. Yesterday, I had a grouper sandwich at Books & Books, and I embarrassed myself by how much I enjoyed it. The grouper must have been swimming around a few hours earlier, it was that fresh. It was fried with mastery by someone who truly cared – although it was the accompanying aioli that made it so out of this world.

My pretensions of holiness have been dropped, so I don't see why I shouldn't enjoy a skilfully made grouper sandwich, but it's bad for a grown man to be so moved by a sandwich. I am a little ashamed of myself for being preoccupied by the sandwich all day, and returning to this end of the Lincoln Road solely to have another.

But when I take my lunch break I discover it's gone from the menu. I now see how wise I was to over-enjoy the grouper sandwich yesterday. Pig it up while you can. I settle for a tuna ceviche and my phone rings.

"You haven't heard, have you?" says Dave.

"Heard what?"

"You're not going to believe this," he continues. "Do you want to guess what's happened?"

It depends a great deal on who's saying to you you're not going to believe something; some people's unbelievable is, actually, very believable and not interesting at all. Dishonest Dave's unbelievable is certain to give the definition a good kicking.

"Tell me."

"No, no. You have a guess."

"Just tell me."

"News like this, you'll have to beg. I want to hear some begging."

"No."

"Beg."

"No. I'd say you want to tell me this news more than I want to hear it."

"You want to hear this news."

"So tell me."

"No, you have to guess first."

"Ludwig van Beethoven, Elvis Presley and Pablo Escobar are alive and well and running a dry-cleaning business with astonishing success in New Jersey."

"Better than that. The Fixico sisters." He pauses for me to say, "Yes?"

"The Fixico sisters…" He gives another long pause. "Have been arrested."

I laugh loudly. For a long time. I can sense Dave is twitching to be asked what for, but I don't.

"Do you want to guess what for?"

"Fraud?"

"We've got fraud. What's better than fraud?"

"I don't know, what's better than fraud?"

"Murder."

Perhaps I shouldn't, but I laugh uncontrollably.

"Wait. Wait," says Dave. "I haven't finished yet. What's better than a murder charge?"

"I give up."

"Twelve counts of murder."

In fact there is a bewildering armada of charges, from unpaid parking tickets through tax evasion to murder. The juiciest revelation was that the Fixicos' start-up capital came from collecting on insurance policies. These insurance policies had been taken out on the homeless of Los Angeles who had a series of fatal accidents under the wheels of cars that didn't stop and which were driven by drivers unknown. I find it hard to believe they managed to collect money like this, since I never managed to get my insurance company to pay for genuine holes in my roof.

"One charge of murder," says Dave. "Any blockhead can dodge. Two or three charges of murder – a fancy lawyer can money you out. Twelve? Twelve? You're kissing goodbye, saying sayonara, auf Wiedersehen, aloha and adieu to the world on the other side of the bars. Yeah. How long have you been working for them?"

"Almost three weeks."

"Tyndale, you are too dangerous to know."

Of course, you'll say to me, Tyndale, my old china, the police must have been on their trail for years, building the case. Okay, but I know the truth.

I dry my eyes. Bitch all you want about life, we all get a few laughs. I drop the boombox and the leaflets in a bin. They're not needed any more.

I reach into my shirt pocket. Calvin.

"Tyndale, how are you?" asks the Hierophant. He was always thin, but he's still managed to lose some weight. However, the old marine swagger is back. He squeezes past the boxes in the hallway.

The house has been sold and Sixto has crammed everything into boxes. He wanted a change of scenery and moving away will also help avoid awkward questions about money, should any emerge from Latin America. I don't know what to do. Having someone to destroy was nice, it provided a reason to get out of bed.

"For someone who died," says the Hierophant, "you're looking good."

My resurrection made no incursion into the world. Only a few dozen people know about it: Sixto, Didsbury, Dr Greer, Virginia, the various journalists I pestered. I can't see what I did wrong. Even now, every other day or so, there is a reference to Gert and his mug in a paper, magazine or website somewhere; but I've never found one line about me. Perhaps I should have tried to keep the whole thing secret, but you can't appeal. I pulled off a miracle and no one cared.

"You're looking good too, Gene," I say, because it's mostly true.

"I'm okay. I'm an old man. There's no getting away from it. You tell kids how tough old age is, but they won't listen to you – they keep on getting older. You get old, you get maudlin. I don't watch television any more. I don't read the papers any more. I can't bear news, because it's all about the suffering. I can't take it any more. I see a poster for some kid's missing dog and it breaks me up – that's how old I am. I can't even enjoy the sports channels any more, because sport at its worst means someone breaks a leg, and at its very best even sport means someone loses."

He pulls out a copy of Scientific American from his jacket.

"This is all I read now. Science is safe. Muons don't moan."

Sixto's been generous, I have a little capital. I have survival money for a year. I also still have my persistent and embarrassing medical condition. What I don't have is any idea of what I should do next.

"We miss you at the Church, Tyndale," says the Hierophant. "What a man does with his time is his business. I don't know why we haven't seen you lately, but I came round to let you know that I'm not sore or disappointed with you for giving your services to the Fixicos. Lots of people were taken in. You're always assured a warm welcome at the Church of the Heavily Armed Christ. And we are now the seventy-second most happening church in the country."

Fash's money has helped of course. Air conditioning has been installed. Youth activities established. Mike runs a boxing club which has proved popular. "Kids love organized violence." The Hierophant has a science club, basic physics and chemistry (blowing things up). A weekend barbecue has provoked a huge turnout from the older worshippers, and the cakes at the new Bible-study class have received rave reviews in the local press and have helped a number of former muggers change their lives. The Locketts have very publicly expressed their thanks to the Church for getting treatment for Esther, who seems to be in the clear.

"We're looking at bigger premises," explains the Hierophant. "The Temple of Extreme Abundance will probably be moving on."

"Gene, it was great working with you. I learnt a lot from you – you helped me a lot, but I've got other plans now."

I'm worried for a second that he'll ask what my plans are, as I couldn't make up anything convincing. He gives a smile and leaves.

Napalm has already moved out. Without saying goodbye. I'd like to pretend that I don't care, and I don't care a great deal, but it's always disappointing when you've extended your hand to someone and it isn't noticed. I shall take time to explore that disappointment more fully later on.

The door to Gulin's room is opened, and her stuff is all neatly boxed up. I don't have much in the way of packing to do, but it occurs to me it's time to do it and to make a decision. I'm wondering whether I'll see her before she leaves, when I hear steps and she appears.

"Hi," she says, pleased to see me. It is a small, but real pleasure, to see that someone is pleased to see you. "How you doing?"

"Okay," I reply. "When you moving?"

"Soon. Why don't you ask me if I have any news?"

"Do you have any news?"

"Yes. I'm a millionaire." I wait for the punchline, but there isn't one. "My boss has left me a ranch. Fifty acres."

I laugh. I don't know why I find it so funny, but I do. I laugh and laugh. She's beaten the system. It's the best news I've heard for years.

I can see why he left her something so generous. He left his family in Illinois when he was sixteen, never had contact with them again, he came out to Florida on his own, built up a chain of movie theatres. That he was gay might have been a factor, because it was a different era, the Forties, when having a fruit for a son was worse than having him eaten by wolves, but maybe it wasn't that. Sometimes it just doesn't work. He saw himself in Gulin, someone who was completely unsupported, completely on her own, because very few of us are without some backup, some family, some membership, some savings. Very few of us have the courage to step right out into the unknown. I don't. I came here because I had nothing to leave behind. I spoke the language. I had some money.

"I'm a millionaire," she says, "but I'm broke." Gulin's got the ranch, fifty miles outside of Miami, but no money to pay all the overheads. I'd sell the whole caboodle immediately, but as has been observed, I'm often in the company of the wrong decision. "I need to find a way of making money. There used to be a chicken farm on the property."

One of the great shortcomings of life is the lack of captions, that there is no punctuation, no musical sting to warn you when something important is happening. The very important events usually appear as indistinct from the unimportant events. Friends or relatives put on their coats and leave, they close the door quietly, as they have done hundreds or thousands of time before and you have no inkling that that will be the last time you'll see them, that that particular walking-out, number three hundred and sixty-two, will be the one that will change everything, even though it looked exactly the same as the other three hundred and sixty-one.

I'm glad I have a chance to say goodbye to her properly.

"I could use a lodger. You interested, Tyndale?"

Orinoco is put on the back seat. Being boxed up upsets some cats, but Orinoco, as always, is calm and, while cooperative, dignified, like a celebrity signing an autograph. Orinoco has to be the reincarnation of some wisdomist. Every time I look at Orinoco I feel inferior – because the cat has clearly got things figured out.

Keep cool. That's all you can do. Keep cool and wait. Wait for your opportunity. There's always a danger that coolness can collapse into capitulation, but all you can do is keep cool and wait for your opportunity. Maybe I've missed some, and maybe the ones I've taken wouldn't have been the ones I'd have chosen, but I've had some fun. Crusher of lighting companies, destroyer of multinational criminal organizations, swatter of sanctimonious swindlers, that's me. At least one was a mission, and it's nice to have a mission accomplished.

Keep cool. Or at least sham cool. Sham cool and true cool, they're almost the same. What's our future? Orinoco and I, we laugh. I finger the diamond I've had fitted in my left ear as a memento of Miami, and the lesson I hope I've learnt here: be cool, be hard, be patient as a diamond waiting in the ground.

"Is Orinoco any special breed?" I ask.

"Just your black cat. I got him from a rescue centre. Some heartless person had abandoned him," says Gulin.

As I manoeuvre my suitcase in the car, I have a strange sensation, something I haven't experienced for so long, I've almost forgotten it: I'm home.

We've said our goodbyes. Dishonest Dave gave me a compilation disc which we play as we head south towards Florida City. A singer I don't know sings about being lucky. It occurs to me that perhaps bad luck, the nasty, unscenic sibling of good luck, can shepherd you to your destination too.

"Idiot," comments Gulin, as an idiot cuts in front of us, but it's an observation not a curse. Gulin is a gifted driver, effortless but masterful. There's nothing like driving in a comfy, powerful car, in sunshine, to give you the feeling that you're getting somewhere. Despite my persistent and embarrassing medical condition, I ponder my future and eternity with amusement. My future? I'm wearing a sharp, short-sleeved silk shirt that Fash gave me, appropriate to an upender of realms, a man who has taken out entire empires single-handed, not that anyone will know or believe it; but I don't care. The sun is shining, I don't care. This might be extremely superficial, but the extremely superficial, like a tissue, can often get the job done.

I ponder eternity. If you think about it, eternity can't be a long time, because time has been removed from the mix. Eternity might feel momentary, like putting on a pair of sunglasses, or like a drive in the sunshine, while you wear a sharp, short-sleeved silk shirt. Honestly, what good is the world? Why does it have to be so big, crowded and messy, when it boils down to a handful of characters, and maybe just one?

Somehow Gulin always cheers me up. There's an infectious optimism about her. No, not that, not optimism, because it's not that everything will be fine. She's not that foolish. No, there's a can-do will about her. Whatever comes, it can be managed – and you really can't ask for anything more than that.

Keeping her eyes on the road she asks:

"So, Tyndale. Have you ever thought about children?"